ACCI

"I don't think Fr ink
he was murdered," A ice
Chief, Nick Thorn.

She watched a look of incredulous disbelief spread across Thorn's face. She waited, knowing he was going to explode. He always exploded when she cried *murder,* while he maintained *accident.*

"How could anybody in her right mind leap to such a ridiculous conclusion? We *saw* Frank lose control of his truck, sail over the sand dunes, then plunge headlong into Whatsit River. Dead men don't drive trucks, Hazard. The only one who went off the deep end was you!"

"Frank Lemon," Amanda insisted, "was either dead, or unconscious, when we chased after him."

"Oh, sure," Nick said, and snorted. "Frank drove in his sleep—eternal or otherwise. Right, Hazard. Sure, I'll buy that. Why shouldn't I? Makes perfect sense to me. And what clue, or dare I ask, tipped you off?"

Amanda stared him squarely in the eye. "The steering wheel was tilted to the 'down' position."

Thorn stared at her as if she were a strange creature who had beamed down from the mother ship. "That's it?"

"When I find Frank Lemon's killer, I insist that you apologize for not taking my suspicions seriously," she said on her way out the door.

"Hazard, wait a minute—"

Amanda didn't wait. She was going to solve this case, and Thorn would be sorry, indeed, that he doubted her!

Other Amanda Hazard mysteries
by Connie Feddersen

Dead in the Water
Dead in the Cellar
Dead in the Melon Patch
Dead in the Dirt
Dead in the Mud

Dead in the Driver's Seat

An Amanda Hazard Mystery

Connie Feddersen

Kensington Books
Kensington Publishing Corp.
http://www.kensingtonbooks.com

KENSINGTON BOOKS are published by

Kensington Publishing Corp.
850 Third Avenue
New York, NY 10022

First Kensington Paperback Printing: June, 1998
10 9 8 7 6 5 4 3 2 1

Printed in the United States of America

This book is dedicated to my husband Ed and our children Jeff, Jon, Jill, Kurt and Christie with much love. And to our granddaughter Brooklyn Walls.

One

According to Amanda Hazard, CPA, every accountant needed a vacation after enduring the hell of income tax season.

Amanda pulled into the driveway of her rented farmhouse and smiled appreciatively. It was good to get away from the office—and good to be home again.

For the past two weeks Amanda and her paternal grandfather had been cruising down Highway 81, through Oklahoma and into Texas. They stopped at antique shops in the small rural towns of Union City, Minco, Pocasset—to name only a few. Pops had gone on such an extensive buying spree that Amanda had to rent a U-Haul trailer at the Oklahoma-Texas border to tote home all his treasures.

"I can't wait to repair and refinish my finds," Pops said as he shouldered open the door of the Toyota. He glanced at Amanda through his wire-rimmed glasses. "As for you, Half Pint, you should start looking for another vehicle. This tin can of a car quit us twice in Texas. Besides that, these foreign cars aren't worth a damn on these gravel roads you buzz around, going to and from Vamoose."

Amanda silently agreed. Zipping up and down the rough country roads in small-town America, visiting her elderly clients, had taken its toll on her Toyota. Her ex-fiancé, Nick Thorn, continually insisted that she purchase a four-wheel-drive pickup . . .

Amanda refused to let herself become sidetracked by thoughts of Thorn and their on-again, off-again wedding plans. She had spent the past two weeks mulling over their relationship but still hadn't resolved the dilemma.

"I'll look around for a truck, first thing in the morning," Amanda said as she climbed from the car. Bruno, the Border collie, and Pete, the three-legged mutt, scampered off the porch to greet her. Amanda gave her pets a fond pat on the head.

"No, first thing *now,*" Pops insisted as he unfolded his aluminum walker and heaved himself to his feet. "We'll unhitch the trailer and you can shop around after I fix us a sandwich."

Amanda glanced at her watch. It was high noon. She supposed it wouldn't hurt to browse around Vamoose's one and only used car lot, after detouring by the office to see if her secretary, Jenny Long, had everything under control.

By the time Amanda unloaded the antique sewing machine, rusty milk can, drop-leaf table (missing a leg), and a dozen other items in various states of disrepair, Pops had the sandwiches prepared.

The old farmhouse smelled moldy after being locked up for two weeks, Amanda noticed as she came through the back door. She opened the windows on her way to the kitchen.

"There wasn't much to choose from in the fridge," Pops said as he plunked down at the table. "Tuna salad is the best I could come up with. But I was getting tired of eating out."

Amanda never got tired of eating out. She wasn't known for her culinary skills, as her ex-fiancé had brought to her attention often enough.

Pops bit into his sandwich, then stared curiously at Amanda. "Well, girl, have you decided what to do about the chief of police and that new county commish, Sam Harjo, who have been chasing after you?"

Amanda inwardly winced. Her vacation was over, but she was no closer to solving the dilemma that had arisen while she was solving the case that left Dusty Brown dead in the mud. Maybe marriage simply wasn't in her future. She had one failed marriage, and a broken engagement, to her credit. Maybe she should accept the county commissioner's interest in her and keep her relationship casual for the next year—or three.

"Well?" Pops persisted. "Is Nick Thorn completely out of the picture or not?"

Amanda chewed and swallowed her bite of sandwich before replying. "To tell you the truth, Pops, I can't decide what to do about Thorn."

Pops' wide grin displayed his mouthful of dentures. "Of course you can make a decision. You took a two-week vacation to think things over. Now that you have been there and done that, you are going to have to deal with both men."

"You're the man in my life, Pops. I think maybe I should stick with what's working."

Pops snorted at her evasive answer. "I didn't bring up the situation while we were on the road, so you could think it through by yourself, but now that we're back in Vamoose you'll have to deal with both of those men. And do you wanna know what I think?"

Yes, she did. Pops had seventy some-odd years of experience under his belt. "Just what do you think I should do, Pops?"

Pops propped his elbows on the table and stared directly at Amanda. "Sometimes, Half Pint, you just gotta wait for a sign. Then you'll know what's best. Analyzing your dilemma to death isn't the answer. You just have to go with your feelings. You've been a numbers cruncher so long that you've started thinking that everything has to add up."

Amanda ate her sandwich and contemplated her grandfather's advice. Wait for a sign? Well, maybe she should give it a shot, she decided. For sure, fourteen days of stewing about Thorn and Harjo had resolved absolutely nothing.

The phone rang just as Amanda polished off her Diet Coke. She strode off to answer the call.

"Hi, doll, it's about time you got back."

It was Mother. Amanda gnashed her teeth.

"Now that you've had time to think things through, I hope you have decided to break off your relationship with that country hick of a cop you were going to marry. It's obvious to me that this relationship is never going to work. That disastrous wedding shower testifies to that! So . . . are you going to write off that cop as the second mistake of your life, doll?"

Amanda counted to ten. Dealing with her overbearing mother was always an exercise in patience. "I'm waiting for a sign," she said calmly, deliberately.

"A sign? What are you talking about?"

"Pops said I should wait for a sign."

"And you're taking advice from a nearsighted, bald-headed, senile old man?" Mother said, and scoffed. "How is my father-in-law, by the way?"

Amanda glanced back at Pops who was clearing the table. "Pops is in antique heaven. He snatched up some priceless treasures for little or nothing while we were on vacation."

"More junk, you mean," Mother sniffed. "Well, I don't want more of that stuff hauled back to my house."

"Not to worry, Mother, I wasn't thinking of sending Pops back to live with you and Daddy. Pops loves it out here in the country."

"And the boondocks is where that cantankerous old

goat belongs," Mother yammered. "When he is staying with us, all he does is try to drive me crazy."

It wouldn't be a very long drive, Amanda thought to herself. "Sorry, Mother, but I have to go. I want to look for a new vehicle this afternoon."

"Good. Get something with some class and style—like a Lincoln or Caddy."

"I was thinking more in the line of a pickup."

"A pickup!" Mother yowled. "Good gad, you're turning out to be as much of a hick as that Thorn character. Forget the truck and buy a luxury car."

Amanda hung up the phone, wondering if the day would ever come when Mother would back off and let her run her own life.

Probably not. Mother, bless her heart, was a control freak.

On the way to the used car lot, Amanda detoured to her office on Main Street. She was pleased to find that her secretary had the business shipshape. These days, Jenny Long was taking her job very seriously. The accounting classes she was taking at night were paying off: Jenny had become as alphabetically organized as Amanda. Everything in the office was in its place, and Jenny was at the computer, recording information for one of Amanda's clients.

Well satisfied, Amanda turned her attention to the acquisition of a new pickup truck.

She stared at the lemon-yellow archway where a huge sign that read: LEMON'S USED CARS flapped in the breeze. Colorful banners were strung around the car lot, and shiny vehicles were lined up for passersby to see. Amanda pulled into the lot, hoping this quest for a new truck would be quick and painless. She had no patience with long-winded, wheeler-dealer salesmen.

Amanda glanced around the lot, surprised that high-intensity salesmen weren't dogging her footsteps. All she saw was the silhouette of a tall, lean auto mechanic who was strolling around a car that was parked inside the workshop.

Amanda heard loud male voices coming from the small metal building that served as an office. A woman's shrill voice rose above the shouting men. It sounded as if the woman was trying to calm down two angry men—and failing miserably. Amanda strode off to see what the hub-bub was all about.

The instant she opened the door, the quarrel ended. She glanced at the chubby-faced Frank Lemon, owner of the dealership. Frank, who was dressed in a cream-colored suit and a tie that displayed an assortment of antique cars, reminded Amanda of the Boss Hogg character from the "Dukes of Hazzard." A cigar was clamped between his gritted teeth, and he was glaring ferociously at his son-in-law, Ernie Niles.

Ernie, decked out in khaki Dockers and a hunter green Polo shirt, was glowering right back at Frank.

Amanda took one look at the men's flushed faces and decided the heated argument hadn't been resolved, merely postponed because of her arrival.

The secretary was wringing her hands and glancing back and forth between the two men who stood rigidly in the corner of the office. Amanda took one look at the secretary and wondered if any of the woman's ample assets had come as standard equipment. Amanda seriously doubted it. The long, rose-tinted fingernails were definitely acrylic, the eyelashes were fake. The red hair was the bottle variety. A cotton-knit sweater showcased the secretary's 38-D's, and the trim-fitting skirt hugged contoured hips—magic worked by a tight girdle, no doubt. The woman's artificial tan indicated she devoted a major portion of her paycheck to a health club membership. The only thing about her that didn't appear to be fake was her anxiety.

"I'm looking for a pickup truck," Amanda said, to break the stilted silence.

"We'll finish this discussion later, Ernie," Frank muttered before he spun on his heels. He clamped a meaty hand around Amanda's forearm and ushered her outside.

"Did you and Ernie have a difference of opinion?" Amanda asked as Frank shepherded her down the second row of vehicles.

"Nothin' for you to worry your pretty head about, little lady." Frank popped a blood pressure pill in his mouth, then pasted on a cheery smile. "Now then, how much do you want to spend on a new truck?"

Amanda discreetly stepped back a pace when Frank breathed on her. The smell of whiskey was so strong it nearly knocked her over. She wondered how Frank's medication would interact with the alcohol he had obviously consumed. Not a good combination, to her way of thinking.

"I don't want to spend more than I have to," Amanda said belatedly. "I consider vehicles to be necessary evils in our mobile world."

Frank chuckled heartily, then slapped Amanda on the back. "Nonsense, little lady. The vehicle you drive is a statement that testifies to your success and position in the world. Your car is what you are."

Frank Lemon reminded Amanda of Mother. Image, not cleanliness, was next to Godliness, in the gospel according to Mother.

"Then I'm a truck," Amanda stated proudly. "I want something that will get me up and down these rough county roads. I need a rugged, dependable vehicle. The closest thing you have to an armored tank will be acceptable."

Frank snickered and slapped Amanda on the back

again, causing her to stumble off balance. "Then a truck it will be, Mandy, m'girl. Let me show you what we've got."

For the next fifteen minutes Frank led Amanda around the lot. He rattled off the selling points of several trucks, none of which suited Amanda's tastes. Although most of the trucks had surprisingly low mileage—and that made her instantly suspicious—the exterior and interior colors didn't appeal to her. Bland tan, lime green, or flashy pink with ground effects simply had no interest . . .

Amanda's gaze landed on a shiny red 4X4 extended cab truck parked near the auto body shop. Now here was a truck that had her name written all over it! The extra seat would give her needed room to carry Pops' walker, groceries and the client files she often took home from the office.

Amanda gestured toward her dream truck. "That is exactly what I'm looking for."

Frank, puffing on his stogie, pivoted to stare in the direction she pointed. "That's my personal truck, hon."

Amanda's arm dropped to her side, her shoulders slumped in disappointment. "Darn, I should have known the pick of the lot was already taken."

"But . . . being the good salesman I am, I contend that everything has a price, my own truck included. If that big beauty is calling out to you, then you can take it for a spin."

Amanda strode over to inspect the extended cab pickup at close range. The vehicle gleamed in the bright sunlight. When she sank down on the bucket seat, and looped her hands over the steering wheel, visions of driving around Vamoose in this snazzy truck popped instantly to mind.

"This is a country Cadillac if ever there was one," Frank said as he levered his hefty body onto the passenger seat. "This baby has all the bells and whistles." He indicated the console with its built-in cup holders, the comfort-adjustment control button for the seats, and the automatic windows and locks.

Frank glanced around the interior of the truck, then stared pensively at Amanda. "Yes siree, I think you're right, Mandy. This is your kind of truck. You look like you belong beneath the wheel. Crank her up and listen to Big Red run."

Amanda fastened her seat belt, then repositioned the steering wheel that was tilted upward to accommodate Frank's barrel-shaped belly. When she switched on the ignition the engine purred like her tomcat. Amanda liked this beautiful beast from the get-go.

As she drove down Main Street, Frank reached out a bejeweled hand to tune the radio to the country station. "State-of-the-art stereo with equalizer," he pointed out. "We're talking plush, Mandy. You've also got full-equipped, heavy-duty rear-wheel suspension, a high-dollar towing package, mag wheels, the whole nine yards. If you want a truck that will withstand the wear and tear of county roads, and allow you to see over the overgrown weeds that clutter country intersections, this baby is absolutely perfect for you."

Amanda accelerated as she passed the city limits sign that read: If you like it country style, then Vamoose. The truck shifted gears smoothly and sailed down the highway. Amanda tried out the cruise control to ensure the gadget functioned properly.

A thick fog of smoke filled the cab when Frank puffed on his cigar. Amanda pressed the button on the door to roll down the window. She didn't want to risk having her vision impaired by a smoke cloud that could result in a collision.

"You can feel all three-hundred-fifty horses galloping beneath you, can't you?" Frank said as he lounged in his bucket seat. "Handles like a dream, doesn't it, Mandy?"

Amanda nodded, afraid to speak for fear of taking in too much smoke.

"Tell ya what I'll do, little lady. If you want this truck, I'll make you a whale of a deal. I'll sell you Big Red if you'll agree to do my accounts for a year. Then I can fire that incompetent secretary who screws up my book work. That air-head female fouls up registration forms so often that I spend my spare time correcting her errors and explaining the mistakes to the state office of vehicle registration. I've had enough of Irene Pratt sashaying around my office, causing more trouble than you can imagine!"

"What kind of trouble?" Amanda asked as she turned onto a gravel road for a test drive.

Frank muttered unintelligibly as he puffed on his cigar.

"Is that what the argument I interrupted was all about? Does Ernie want to keep Irene and you don't?"

"Yeah, something like that. But as far as I'm concerned, they can both take a hike, those two—"

Frank slammed his mouth shut as Amanda made a U-turn and headed back to the highway. She wondered what Frank had started to say—and didn't. The car dealer refused to elaborate. He clamped his lips around his smoldering cigar and blew smoke.

"I plan to trade in my Toyota if I buy this truck," Amanda said as she cruised past the outskirts of town.

"You mean that tin can of a car with bent fenders and paint dings from flying gravel?" Frank asked, then scoffed.

Amanda frowned darkly. She was being subjected to the customary salesman routine. According to this car dealer, her trade-in was a broken-down bucket of rust that barely sufficed as scrap metal. But Amanda would have none of that! Frank Lemon was not going to praise this truck and criticize her Toyota!

"The Toyota has a few minor problems that will cost very little to repair, and it gets excellent gas mileage," she insisted. "And yes, I admit that the car needs minor body work, but it has never been wrecked. It has held its value and the interior is in mint condition—"

Frank held up his hand to forestall her. "Don't blow a gasket now, hon. I'll test drive your Toyota and tell you what it's worth to me."

Frank would probably shoot her a price that was far less than blue book value, Amanda thought to herself.

When Amanda reentered the car lot, the man she had seen in the auto body shop was standing outside, taking a smoke break. His grimy clothes and slicked-down hair suggested that he spent a great deal of time wallowing in automotive grease.

"I would like to have a word with you, boss," Freddy Lassiter requested.

Frank excused himself and waddled over to the mechanic. Amanda brushed the cigar ashes off the upholstery, then tried out the windshield wipers and mist cleaner. Everything on the truck seemed to be in proper working order.

Loud voices erupted from the workshop. Amanda glanced up to see Freddy Lassiter and Frank Lemon standing toe-to-toe. Amanda wondered if it was difficult to work for Frank Lemon. The car dealer seemed to go from one heated argument to another—in between tipping the bottle she had noticed peeking out of the pocket of his jacket.

Face flaming, Frank stormed from the garage. Smoke rolled around him. The instant he saw Amanda staring speculatively at him, his annoyed expression transformed into a sunny smile.

"Let me have your keys and I'll take your Toyota for a quick spin around town."

Amanda handed over her keys, then watched Frank squirm beneath the steering wheel. He tilted the lever upward to accommodate his rounded belly and whizzed off without fastening the seat belt.

"Are you thinking about buying Frank's truck?"

Amanda pivoted to see Freddy Lassiter wiping his hands on the red rag that had dangled from his back pocket a few minutes earlier. His tousled blond hair fell over one eye, reminding Amanda of James Dean.

"I'm definitely considering it," Amanda replied.

"Nice truck," he mumbled. "But then, it's nothing but the best for Frank. He likes to ride in style."

Amanda couldn't be certain, but she thought she detected bitterness in the young man's voice.

She spun around when she heard a roaring engine and squealing tires. Frank had returned, taking the corner at excessive speed. He stamped on the brake and the Toyota ground to a halt.

Puffing on his cigar, Frank ducked his head and wormed from the compact car. Amanda girded herself up to negotiate the trade-in transaction. When Frank breathed on her, she noted that his mouthwash was considerably stronger than it had been when he buzzed from the lot in her Toyota. Apparently, he had taken a few belts during the test drive.

For the next fifteen minutes Amanda and Frank haggled over the price of the red truck and her Toyota trade-in. Amanda held her own with the car salesman, and even walked off once. Frank called her back, then made a lower offer. In the end, Amanda promised to figure Frank's income taxes and handle his accounting for a year. In return, Frank gave her his rock bottom price.

Buyer and seller came away from the negotiations well satisfied.

Beaming with pleasure, Amanda drove home to retrieve her car title and clean her personal belongings from the compact car. Frank promised to spiffy up the big red truck and have Freddy Lassiter check under the hood. All in all, Amanda decided her afternoon had been a huge success. This time tomorrow she would have the paperwork completed and she would be cruising around Vamoose in her new 4X4 fire-engine-red truck.

Hazard was back in town.

Nick Thorn had been given the news at least a half-dozen times during the afternoon. It seemed everyone in Vamoose was waiting to see if he intended to patch up the broken engagement or stand back and let Sam Harjo, the new county commish, beat his time.

Recently showered, dressed in cowboy boots and his police uniform—Hazard had a soft spot in her heart for a man in a uniform—Nick stared at his reflection in the mirror. He wasn't going to delay welcoming Hazard back from her vacation—he couldn't, not while Sam Harjo was eager to take his place in her affections.

Resolved to making a new start, Nick strode outside and climbed into his squad car. As he drove toward Hazard's rented farm, he mentally rehearsed what he planned to say. He would be charming, polite, attentive and respectful. He was not going to let the jealous green monster nip his butt, either, he promised himself. If Hazard had developed an interest in Harjo, then Nick would simply out-charm the commish. Although Nick's mom didn't think a marriage between him and Hazard would work out satisfactorily, he had high hopes. After all, Mom didn't think any woman was good enough for her two darling sons.

Nick pulled into the driveway and waved at Pops, who was making his way to the converted granary in the barn that had become his workshop. Pete, the three-legged dog, was lounging on the porch. Pete lifted his head, glanced in Nick's direction, then settled down for another nap.

Before Nick could knock on the front door, a bark

erupted from inside the house. Bruno, the Border collie that had adopted Hazard while she investigated the Dead in the Mud Case, was as protective as ever, Nick noted.

The door swung open and Nick pasted on his best smile. "Hi, Hazard. I came by to welcome you back from your vacation." He gestured toward the U-Haul trailer that was parked near the barn. "Pops must have come home with scads of antiques to refinish."

Nick looked into Hazard's eyes, gauging her reaction to him. She was being politely reserved, while he made small talk. At least she hadn't shouted him off the porch. It was a start.

"May I come in?" Nick asked, flashing his killer smile.

Hazard stepped aside, but the Border collie growled a warning.

"Down, Bruno, it's only Thorn," Hazard said.

Nick strode inside, noting the gifts from their wedding shower still stacked in the corner of the living room. Hazard hadn't returned the items.

Another good sign, thought Nick.

Hazard looked him up and down. "You must be on duty tonight," she said, then glanced away.

"Deputy Sykes is taking some time off." Nick sank down on the recliner, then smiled again. "So . . . how was your trip?"

"Fine."

Damn, but he felt awkward. Conversation between him and Hazard had never been so stilted. But it was his own fault. He had asked for the engagement ring during a momentary lapse of sanity. The ring had been burning a hole in his pocket ever since.

"Were things quiet in Vamoose while Pops and I were gone?" Hazard asked as she took a seat at the far end of the sofa—as far away from Nick as she could get.

Nick shrugged casually. "I made a few arrests, gave three traffic tickets, a citation for DUI and put a stop to a race between a couple of high-school hot-rodders who were trying to burn up the road. I investigated a stolen vehicle that had been stripped of its parts, doused with gasoline and burned. Other than that it's been a relatively uneventful two weeks." Nick paused, then added quietly, "I missed you, Hazard."

She didn't comment, just let his confession hang in the uncomfortable silence. After a moment, she leaned forward to rearrange the stack of magazines on the coffee table.

"I bought a truck this afternoon," she announced. "We'll wrap up the paperwork in the morning. I'm trading in my Toyota."

"Are you? What kind of truck did you get?"

"A big red 4X4."

Nick nodded approvingly. "Good. These country roads are hard on vehicles. You need something stout and sturdy. Where did you get your truck?"

"From Lemon's Used Cars."

Nick couldn't help himself, he groaned aloud. "I hope you're kidding. Please tell me you're kidding. Frank Lemon is a shyster and a drunk. He's the one I picked up for DUI this week. I told that potbellied old goat that if he kept mixing his drinking and driving I would haul him to jail and leave him there until he dried out."

"Frank gave me a good deal," Hazard said defensively.

"Nobody gets a good deal when she buys a Lemon," Nick shot back. "You should have consulted me first. I would have helped you select and negotiate for your truck."

It was the wrong thing to say. Hazard threw back her shoulders, her eyes flashed and her blond hair rippled as she turned her hostile glare on Nick. "Watch it, Thorn. When you broke off our engagement you forfeited all rights to add input into my decisions. I'll have you know that the big red extended cab truck was an absolute steal.

It isn't costing me two arms and both legs. In fact, I think I got the better end of the deal with Frank Lemon."

Nick scoffed. "You may think so now, but when your truck starts falling apart, you'll wish you hadn't dealt with Lemon. You won't be the first person to complain about vehicles that run just long enough to hand over a check and sign the title and registration forms. You should have driven down to Pronto to shop around before you made the deal."

Hazard bolted to her feet, clearly put out with Nick for spouting his opinions. He wished he had kept his trap shut. His attempt to mend broken fences wasn't going as well as he had hoped.

"Let's get something straight, here and now, Thorn," she huffed. "I still make my own choices and I have no complaints about buying a Lemon. I think you better leave before you ruin my good disposition."

"I think I should, too." Nick rose to his feet. "I thought maybe we could drive over to Oklahoma City and catch a movie. You know, start over and put the past behind us."

"There isn't a movie out right now that I want to see," she said stubbornly.

"Then maybe we could have dinner and go dancing."

"I'm not hungry and my feet hurt."

Nick was being as nice as he knew how, but Hazard's contrariness was starting to piss him off. "Look, Hazard, I came over here to let you know that I don't want to call it quits. If you don't want to work out our differences then you better come right out and say so. What's it going to be?"

Hazard stared at him for a long, pensive moment. Nick held his breath, wondering if blurting out that ultimatum was the dumbest thing he had ever done. Then, on impulse, he decided to go for broke.

He walked over and pulled Hazard into his arms. He gave her a kiss that stole the breath right out of her. If

Sam Harjo was beating Nick's time, then the handsome commish would have to compete with a kiss that carried enough heat to melt lava.

When Nick released Hazard as abruptly as he had embraced her, she wobbled on unsteady legs and braced her hand on the wall for support.

"Well?" he asked, his voice unsteady. "Are you hungry yet? Do your feet still ache?"

Hazard stared dazedly at him—and that pleased Nick immensely. At least he hadn't lost his touch, he thought. Sparks still flew like fireworks on the Fourth of July when they kissed. There was still hope.

"Dinner and dancing will be fine," she wheezed.

"Good. How about tomorrow night?"

She nodded agreeably.

When Nick ambled out the door, Hazard followed him. Darkness had settled over the countryside and the full moon resembled a fluorescent orange balloon hovering on the eastern skyline. A lover's moon, thought Nick. Too bad it was too soon for that. He had already pushed his luck by stealing a kiss.

"Damn it, that's my new truck!" Hazard erupted beside him.

Nick glanced sideways to see the silhouette of a four-wheel-drive truck, its bright headlights flaring, as it flew over the hill and stirred up a cloud of dust from the gravel road.

"You bought Frank's personal truck?" Nick asked, surprised.

"Yes, I did, and he's out here giving it one last spin at high speed. If he winds up in the ditch and wrecks my truck he'll have hell to pay!" she spouted off.

"Damn that idiot," Nick muttered as he jogged toward the black-and-white. "I told Frank to stay off the roads while he's boozing it up. And he's obviously boozing it up. Not only can't he walk a straight line, but he can't drive one, either. I warned him that I would have him behind bars, and I meant business!"

Hazard darted toward the passenger side of the squad car. "I intend to protect my new interest. When you stop Frank, I plan to be here with you," she insisted. "Gun it, Thorn!"

Nick flicked on the flashing lights and siren and rammed the squad car into gear. Gravel flew as he gave chase. "Frank better enjoy his joy ride, because it will be his last. I'm suspending his damned license this time!"

Amanda fastened her seat belt as Thorn chased the speeding truck that swerved from one bar ditch to the other. Twice, she thought Frank was going to veer off the road and ram Big Red into the barbed-wire fence. Miraculously though, the drunken driver managed to keep the truck between the ditches at seventy miles per hour.

Gritting her teeth, Amanda braced her arm against the door as Thorn whizzed around the corner of the intersection. Dust rose like a gray fog as Frank Lemon zoomed down the country road.

"He's going to peel the rubber off my tires in this thick layer of gravel," Amanda fumed. "That does it! I'm going to make Frank knock off another four hundred dollars for a new set of tires."

Amanda swore Frank had to be pushing eighty miles an hour. The dust cloud he sent up made it impossible to see anything except a dim view of his taillights. He ran three stop signs in his attempt to outrun Thorn's squad car.

"What the hell's wrong with him?" Thorn scowled as he increased his speed. "He knows that I know where he lives. Frank must be drunker than a skunk if he thinks I'm going to let him get away with this."

For five minutes Thorn gave chase and cursed each time

the truck swerved dangerously on the country road. Amanda could hear gravel thumping against the underside of the squad car. She could easily imagine what flying gravel was doing to the paint on Big Red. The sides of her truck would be pitted and the wheels would be out of line after this wild chase down rough gravel roads. She was going to make Frank Lemon knock off another thousand!

"Hell's bells!" Thorn growled. "He's heading for the highway to cross Whatsit River Bridge. If Frank causes a pile-up, I'll kill that crazy fool myself! Damn it, he'll probably be the only one drunk enough to survive a head-on collision."

Amanda planted her feet firmly on the floorboard when Thorn mashed on the accelerator. She glanced at the speedometer. They were doing ninety in loose gravel, sending up a second fog of dust that hung in the still evening air. The squad car's headlights reflected off the dust particles suspended in front of them. Amanda could barely see Frank's taillights in the distance. Damn, he had to be doing one hundred! How he managed to keep the truck under control in his intoxicated condition was beyond Amanda. Undoubtedly, he was too drunk to be scared, but Amanda wasn't. High-speed chases—especially on gravel roads—were unnerving.

"Hold on, Haz, this is a rough stretch of road," Thorn said without glancing at her.

The car bounced over the low water bridge, then zoomed up the hill toward the highway. Amanda could see Big Red on the pavement ahead of them. The truck swerved when it met the headlights of oncoming traffic. Amanda held her breath and prayed that Frank's daring getaway attempt wouldn't cause some innocent victim to lose his life.

With lights flashing and sirens still screaming, Thorn turned onto the highway. He was gaining on Big Red when the truck suddenly careened sideways. In stunned shock,

Amanda watched the swerving truck miss the curve that would have carried it safely over the river bridge. The beams of Frank's headlights soared skyward, then downward. The truck bobbled over the sandy knolls beside the river. In the distance, Amanda could see it plowing through the thick underbrush and scraggly trees that lined Whatsit River. Frank was putting so many scratches on her dream truck that it was going to require a paint job. Damn the man! Didn't he know when to quit? When she and Thorn caught up with Frank she was going to insist that Frank trade her even for her Toyota . . .

Amanda's spiteful thoughts trailed off as she watched her truck soar over the cliff and nose-dive into the river.

"Hurry up, Thorn! Frank will drown if we don't get to him quickly."

Thorn mashed on the brakes as he veered down the sandy path Frank had taken. When he ground the squad car to a halt, Amanda leaped out, listening to the hiss and sputter of the hot engine that had been doused in water.

"Well, damn it all," Nick muttered as he rushed toward the scene of the mishap. "Hazard, go back to the car and get the rope in the back seat. I don't want to sink in the quicksand while trying to save that idiotic drunk."

Huffing and puffing, Amanda retraced her steps. When she returned with the rope, Thorn was climbing into the bed of the upended truck. His flashlight reflected off the water that seeped into the cab through the partially opened window.

"No need to hurry now," Thorn muttered. "Call the dispatcher and request Watts's towing service. Then call the medical examiner. Frank Lemon just took his last joy ride."

For an instant, Amanda simply stood there, absorbing the horror of the situation. Frank, owner and proprietor of Lemon's Used Cars, was dead in the driver's seat. He had made his last, sale, smoked his last cigar, and guzzled his last drink of Jack Daniel's. He had also wrecked Amanda's dream truck.

Frank Lemon was on his way to that big used car lot in the sky . . .

Two

When Amanda returned to the scene of the disaster, Thorn was still trying to retrieve Frank Lemon's body from the waterlogged cab of the truck. But the doors were jammed and the window wasn't open wide enough for Thorn to reach his brawny arm inside.

Since Deputy Sykes was on vacation, Amanda had placed a call to the Vamoose County Sheriff's department, requesting assistance. Thorn needed professional backup and he also needed to get out of his wet clothes. His uniform stuck to him like paint, and he was gasping for breath.

Amanda whirled around when headlights spotlighted her. Cecil Watts's tow truck lumbered down the steep incline. The hook of the tow chain swung like a gigantic fishhook.

"Hook me up, will ya, Chief," Cecil hollered as Thorn scrambled over the truck bed. Hurriedly, Thorn attached the hook to the heavy-duty steel bumper. Metal creaked and groaned as Big Red inched from the river. By the time the pickup was sitting on all four wheels—one of which was bent completely out of shape—the medical examiner and the deputy from the sheriff's department had arrived on the scene.

As water seeped around the door and dribbled into the sand, Amanda peered into the cab. Frank was sprawled, facedown, half on and half off the console between the bucket seats. A soggy stogie lay on the floorboard beside an open bottle of Jack Daniel's which gurgled with water.

"What happened here, Thorn?"

Amanda glanced at the sheriff's deputy, who stood at attention, like a soldier on parade. While Thorn explained the events leading up to the accident, Deputy Joe Payne took notes and fired questions. Amanda didn't like the looks, or the sound, of Deputy Payne. He appeared to be the no-nonsense, ex-soldier kind of cop whose gruff voice and brisk manner held no reassurance. Amanda was glad Thorn was dealing with the gung-ho, GI-Joe deputy, not her. She would have lost patience with Payne's accusing questions from the get-go.

While the coroner did his thing, Thorn glanced at Amanda. "Cecil Watts is going to give you a ride home before we wind things up here, Hazard."

"But—"

"You were cruising the country roads with a civilian on board?" Payne said, then snorted disdainfully. "Come on, Thorn, any fool knows better than to do that."

"Now listen here, Payne—" Amanda closed her mouth when Thorn tossed her a silencing glance.

"There were extenuating circumstances," Thorn said.

Payne smirked as he jotted down more notes. "Yeah, like I haven't heard that before."

Cecil Watts took Amanda's arm to assist her up the steep slope. "C'mon, 'Manda. Chief said for me to take ya home. I gotta get back here so I can tow the truck to my shop."

Reluctantly, Amanda climbed into the tow truck. She felt as if she were abandoning Thorn to the obnoxious Payne. Damn, weren't cops supposed to be on the same side? That county deputy behaved as if Thorn was on trial for murder, what with all his ridiculous questions. Amanda could only hope that poor, lovable Thorn had the patience to deal with him.

She mentally kicked herself all the way home for placing that phone call.

Amanda reflected on her encounter with Thorn at her house. She wondered if his arrival, and his attempt to smooth over the rocky events leading to their *dis*-engagement was the kind of "sign" Pops had mentioned. She wasn't sure, but she didn't think so.

As physically appealing as Thorn was—and always had been to her, in his police uniform—that was not the issue here. Thorn was one hot, virile hunk of country cop, but the conflict that rose between them while she investigated the Dead in the Mud Case was the issue. Thorn presumed Amanda had been fooling around with Sam Harjo, who was the spitting image of Clint Eastwood in his spaghetti Westerns.

Jealousy had gotten the better of Thorn, and he had behaved unreasonably. His lack of trust, his infuriating habit of discounting her innate suspicions during investigations, were the crux of the problems between them.

As far as Amanda was concerned, the "sign" had not yet made itself clear to her. Until it did, she was going to play it cool.

Except for that scorching kiss Thorn planted on her lips, she silently amended. She tamped down the tingles and focused her thoughts on the untimely accident that had totaled her soon-to-be-acquired truck and left Frank Lemon with a new mode of transportation—a hearse.

Amanda wondered how the employees of Lemon's Used Cars would react to the news. No doubt, Irene Pratt would be relieved to know she wouldn't be fired, not with Ernie Niles in control of the dealership. No, Amanda decided, Frank Lemon probably wouldn't be missed much at the car dealership.

Amanda awoke to the smell of sizzling bacon and percolating coffee. Pops, it seemed, was up and at 'em, anxious to begin a full day of repairs on his antique treasures. Amanda preferred to lounge in bed, recovering from the long hours of driving home from vacation and the shock of watching Frank Lemon plunge into the river.

Reluctantly, she pried herself loose from the cozy nest of her bed and staggered to the shower. A few minutes later, she was halfheartedly prepared to face the day. Although she was customarily a morning person, her butt was dragging today. She supposed that spending the past two weeks worrying about her relationship with Thorn was partially responsible for taking the starch out of her.

Amanda tugged on her pantyhose and silk blouse, then combed her hair. She was halfway to the bedroom door before she realized she was too indecently dressed to eat breakfast with her grandfather. Pivoting, she snatched up her plum-colored skirt and left the hem of her blouse dangling.

The sound of a second male voice in the kitchen caused Amanda's brows to beetle curiously. It sounded like Thorn. What was he doing here at 7:30 in the morning?

Amanda decided the only way to answer that question was to walk into the kitchen and ask him.

"Thorn, what are you doing here at 7:30 in the morning?"

"Good morning to you, too, Hazard," Thorn said before he took a cautious sip of coffee.

" 'Morning," Amanda mumbled as she sank down in the chair Thorn politely pulled out for her.

"Pops was telling me about all his finds in the antique shops from here to the gulf," Thorn said as he sprawled his long, muscled legs out in front of him.

Amanda frowned, bemused. Thorn was wearing a faded black T-shirt and jeans that had seen better days. "I thought Deputy Sykes was on vacation. Why aren't you in uniform?"

"I have a replacement," Thorn said, then nodded gratefully when Pops set a plate of bacon, eggs and hashed brown potatoes in front of him.

"What does that mean?" Amanda questioned. "Does Vamoose have another deputy?"

"Not exactly," Thorn murmured, staring at his plate.

Amanda was in no mood for guessing games. "What's going on that I don't know about, Thorn?"

"Give the man a break, Half Pint," Pops interjected as he levered from his walker and plunked into his chair. "Thorn doesn't need to be grilled on an empty stomach."

Amanda clamped her mouth shut and let Thorn eat in peace while Pops made small talk to break the brittle silence that hovered over the kitchen table. When the meal ended, Amanda cleared the table, then turned her gaze on Thorn. "Now that you have been well fed, what's this business about your replacement?"

Thorn focused his dark-eyed stare on Amanda. "I have been temporarily relieved of my position as Chief of Vamoose Police Department, pending an investigation of Frank Lemon's death."

"What?" Amanda and Pops howled in unison.

Thorn nodded grimly. "Deputy Payne-in-the-ass, the same cop who has been substituting for Benny Sykes and me the past two months, so he could make extra money, filed a report that implied misconduct on my part. Payne maintains that my high-speed chase, with a civilian on board, was against regulations. The sheriff called to inform me that I was taking a forced vacation. 'This is a good time to catch up on the farming chores that policing the Vamoose beat have caused you to postpone,' he said."

"That is ridiculous!" Amanda erupted in outrage. "In the first place, I don't consider myself a civilian, not after investigating five murder cases. And secondly, I'm your ex-fiancée!"

"That doesn't count in Payne's book," Thorn grumbled. "If you ask me, that ex-GI has delusions of replacing me permanently. And why am I not surprised that Payne maneuvered the sheriff into putting *him* in charge of investigating the Lemon incident?"

"Well, you can bet your bottom dollar that I will have a few things to say to the sheriff about this injustice!" Amanda replied.

"A few things, Hazard? When, in your life, have you only had a few things to say on any subject?" Thorn gave his raven-colored head a shake. "Not this time, Haz. The sheriff knows we are . . . *were* . . . engaged. He will view your comments, in my defense, as partial."

"And what would you call Payne's comments?" she shot back. "Look what he has to gain by casting suspicion on you! The man will twist the accounts of this incident to make you look bad, then he'll be right here, in your face, anxious to take your place! When I get through speaking my piece to the sheriff he will demote Payne—"

Thorn flung up his hand. "Hazard, back off. That's not the way to handle this situation." His cocoa-brown eyes locked with Amanda's angry gaze. "I have a favor to ask of you, Hazard."

Amanda watched Thorn squirm awkwardly in his chair, then stare at the contents of his coffee cup as if it held all the answers to the problems of the universe. Clearly, whatever Thorn intended to ask, wasn't going to be easy for him.

Finally, Thorn leaned his elbows on the table and stared unblinkingly at Amanda. He inhaled a deep breath that made his massive hulk of a chest swell to excessive proportion. "I want you to conduct one of your unauthorized investigations in this case. I want you to glean information in all the unorthodox ways you always do. I want you to gather evidence that indicates that Frank Lemon had a drinking problem and that extenuating circumstances put him on that high-speed run that resulted in his fatal accident. The only way to clear my name, and restore my reputation as a law officer, is to prove that Frank's state of intoxication and irrational emotional mood were responsible for the traffic fatality.

"Will you do that for me, Hazard? Will you conduct an investigation that might salvage my job?"

Amanda stared at Thorn in stunned astonishment. Never before had Thorn asked her to apply her natural-born detective skills when she happened on a corpse in Vamoose. She had stumbled onto bodies in a water tank, in a cellar, in a melon patch, in the dirt and in the mud. And each time Thorn had ordered her to back off, ordered her not to stick her bloodhound nose into police business.

And now, like a bolt from the blue, this big, ruggedly handsome stud of a police chief was *asking* her to open an investigation.

A jolt of pride, satisfaction and pleasure gushed through Amanda. She glanced at Pops, who was propped against the kitchen counter, grinning at her.

It struck her that this was the "sign" Pops had told her to wait for. This was the crystal-clear indication that Thorn respected her analytic intelligence, her perseverance. He recognized her ability to dig up clues, even if she relied on unconventional methods to gather facts and evidence.

Overcome with emotion, Amanda bounded from her chair. "Oh, Thorn, you know I will do everything I can to clear your name. I will make this case my first priority."

In her elation, Amanda flung herself at Thorn and hugged the stuffing out of him. Unfortunately, her enthusiasm was too much for the chair Thorn was sitting in. It reared up like a misbehaving horse when she hopped on Thorn's lap. Thorn squawked as the chair crashed back on the vintage green linoleum, leaving Amanda sprawled on top of him.

Pops muffled a chuckle beneath a cough, grinned widely, then grabbed his aluminum walker. "If you'll excuse me, I'll go soak my dentures and replace the batteries in my hearing aids."

When Pops clomped off, Amanda stared down into the bronzed features that denoted Thorn's Native American heritage. Two weeks of fretting about their relationship melted away, leaving her with the simple, conclusive fact that she was still absolutely crazy about this gorgeous country cop. The new county commissioner was quickly forgotten. Thorn was the man for Amanda. Intuition had told her that, but she had allowed petty conflicts and stubborn feminine pride to override that one irrefutable truth.

Nick squirmed beneath Hazard's shapely body, which was meshed to his. That old, familiar flame burst to life, sending his testosterone count through the roof. Hazard was back in his arms again, showering him with kisses that indicated he had said the right thing to her—for once. He hadn't wanted to involve her in his problems, knowing she must be at least two weeks behind in her work at her accounting office. But he needed her expertise, needed her to uncover facts in her unorthodox manner that caused veteran law officers—like himself—to howl in dismay. But this time Nick was willing to accept whatever help Hazard could provide in his effort to get reinstated as police chief.

He needed Hazard—period. Nick decided, right there and then, to take complete advantage of Hazard's grand mood. He was going to go for broke again, going to humble himself and *beg,* if that's what it took.

"Hazard, I have one more favor to ask."

"Name it, Thorn."

Nick reached into the pocket of his jeans to retrieve the engagement ring he had been carrying around with him for more than a month. He held up the glittering diamond.

"Will you take this back, Hazard? Will you put it back

on your finger where it belongs and do me the honor of marrying me? You know I'm crazy about you. Through thick and thin, happy or annoyed, I have always been crazy about you. Please say you'll get through the hassle of the wedding and come live with me 'til the day I die. This is for keeps, Hazard. Even if your mother and my mom think we're making the biggest mistake of our lives, let's prove them wrong."

"Oh, Thorn!" Amanda exclaimed.

And then she did the darnedest thing. She cried! Nick could count, on one hand, the number of times he had seen Hazard dissolve into tears. Ordinarily, she wasn't prone to springing leaks. This cast-iron daisy, with a mile-long sentimental streak that she didn't want the men of this world to know she had, was crying. Her tears were splattering on his ragged T-shirt.

"Is 'Oh, Thorn!' a yes or a no, Hazard?" he asked, staring intently into her watery blue eyes. "I'm not only down on my knees here, I'm flat on my back. You hold my personal and professional life in your hands. Are we going to get through this investigation and wedding together or aren't we?"

Hazard put the ring on her finger, then practically squeezed him in two. "It's a y-yessss," she breathed raggedly.

Smiling, Nick cupped her tear-stained face in his hands and kissed her. Then, while Pops was ensconced in his bedroom, soaking his store-bought teeth and replacing the batteries in his hearing device, Nick and Hazard made it, right there on the vintage green linoleum.

Nick didn't care that Hazard set off every smoke alarm in the house when she tried to cook a meal. He didn't care that she outclassed him by a country mile and that she could spit words at him that he had to look up in the dictionary, after one of their arguments. He didn't care that she was so organized that she alphabetized her kitchen and medicine cabinet. All that mattered to Nick was that they had resolved their differences and all was right with the world.

Nick thanked his lucky stars that he and Hazard were back where they belonged.

Still walking on air, Amanda dried off from her second shower of the morning. Thorn had left the house with a smile on his face and a swagger in his walk. Pops was still in the bedroom sorting his socks—or whatever he had found to occupy his time.

Amanda felt like a new woman. Her life had been out of sync when she and Thorn were at odds. Now, the engagement ring was back on her finger and Thorn had given her the go-ahead to investigate the accident that had left him suspended from his duties as police chief.

She would show that Deputy Payne a thing—or three—about investigation, she promised herself. She would run circles around that hot-shot cop who had visions of taking Thorn's place in Vamoose.

When Amanda confronted the sheriff, she intended to have facts galore. She already knew that Frank Lemon had encountered two conflicts the day of his death, because she had witnessed both of them. Frank Lemon could have been in a state of mental turmoil the night he died. That, Amanda told herself, was why he had tried to outrun Thorn's squad car. That was what caused the car dealer to end up dead in the driver's seat.

Now that Amanda thought about it, she suspected the whiskey, the blood pressure pills, and the cigars that Frank chain-smoked, might have interacted. He might have passed out while he was behind the wheel. She would call the medical examiner and wheedle information out of him, she decided. He was a friend of Thorn's, after all, and she knew she could count on the man to divulge facts when he learned that Thorn's job was in jeopardy.

But, first things first, Amanda reminded herself. She had to hitch up the U-Haul and stop by Thatcher's Oil and Gas to fill up her Toyota. Thaddeus Thatcher was an excellent source of information in Vamoose. She would see what the service station owner had to say about Frank Lemon.

Dressed in designer jeans and colorful Western blouse, Amanda poked her head inside Pops' bedroom to tell him good-bye. Pops nodded approvingly when he saw the ring sparkling on Amanda's left hand.

"My money was on Thorn, Half Pint. I guess you got the sign you have been waiting for."

Amanda returned her grandfather's wry smile. "Thanks for the good advice, Pops. I don't know what I'd do without you."

"Does this mean I can stay down on the farm for a while longer?"

Amanda nodded. "Rest easy. I'm not sending you back to deal with Mother until you want to go back to the city. In fact, you can live with Thorn and me. You can visit Daddy and Mother when the mood strikes you. Thorn has a spare bedroom, and I know he won't mind having you around, because he likes you."

Pops frowned. "I don't think it's a good idea to crowd in on newlyweds' space. You're getting enough interference from Thorn's mom and your mother as it is."

Amanda waved off her grandfather's concern. Considering the fabulous mood she was in, nothing could burst her bubble. "Don't worry about a thing, Pops. Just go repair your antiques and enjoy yourself. I'm going to spend the day digging up facts about Frank Lemon. If you need anything, call my secretary at the office. I'll check in with Jenny every couple of hours."

With a wave and a smile Amanda strode off. There was

nothing—and she meant nothing—that she wouldn't know about Frank Lemon before she was through with this investigation. She would question everyone who had the slightest association with the wheeler-dealer used car salesman. Deputy Payne-in-the-butt would be eating her dust, because that GI-gung-ho-Joe Payne would be several giant steps behind her. She would know everything he knew—and even more. There was no way in hell that she was going to let that sneaky cop twist the facts to his benefit. And if the scheming, conniving cop got fired over this investigation, then all the better.

There was nothing Amanda hated worse than a dirty cop who had his own hidden agenda. Deputy Payne must have set his sights on the sleepy little haven of Vamoose while he was earning extra wages as a substitute police officer. But Payne would rue the day he butted heads with Amanda Hazard. He would also regret the day he messed with *her* man. Amanda was on a crusade for truth and justice, and Deputy Payne had damned well better stay the hell out of her way!

Amanda frowned pensively as she drove through Vamoose. Lemon's Used Cars was open for business. She had expected the bereaved family to shut down for a couple of days. Apparently, Ernie Niles planned to make a few sympathy sales. She made a mental note to stop by to see Ernie after she fueled up her car. She was curious to see how the employees of Lemon's Used Cars were dealing with the passing of the owner and proprietor.

Thaddeus Thatcher hiked up his navy blue breeches as he ambled from the station to wait on Amanda. "Howdy, li'l girl. Heard you had an eventful evening."

Amanda nodded as Thaddeus crammed the nozzle into her fuel tank. "I guess you heard the ridiculous news that

Thorn has been suspended from duty because of that high-speed chase."

Thaddeus' eyes popped. "What?" He glanced toward the squad car that cruised down Main Street.

Amanda glared at the man behind the wheel.

"Is that why that sheriff's deputy is driving Thorn's black-and-white?"

Again, Amanda nodded. "Deputy Payne has set his sights on Thorn's position. If he can prove wrongdoing on Thorn's part, Payne will step in as interim chief."

"Why, that's the craziest thing I ever heard," Thaddeus snorted. "Ole Frank was known to booze it up. Thorn was on his case, because Frank had been hitting the bottle with alarming regularity the past month. Don't know what burr the man had under his saddle, but he was chain-smoking cigars and carrying a pint of Jack Daniel's in his pocket. I'll bet he made the run to Pronto's liquor store at least once a day."

Amanda stored the information in the file cabinet of her mind, wondering what had driven Frank to heavy drinking.

"Thorn warned Frank to stay out of his truck while he was snockered," Thaddeus continued. "The chief cautioned everybody in town to drive defensively when Frank was on the road. You would think Ernie Niles would have taken Frank's keys away from him, or at the least, driven his father-in-law home from the dealership."

Amanda could imagine how well that would have gone over. Frank seemed to be the domineering kind of man who wouldn't appreciate having his son-in-law in control.

Thaddeus removed the gas nozzle and screwed the gas cap in place. "If you'll pull around back, I'll unhitch the U-Haul for you. Gertrude is in the office, so you can fill out the paperwork for the rental."

After unhitching the trailer, Amanda strode inside to find Gertrude Thatcher poring over her tax forms.

"You're just the person I need to see," Gertrude said, glancing up. "These confounded rules and regulations are giving me a headache. I have to figure gas sales tax and get my accounting ledger in order before the auditor arrives next week. Somehow or another I've lost track of a truckload of fuel that Thaddeus delivered to one of the farmers in the area. I still can't figure out who it might be."

Amanda's practiced gaze swept down the tax form. In two minutes, she pointed out Gertrude's oversight.

"Heavens to Betsy, it was staring me right in the face," Gertrude exclaimed. "Thanks, Amanda, you're a lifesaver."

While glancing over Gertie's thin-bladed shoulder Amanda noticed the exceptionally high tax paid by Lemon's Used Car dealership. High taxes indicated excessive amounts of fuel. Amanda was under the impression that cars sitting on lots had only a quarter of a tank of fuel in them—enough for an occasional test drive.

Amanda quickly calculated the approximate number of cars on the lot and multiplied by the price of fuel per gallon—give or take a few gallons. In her professional estimation, the amount of fuel tax paid by Lemon was exceedingly high. She wondered if the employees of the car lot were filling their personal vehicles from the deliveries Thaddeus Thatcher made to the lot. She should check on that when she retrieved the accounting ledgers from Irene Pratt, the incompetent secretary who worked for Frank Lemon.

Near as Amanda could tell, there was considerable turmoil beneath the asphalt surface of Lemon's Used Cars. If employees were guilty of tax evasion and embezzlement she would find out when she studied the accounts.

"Sure is too bad about Frank Lemon," Gertie said as she smoothed a recalcitrant strand of dark hair back into the no-nonsense bun that rested on the nape of her neck.

"I'll bet his wife and daughter are beside themselves. Frank handled all the business. Ima and Loraine won't know where to start. I guess they'll have to rely on Ernie to manage the dealership."

Ima Lemon? Catchy name, thought Amanda. She would stop by to offer condolences to the family—and see what turned up.

Gertie waved a form—in triplicate—at Amanda. "Just sign your John Henry on the dotted line. It's just a formality that states that you returned the U-Haul in good condition," she explained. "I was reluctant when Thaddeus decided to add the U-Haul trailers to our service station business, but we've made decent money from the franchise."

Gertie frowned thoughtfully. "That reminds me, I need to call Ernie to check on the U-Haul truck Frank rented. Frank made arrangements to lease the truck on a monthly basis, for short runs and overnight business trips. I better check on it now that Frank is gone."

"Why did Frank need a U-Haul?" Amanda asked.

Gertie shrugged. "I don't know. Maybe he used it to haul inoperative cars he purchased. After that Ryder truck was used to blow up the Murrah building in Oklahoma City, franchises have tried to be more careful about who leases what. I guess I should have inquired about Frank's U-Haul. Never can be too cautious, I suppose."

Amanda supposed Gertrude Thatcher was right. That tragic explosion in the city was a hard lesson to learn.

Tucking the carbon-copy receipt in her purse, Amanda strode off to pay Thaddeus for her fuel. As she drove away from the station she saw Deputy Payne parked in the lot at Last Chance Cafe. She had the unmistakable feeling that this supposed investigation Payne was conducting would be filled with fictitious facts which would facilitate his reassignment as interim police chief in Vamoose.

The man didn't seem to be doing more than making

his presence known in town, thought Amanda. Payne certainly wasn't buzzing around, interviewing people who could attest to Frank's drinking and health problems.

Forget about Payne-in-the-butt, Amanda scolded herself. Do the job Thorn asked you to do. Payne will get what he deserves in due time.

Nobody messed with Amanda Hazard's man and had the chance to boast about it!

Three

Under the pretense of looking for another truck to replace the one totaled in Frank's wreck, Amanda pulled into Lemon's Used Cars. Freddy Lassiter was sprawled beneath a Buick LeSabre, repairing malfunctioning parts. Ernie Niles, dressed in Dockers and a cream-colored Polo shirt, was showing a fiery-red sports car to an elderly man.

Amanda took a closer look, stunned to realize that her client, Leon Pike, had entered his second childhood. What did Leon need with a flashy sports car, in which the cramped space would cause his arthritis to flare up?

"You won't find a better deal anywhere on a car like this," Ernie insisted as he opened the door and gestured toward the plush red leather interior. "This little beauty has power and style written all over it, Leon."

Yes, and Ernie Niles had Sales Shark written all over him, thought Amanda. He had no business trying to sell that sports car to Leon. The old man would never be able to crawl from the bucket seat. Besides that, Leon couldn't afford that racy hot rod, not on his fixed income. Amanda knew that for a fact, because she handled Leon's income taxes.

Just what kind of operation did Ernie have going here? she wondered. According to Thorn, Lemon was a shyster. Ernie Niles appeared to be no better than his father-in-law.

He didn't care about his clients, only about making a profitable sale.

"Hi, Leon," Amanda called out, then waved in enthusiastic greeting. "Are you car shopping, too?"

The gray-haired man pivoted and stared at her through his thick glasses. "Ernie thinks I'd look good in this sports car."

Amanda asserted herself in her client's behalf. "I think you would be happier with that four-door sedan." She gestured to a more suitable car on the lot. "Better leave that cramped little model to the younger crowd, Leon. There won't be room for the passengers you like to drive to the bingo parlor in Adios every Thursday night."

Leon rubbed his chin pensively. "Never thought about that."

Ernie glowered at Amanda for interfering with his sale.

Amanda ignored him as she curled her hand around Leon's frail arm. "Now here's a car that you and your friends could sit in comfortably." She escorted him toward the bronze-colored Oldsmobile. "The price on the windshield is an important consideration, too," she added tactfully.

"Ernie said that was an old man's car, a man much older than my years," Leon repeated.

Leon was in his late seventies—very late seventies. Truth be known, the old man probably didn't need to be behind the steering wheel at all. Fortunately, this senior citizen only made short trips to the store, to church, and to the bingo parlor. How was Amanda going to remind Leon that he was getting on in years without offending his pride?

"I think it all boils down to taste and practicality," Amanda said. "You should buy what suits your needs. Take me for instance, I own a Toyota that was left over from my days of working and driving in the city. Now that I live in Vamoose, and travel gravel roads, I need a vehicle that suits my present situation. This car"—she pointed to the four-door sedan—"satisfies the needs of a man who carries passengers his own age."

Leon studied the car for a long moment, then nodded his head. "Gimme the keys, Ernie. I want to try out this car."

Scowling, Ernie produced the keys. When Leon drove off at a whopping ten miles an hour, Ernie rounded on Amanda. "I would appreciate it if you would let me handle the sales around here. This is my business operation, not yours."

Amanda's brows furrowed disapprovingly. "As I recall, this is still Frank's business. Out of respect for your departed boss, and father-in-law, I'm surprised you didn't have the decency to close down for a few days. If I didn't know better, I would say that you're glad Frank is gone for good."

Ernie puffed up like a disturbed toad. "How dare you say that! Frank and I got along famously."

"No, you didn't," she contradicted. "I was here yesterday when the two of you were biting each other's heads off. Frank told me he would like to be rid of you and Irene Pratt, so don't try to feed me a crock of bull."

Ernie assumed the same argumentative stance he had taken yesterday, while doing verbal battle with Frank. "What are you implying here, Hazard? That I'm somehow responsible for Frank's fatal accident? Well, it's not so. When Deputy Payne came by to question me—"

Damn, thought Amanda. Leave it to Payne to interview people who could produce the kind of conclusions the deputy was after. Ernie probably had a lot to hide and he would be willing and eager to place the blame on Thorn.

"I told Payne that Frank wasn't behaving any differently than usual. He was the same yesterday as he was last week," Ernie insisted.

"So you're saying that you and Frank had the same

argument yesterday that you had last week? The one about firing Irene for incompetence?"

The question caught Ernie off guard. His mouth opened and shut like a rural mailbox. When he finally recovered his composure, he glowered at Amanda.

"Now, hold it right there, Hazard. I know about your reputation, don't think I don't. When somebody dies around here, you start looking for opportunity and motive. Only this time you are looking to lay the blame everywhere except at Thorn's feet. Payne told me that you and Thorn were in the squad car that caused Frank to lose control of his truck and plunge into the river. If you hadn't hounded Frank, he would still be alive."

Amanda was going to choke Payne for planting those thoughts in Ernie's head. It was just as she suspected. That conniving deputy was leading witnesses in order to acquire the conclusions he wanted.

"I was there, Ernie, you weren't," she told him. "Frank was driving down the gravel road in front of my house like a maniac. When he spotted Thorn's squad car, he took off like a tornado. As I see it, Frank's conflict with you, a member of his family and his business associate, led to his untimely death. You and Irene put that bottle in his hand and his heavy foot on the accelerator by upsetting him with arguments."

"What do you mean *me and Irene?*" he huffed.

Amanda took a mental step backward. Ernie's defensive reaction caused suspicion to float to the top of her mind. Was something going on here that she didn't know about?

"I think I'll have a word with Irene," Amanda said, spinning on her boot heels.

Ernie grabbed her arm to detain her. "You leave Irene out of this, you hear me, Hazard?"

"Why should I?" she countered, worming her arm loose. "Irene's incompetence with registration forms and accounting ledgers was giving Frank fits. He told me so himself."

"Irene is not incompetent!" he all but shouted.

Amanda studied the car dealer for a ponderous moment. What was it that he didn't want her to know?

When Leon Pike returned to the lot, Amanda saw her chance to skedaddle. "I'm sure you'll want to talk to Leon about the sedan," she said as she wheeled away.

"You leave Irene alone," Ernie hissed at Amanda's retreating back.

Amanda didn't heed the warning. She made a beeline toward the metal office building.

Amanda grabbed the doorknob, then glanced over her shoulder to see Ernie scurrying toward the bronze sedan. No doubt, this would be the quickest car deal Ernie ever made—and the best deal Leon would get. Ernie was anxious to conclude the deal so he could rush into the office to protect Irene from Amanda.

Intent on making good use of the few moments of privacy Ernie would allow, Amanda breezed into the office to see Irene applying a fresh coat of lipstick. What had happened to the last coat? Amanda wondered.

She was beginning to have serious suspicions about the nature of the relationship between Ernie and Irene. Very serious suspicions.

"May I help you?" Irene asked as she shoved the tube of lipstick into her purse, then dropped it into the bottom desk drawer.

Amanda couldn't see the contents of that bottom drawer, but she assumed it held Irene's personal belongings. Amanda would like to take a gander at that particular drawer. She might turn up some interesting information for this case.

She glanced speculatively at Ernie's desk, wondering if his bottom drawer was also reserved for personal items—say a stack of contraceptives for those spontaneous moments of privacy, while Frank was out drinking and driving?

Is that why Ernie was dead-set on keeping Irene at the office? Did Frank suspect his son-in-law was cheating on his daughter? And was the turmoil of dealing with his two-t—?

Amanda's thoughts screeched to a halt. She recalled what Frank started to say yesterday, while she was test driving Big Red. Frank had said "two—" and then slammed his mouth shut. He must have meant to say: two-timing son-in-law. He must have known that Irene and Ernie were having an affair. At the very least, he must have suspected it.

Having once been the victim of a two-timing husband herself, Amanda was extremely sensitive to the subject. As far as she was concerned, wedding vows were sacred. Anyone who fooled around and committed the cardinal sin did not deserve her respect. Amanda wasn't going to cut this sexpot secretary any slack whatsoever.

"Yes, you can help me," Amanda said. "I'm curious to know if your affair with Ernie was the real reason Frank wanted to fire you. Or if it was the combination of your incompetence in bookkeeping and immoral conduct that compelled him to let you go?"

Irene's face paled beneath the thick coat of Estée Lauder makeup. The only visible color was the cherry-red lipstick she had recently applied.

Bullseye, thought Amanda. Her first torpedo scored a direct hit. Irene wasn't incensed by the question, she was shocked.

"I—" Irene's breath came out in hitches, making it impossible for her to speak. "I—" Her second attempt also failed.

"I'm sure you are relieved that Frank is no longer around to threaten your job security. In fact, I wonder if you and Ernie didn't conspire to drive him to drink, especially when you knew he was popping blood pressure pills at alarming intervals. You expected him to kick off sometime soon, didn't you?"

Amanda wished she had cut her long spiel shorter, for Ernie came through the door in time to catch the drift of her accusations. His face flamed with fury as he stalked over to take a defensive stance behind Irene, whose complexion was still the color of vanilla yogurt.

"I told you to lay off, Hazard," Ernie gritted between clenched teeth. "I will not have you flinging unfounded accusations at Irene. She has nothing to do with Frank's unfortunate death. You're simply trying to divert blame away from you and Thorn, is all. It's *your* fault Frank is dead, not ours. *You* caused it!"

His arm shot toward the door. "Now get the hell out of here before I call Deputy Payne to have you escorted off my property."

Amanda strode across the small office, then paused at the door. "One more question," she insisted. "You were well aware that Frank had been drinking heavily and you knew that he had been stopped and reprimanded by Thorn. If you weren't hoping your father-in-law would wrap his truck around a tree, or nose-dive into the river, why didn't you offer to drive him home from work? Didn't your after-business-hours activities allow time for that?"

Ernie's face exploded with so much color that Amanda swore he would burst an artery. "Get out and stay out!" he bellowed at her.

Amanda got out, but she knew she had only just begun to explore the activities of Ernie Niles and Irene Pratt. In fact, she was going to consult Vamoose's most reliable gossip. Velma, the gum-chewing beautician, knew the background of every citizen in the county. Amanda would get the scoop on Ernie and Irene, and everyone else who associated with Frank Lemon.

"I decided to buy the sedan," Leon Pike said as he passed Amanda on his way into the office.

"Wise choice," Amanda complimented.

"I got one heck of a deal, too." Leon beamed in satisfaction. "Ernie took my first offer."

Amanda wasn't surprised to hear that. The car dealer was in a flaming rush to protect Irene from Amanda's grilling interview. Before long, she would have enough information to convince the sheriff that it was stress and strain in Frank's personal and professional life that had provoked him to attempt to outrun Thorn . . .

Amanda pulled up short when she recalled something Thorn had said to her during their high-speed chase down gravel roads.

What the hell's wrong with Frank? Does he think I don't know where he lives?

That question hounded Amanda all afternoon, while she caught up on her bookwork in the office, checked on Pops, and placed a call to the medical examiner. Why hadn't Frank pulled over when he saw Thorn's flashing lights? As Thorn also said: "There was nowhere for Frank to run."

Something didn't add up here. Being a conscientious accountant, Amanda could never be satisfied unless things *did* add up logically and correctly. She had the instinctive feeling that there was more to this case than met the eye—and she would dig it out, one buried clue at a time.

Amanda glanced at her watch, then stared out the office window that gave her an unimpeded view of Lemon's Used Cars. It was 6:15. Irene Pratt had driven off a few minutes earlier. Ernie Niles slipped into a nondescript Chevy that was lined up on the second row of cars. He halted the car long enough to lock the iron gate before he drove away.

Grabbing her purse, Amanda headed for the door. She intended to see if Ernie was going straight home from the office—or making a detour.

Following at an inconspicuous distance, Amanda watched Ernie cruise north of town, then circle back from the west. Sure enough, he pulled up beside Irene's car in the driveway of a modest brick home on the edge of town. Ernie glanced this way and that before he strode quickly toward the front door.

Amanda smiled craftily. At 6:15 tomorrow, she would be waiting to see if this was a daily ritual for Ernie and Irene.

Amanda had the unshakable feeling that Ernie was in the habit of going to bed long before he went home to his wife.

"Hi, hon," chomp, pop. "Long time, no see! How was your vacation?"

Amanda smiled at Velma Hertzog who stood behind The Chair in the beauty shop. Velma was rolling up Millicent Patch's wiry gray hair.

"My vacation was a welcome change after income tax season." Amanda took a seat beside the wooden rack that held a variety of fashion magazines. "Pops found all sorts of antiques to refinish."

Champing on her chewing gum, Velma stared at Amanda's reflection in the mirror. When the Amazon beautician's gaze landed on Amanda's left hand, her fake-lashed eyes widened. "You have the ring back! Thank goodness. I knew you and Nicky were meant for each other.

"You've always been Vamoose's favorite couple." Velma glanced over at her niece who was sorting rollers by size. "Haven't they, Bev?"

"Like, sure!" Beverly Hill enthused. "Aunt Velma and

I were, like, so excited about helping with your wedding plans. And like, poof, the engagement was off. Bummer!"

"So . . ." Velma smacked her gum, her mascara-fringed gaze glittering with anticipation. "When is the big day? You have set a date this time, haven't you?"

All three women in the salon targeted Amanda with gazes as intense as patriot missiles. Amanda went out on a limb without consulting Thorn first. "We're getting married in two weeks. We'll squeeze in the ceremony between Thorn's hay cuttings and wheat harvest."

"Two weeks!" Bev hooted. "Like, Aunt Velma and I will have to get it in gear. We want to have everything just perfect for your reception. Wow, there's tons of stuff to do!"

"That isn't necessary—" Amanda was cut off at the pass.

"Now don't you worry about a thing, hon," snap, crunch. "Why shoot, we have been looking forward to planning your reception. The decorations we made for your shower will be nothing compared to your reception."

"And like, we need to plan Nicky's bachelor party, too," Bev threw in. "We gotta do everything like right, ya know. Can't forget the bachelor party."

"I think Thorn can plan his own b—" Again, Amanda was allowed to wedge in only a few words before her self-appointed wedding consultants interrupted.

"That's right!" Pop, pop. "Gotta have a wingding for Nicky. It's tradition."

Amanda inwardly cringed. She wasn't sure she could convince Thorn to attend a party that and Velma arranged, even if he was the guest of honor. As for Mother, she had had a conniption over the creative decorations at the wedding shower. Amanda shuddered to imagine what Bev and Velma would dream up for the reception.

"Okay, Millie, time to stick you under the dryer." Velma stamped on the lever, returning The Chair to floor level.

"You got any of that hypo-allergenic hair spray, Velma?" Millie asked as she hoisted herself from The Chair, then rearranged her polyester skirt and knee-high pantyhose. "My scalp has been itching something fierce this week."

Velma smacked her gum and smiled. Her full jowls folded up like an accordion. "You bet, Mill. You should have said something earlier. I've got some of that scented herbal conditioner." Her gaze swerved to Amanda. "Matter of fact, I think I'll try it out that experimental stuff on Amanda. She's always a good sport about letting Bev and me experiment on her."

Amanda inwardly shuddered. She had walked out of Beauty Boutique with so many cosmetic disasters that it didn't bear thinking about.

All in the name of scaring up vital facts, Amanda told herself. Velma gestured her toward The Chair. Like a condemned prisoner, Amanda walked over and sat down.

Velma studied Amanda's reflection, then reached out with her meaty hands to rake Amanda's blond hair behind her ears. "What do you think, Bev?" Crackle, snap.

Bev nodded. Her black, Shirley Temple curls bobbed around her plump face like fishing corks. "Yeah, go for something radical. With Amanda's great face and figure, she can wear the latest 'do. We should try out some of that colored glitter again. Like, we have to have the exact match for the signature colors for her wedding."

Amanda groaned to herself. She was doomed to passion pink and Prussian purple.

In a flurry, Bev rustled up the experimental herbal conditioner and dumped it on Amanda's head. God, the stuff smelled like boiled turnips and it made her head burn like fire!

"Stop!" Amanda threw up her hands before Bev could pour another glob of the fizzy solution on her head.

Dumbfounded, Bev and Velma stared at Amanda while she blotted her head with a towel.

"What's wrong?" Velma asked.

"This stuff burns! Do something!"

"Bev, get me a can of Coke. Fast!" Crack, chomp.

Velma grabbed the towel from Amanda and hurriedly blotted the fizzy conditioner. "Mercy, girl, you're really having a reaction."

Velma swiped the cola from Bev the instant she was within arm's reach. Hurriedly, the beautician dumped the soft drink on Amanda's head. For several agonizing minutes the alkali and acid-base solutions battled to neutralize each other. In horror, Amanda watched bubbles burst around her. The pungent smell had her gasping for breath.

"Dang, I haven't seen a severe reaction like this since I can't remember when." Pop, pop. "I guess I better send this case of conditioner back to the manufacturer. Can't have my patrons walking out of here with scalded scalps."

Velma spun The Chair around, then tilted Amanda backward over the sink to douse her head with cold water. The spray soothed the sensation of acid eating away her scalp.

Amanda decided, there and then, that she was going to get every scrap of background information she wanted about Frank Lemon in exchange for all the trouble and pain she had already undergone. This visit to Velma's Beauty Boutique was not going to be a waste of valuable time.

"I guess you heard about Frank Lemon," Amanda said as Velma wheeled her around to face the mirror.

Crackle, snap. "Sure did. Can't believe the sheriff's department relieved Nicky from his duties over that incident. What can that wool-brained sheriff be thinking? He knows Nicky is a damn fine cop—pardon my French."

Velma massaged Amanda's blistered scalp. "Nicky has a perfect record, at least he did until that snooty Deputy Payne showed up. Why, that scamp threatened to arrest me for jaywalking when I hurried over to Last Chance Cafe for my morning cup of coffee! He talked to me like I was an underling in his military squad!"

"Like, my mama said she knew Joe Payne in high school," Bev spoke up, while she scooped up a bottle of fluorescent pink nail polish. "Mama went: 'Joe had his sights set on being a millionaire by the time he was thirty, but since he couldn't make it in his first year of college he joined the army.' "

Amanda filed away the information. She decided Deputy Payne-in-the-butt had been suffering delusions of grandeur since his adolescent years.

"I can't say I'm surprised Frank Lemon ended up the way he did." Velma chewed her gum vigorously as she combed Amanda's wet hair. "He had been hitting the sauce so heavily lately that he was bound to hurt himself. Lucky that he didn't take anybody else with him when he went."

"I'm sure his wife and daughter are all broke up over it," Amanda put in. "According to Gertrude Thatcher, neither woman was familiar enough with Frank's business dealings to assume control of the car dealership."

Bev looked at Velma, who looked at Bev. Then they stared at Amanda and bit back grins.

Amanda frowned. "Am I missing something here? What is it?"

"Like, you must not know Ima Lemon and her daughter Loraine very well."

"No, not personally," Amanda admitted. She gripped the arms of The Chair when Velma tugged the tangles from her hair.

"Well, I'm here to tell ya that is one screwball family." Pop, snap. "This is Frank and Ima's second marriage. Ima was married to Frank's older brother and Frank was married to Ima's younger sister. Fact is, Loraine should be

Frank's niece, except she isn't, if you catch the way I'm drifting."

Amanda's eyes popped. "So Frank got Ima pregnant while she was married to his brother?"

All this time Amanda had been feeling sorry for Frank, who implied that his son-in-law was two-timing his only daughter. Apparently, Frank Lemon was an expert at two-timing, that old coot!

Had Frank been fooling around with other women when he made his overnight trips with the U-Haul truck he rented from Thatcher's Oil and Gas? Amanda wondered. If Frank had cheated on his first wife, why should Amanda be surprised if he did the same thing to his second wife?

"Mama says she is waiting to see if Ima and Floyd Lemon get back together now that Frank is out of the picture." Bev pulled up a stool and lowered her plump body down beside Amanda. While she applied nail polish remover to Amanda's hands, she sadly shook her head. "Mama went: 'Just you wait and see, girl. Ima's sister is gonna have another reason not to speak to her double relatives. Sally Jean is gonna get the shaft, sure as shootin'.' "

No wonder Frank was drinking heavily, thought Amanda. The man's personal and professional life were in a constant state of upheaval. Frank's *sister-in-law* was his *ex-wife,* and his *brother-in-law* was his *brother.* Holy cow, the Lemon family reunions must be sour occasions, she mused.

"Ima Lemon has been buzzing around town in her Cadillac, making the final arrangements." Pop, crackle. "With all this turmoil I'm sure she is in a real tizzy." Velma scooped up her scissors and snipped hair from the crown of Amanda's head. "Then there's that affair that Ernie and Irene don't think anybody knows about." She snickered wryly. "Don't know who those two clowns think they're fooling. Certainly not me. Ernie drives a different car to Irene's house every night after work so they can do the horizontal macarena."

Amanda brushed away the clump of hair that fluttered onto the tip of her nose. She was too intent on gathering facts about the Lemon clan to notice that Velma had chopped off two inches of her hair. "Does Ernie's wife know what is going on behind her back?"

Again, Bev and Velma stared at her, then grinned.

"What?" Amanda demanded impatiently.

Millie leaned out from under the dryer to put in her two cents' worth. Obviously, none of this conversation had escaped her rabbit ears. "Didn't you ever wonder how Deputy Joe Payne knew his way around Vamoose so well? It wasn't just because he was anxious to be back in his hometown. He has been substituting for Nick and Benny Sykes, just to make extra money by pulling night duty.

"My dear Henry, God rest his gentle soul, would have had a hissy if he had seen the deputy's car parked at Loraine's house. He would have turned Joe in so fast that it would have made his swelled head spin like a top!

"Loraine was my granddaughter's best friend in high school," Millie continued. "And just look how Loraine turned out! Of course, with that girl's mixed up family tree sprouting extra branches, it's no wonder."

Amanda's jaw dropped open, despite the flutter of hair that drifted around her, despite the thick coat of fluorescent pink nail polish Bev applied to her right hand.

"How long has this affair between Ernie and Irene been going on?" Amanda asked.

"Right after that hot-to-trot divorcée moved into town." Chomp, snap. "Ernie hired Irene while Frank was on one of his overnight business trips to buy cars from the jobbers in Oklahoma and Texas. Word around town is that Irene can only type fifteen words a minute, if you don't count the mistakes."

"Fifteen words a minute?" Amanda echoed.

"Yeah, like that would have gotten her an F in my high-school typing class," Bev spoke up. "Like, Irene never gets in a rush about anything. She doesn't want to chip her nails on the computer keyboard."

Amanda was incensed. Considering the information she had gleaned about the Lemon family, she was beginning to think Frank's nose-dive into the river might have been suicidal, prompted by the stressful, traumatic events of his life.

As for Deputy Joe Payne, he had several motives for wanting to pin wrongdoing on Thorn. The deputy was involved up to his eyeballs, and he had plenty of incentive for wanting to make Vamoose his turf. If Payne was fooling around with Loraine Niles, while investigating Frank's death, Payne would see to it that Thorn was permanently dismissed from his patrol duties.

That was *not* going to happen, or her name wasn't Amanda Hazard! She would prepare such a detailed profile of Frank's mental and physical condition on the night of his death that the sheriff would have to drop Payne's trumped-up charges of unprofessional conduct. And while she was at it, she would expose Payne for what he was . . .

Amanda's vindictive thoughts scattered when she glanced into the mirror to see that Velma had sheared her hair like sheep wool. Amanda doubted she could get a curling iron around these shingled layers of hair. And worse, there wasn't enough hair left on her head to conceal the blisters left by Velma's experimental, scalp-eating conditioner. She looked like a side-show circus freak! Amanda had no choice but to wear a wedding veil to cover this latest cosmetic catastrophe!

"Bring me that tinted spray," Velma requested of Bev.

"I don't—" Amanda tried to protest.

"It'll look great. Trust me." Pop, crackle.

Amanda almost never trusted anybody who said: Trust me.

"But, Velma—"

Amanda clamped her mouth shut when Bev squirted the tinted spray on her head. Sticky particles drifted over Amanda, gluing her damp hair in place instantly. A putrid color—somewhere between pink and purple—clung to the traumatized strands of Amanda's hair. She wouldn't be surprised if the brittle strands fell like dandruff on her shoulders . . .

And then Velma sprayed glitter. Lord, have mercy! Amanda looked like a third-rate prostitute.

Thorn was going to blow a fuse.

No, he wouldn't, Amanda assured herself. Thorn had asked her to use her unorthodox methods of investigation to clear his name. If she had to deal with this cosmetic calamity, then so did Thorn.

Velma used a hair pick to add fullness to the outrageous 'do and smiled cheerily at Amanda's reflection in the mirror. "This 'do is on the house." Crackle, snap. "It's the least I can do after I fried your scalp with that new conditioner. And don't you worry about the tint. Bev and I will have the color perfected before we give you your wedding 'do."

Amanda hoisted herself away from The Chair and struggled to keep her feet. She couldn't take her eyes off the freak blonde who was staring back at her from the mirror.

"And like, don't worry about the wedding reception, either," Bev insisted. "We'll keep the price of decorations, napkins, cake and plastic eating utensils within a modest budget. My dad's sister runs the Pronto floral shop. Aunt June Marie Flowers will let us buy your bouquet and boutonnières at discount rates."

"June Marie *Flowers* owns the *floral* shop?" Amanda asked.

Bev bobbed her head. "Sure does. Aunt Velma and I will take care of everything, Amanda. All you have to do is show up."

"You *will* show up, won't you, hon?" Velma's unblinking gaze zeroed in on Amanda. "You missed your wedding shower. But considering the circumstances, that was understandable. Disappointing for us, but understandable. But leaving poor Nicky standing at the altar would be unforgivable."

Amanda tried to assure the beautician and her sidekick that she wouldn't stand up Thorn, but her vocal apparatus shut down the moment her stunned gaze leaped from her horrendous hairdo to her painted fingernails. Bev, in another of her faddish frenzies, had painted pig faces on the pink polish. Ten little piggies stared back at Amanda.

Dazed, Amanda wobbled to the door. Bruno barked as she approached the car. Her self-appointed bodyguard, who had insisted on coming along for the ride this morning, didn't seem to recognize her.

"It's only me, pal," Amanda said as she opened the door.

When she plunked onto the seat, Bruno whined, then lay down on his mat.

"Did you change your mind about going everywhere I go?"

Amanda wondered if Bruno was ready to resign from his position. The dog kept staring cautiously at her, and he didn't wag his bobbed tail.

When Deputy Payne cruised past, Amanda dismissed her frustration with her outlandish 'do and shoved the Toyota into gear. It was nearly noon. She was going to follow Payne—at an inconspicuous distance—to see where he went for his lunch break.

Amanda glanced at the parking lot of Last Chance Cafe, noting the new sign that read: Food is our Specialty. She watched Ernie and Irene stroll toward the restaurant. Amanda noticed that Deputy Payne stared at the couple for a long moment before he drove off.

Amanda didn't have to be clairvoyant to guess where

Deputy Payne was headed, now that Ernie was in the cafe and the coast was clear.

Sure enough, Payne turned off onto the gravel road and drove toward the five-acre estate southwest of Vamoose. Loraine Niles, dressed in a string bikini, was sunbathing on the front lawn. She waved enthusiastically when Payne pulled into her driveway.

Amanda had the sneaking suspicion that Joe and Loraine had every intention of giving new meaning to "Let's do lunch" together.

Amanda debated whether or not to let Payne know she was wise to his activities. Pensively, she grabbed the notepad in her purse to jot down the time and place of this—whatever.

Better to hit Payne with both barrels in a surprise attack, she decided. She would document his activities and present them to the sheriff at an opportune moment. No sense giving Payne the chance to rehearse excuses or dream up alibis to cover the "nooner" he was having with Ernie Niles' skimpily clad wife.

Four

Reversing direction, Amanda drove back to town. When she saw Frank's wrecked truck sitting outside Watts's auto body shop, she acted on the impulsive urge to stop. There probably wasn't a single clue to be found in Big Red, but Amanda had vowed to leave no stone unturned in her crusade to clear Thorn of wrongdoing.

Leaving Bruno in the car, Amanda strode around to the front of the truck. The grill assembly was bashed in, the hood was wired shut, and dried moss clung to the dented bumper. The excessive number of scratches had peeled the paint off the passenger door. Amanda opened the door, noting that the hinges had been sprung during the wreck. The door popped and creaked like arthritic joints as she pulled it open wide to survey the sand particles that had settled on the floorboard.

The cigar was still lying on the floor beside the empty bottle of Jack Daniel's. The capsules of blood pressure pills, which Frank kept in his pocket, were wedged beside the seat belt. Amanda picked up the prescription, noting that it had been filled two days before Frank's accident. Yet, there were only six capsules in the plastic bottle.

Hmm . . . Frank must have been popping those pills like breath mints.

"Hi, 'Manda. Come to see what's left of the truck you wanted to buy?"

Amanda pivoted to see Cleatus Watts ambling from the automotive repair shop. His brother, Cecil, appeared from the adjoining auto body shop. A mist of blue paint clung to his hair and powdered his nose. He had that dazed look that indicated he had been overcome by paint fumes while working on a horse trailer.

Cecil shook his head in dismay, then lit a cigarette as he appraised the red, extended cab truck. "Dunno why Ernie insists on having this truck back at the lot. Isn't of much use, unless he plans to strip parts." Cecil blew a smoke ring in the warm spring air as he moseyed toward Amanda. "Can't imagine that you would have wanted to buy this truck in the first place."

Amanda frowned at the comment. Why wouldn't she want this gorgeous, powerful, extended-cab pickup truck? It was the cat's meow, as far as pickups went.

Cleatus strolled up beside Cecil, then motioned for Amanda to take a closer look at the scraped paint on the lower portion of the passenger door. "See this? This truck was originally two-toned black and gray."

Amanda silently fumed. Frank had never once mentioned that he had painted his truck.

" 'Course, I wouldn't have minded that state-of-the-art stereo and equalizer installed in this truck," Cecil said before he took another long draw on his cigarette. "But it isn't standard equipment on this model of Chevy truck. Looks to me like the radio came from a plush Caddy."

Amanda's irritation mounted. Frank Lemon had left her with the impression that this truck was a factory-direct, without customized alterations. Apparently, Frank had customized the truck for his private use and had planned to pawn it off on Amanda The Sucker.

No doubt Freddy Lassiter, the mechanic at Lemon's Used Cars, could verify the changes made in Big Red. Frank must have switched the radio in his wife's Caddy and added the paint job . . .

Amanda's thoughts trailed off when she glanced at the interior of the truck. Her gaze lingered on the steering wheel. The hair stood up on the back of her neck when she realized the wheel was tilted to the "down" position.

"Cecil, did you change the tilt on this steering wheel when you hauled it back to town?"

Cecil blinked. "Who me? No, I haven't messed with this truck, except to haul it here to be impounded, just like the chief told me to do."

Amanda strode around to open the door to the driver's side. An uneasy sensation trickled down her spine as she stared at the steering wheel. How could Frank Lemon have wedged his barrel-shaped belly under the wheel without tilting it upward? She knew he kept it up, because she had moved the wheel to the "down" position before she took the truck for a test drive. She had also seen Frank lift up the steering wheel of her Toyota before he took it for a spin.

How could Frank have squeezed beneath the steering wheel, while driving ninety miles an hour down rough country roads at night? she asked herself. If he had forgotten to change the tilt after Amanda drove the truck, it was little wonder that Frank swerved all over the road and veered down the steep incline to the river.

"Something wrong, 'Manda?" Cecil asked, after watching her stare at the interior of the truck for several minutes.

"That's what I'm wondering," she murmured to herself.

Amanda turned to meet Cleatus and Cecil's curious gazes. "Do me a favor, guys. When you have time, give this truck a thorough going over. If there is anything—besides a radio—that isn't standard equipment, and a coat of paint that wasn't factory-issued, I want to know about it."

"Sure thing." Cleatus tossed his cigarette butt on the ground and mashed it under his heel. "I'm kinda backed up on my work at the moment, but I'll check over the truck when I have spare time." He smiled slightly, displaying the two silver caps on his teeth. "Nice hairdo. I like a woman who isn't afraid to experiment with new looks."

"Ditto, 'Manda," Cecil chimed in.

"Thanks, fellas. I appreciate your efforts to make me feel better about my disastrous 'do." With a wave of farewell, Amanda walked back to her Toyota, wondering if there wasn't more to this case than she originally thought. The downward tilt of the steering wheel had sent her intuitive suspicions into full-scale riot.

Why would a man who had to shift the tilt on a steering wheel—out of necessity—neglect to change the position before cruising around the countryside? It made no sense. And what about the brakes on the truck? she wondered. Could someone have tampered with them? The brakes had functioned properly during Amanda's test drive, but the accident had occurred several hours later.

Amanda stared down the street, watching Lemon's multicolored banners flap in the breeze. Supposedly Freddy Lassiter had checked over the truck the night Frank died. Maybe he had found the brakes faulty—or maybe he had tampered with . . .

Wheeling around, Amanda clambered into her car. It was time she had a little talk with Lemon's mechanic.

Amanda decided she must have developed a formidable reputation in Vamoose, after tracking down five previous murder suspects and ensuring justice was served, because Freddy Lassiter stared warily at her when she arrived at the car lot.

"I want to talk to you," Amanda called, before Freddy could take refuge in the shop.

"Sorry, Hazard," Freddy said as he sank down on the wooden dolly, then rolled himself beneath the Plymouth he was repairing. "I've got work to do. Besides that, Ernie Niles told me to keep my distance from you."

If this greasy-haired mechanic thought he could dismiss her that easily, he was kidding himself. Hands on hips, Amanda glanced around the shop. When she spotted an extra dolly, she strode off to retrieve it, plunked down on it, and wheeled herself beneath the car.

Freddy gaped at her. "Damn, lady, you don't give up, do you?"

"No, and any attempt to avoid me is a waste of time." Amanda closed her mouth when a drop of oil plunked on her cheek. When the oil rolled toward her lips she grabbed the grimy rag that Freddy had wrapped around his left hand. Hurriedly, she wiped her face, smearing grease from cheek to chin.

"Now, why do you suppose Ernie Niles doesn't want you to speak to me?" she asked as Freddy applied a metal wrench to a bolt that held an unidentified gizmo in place.

"I don't know. I'm only following Ernie's orders," Freddy said. He strained to loosen the rusty bolt. Muscles bulged on his arms. "Hold your breath, Hazard."

Amanda snatched a quick breath of air before Freddy scooped up the can of WD40 to blast a coat of oil on the rusty bolt.

Amanda was pretty certain the oil would settle into her hair and mingle with the pink glitter. No doubt, by the time she finished this interview, she would look worse than she already did.

"What do you call that thingamabob you're working on?" Amanda questioned as she stared at the underside of the Plymouth.

"It's the oil pan." Freddy applied muscle to loosen the bolt. "The gasket is getting old and drying out, which in turn, causes the car to leak oil. If I don't replace this seal the engine will eventually lock up."

"Do brakes malfunction without hydraulic fluid, same as engines without oil?" Amanda asked.

Freddy tilted his head sideways and stared warily at Amanda. "Sure they do. Why do you want to know? Are you thinking of becoming a mechanic?"

Amanda flashed the grease monkey a greasy smile, hoping to put the man at ease. "My inquiring mind wants to know. My inquiring mind also wants to know how many heated debates Frank and Ernie had over the fact that Irene Pratt is beating Loraine Niles' time."

Freddy scooted sideways when a stream of oil dripped on his shoulder. "Why are you dredging up stuff like that now?" he asked as he loosened the base of the seal. "If Ernie and Irene want to screw up their lives, I figure it's their business."

"Frank didn't share your live-and-let-live policy," Amanda parried. She paused, watching the speed and efficiency with which Freddy's nimble fingers worked. She was impressed. This mechanic didn't mess around. "After all, Loraine is Frank's daughter. Naturally, he would be concerned about her."

Freddy snorted as he wiggled the faulty seal, then let it drop neatly into his hand. "Save your sympathy for someone who deserves it, Hazard. In my opinion, which doesn't count for much around here, Loraine isn't concerned about what Ernie does, or who he does it with. When I see them together they aren't the least bit lovey-dovey."

"No, probably not," Amanda agreed. "Deputy Payne stopped by to see Loraine at lunch. I think they might be sharing more than a sandwich."

Startled, Freddy stared at her. "No shit?"

"No shit."

Freddy chuckled as he reached for the new seal. "So that's Payne's angle. I wondered why he was grilling me with questions about the condition of the truck Frank drove into the river. He is convinced that you and Thorn were responsible for the fatal mishap."

"And what, or who, do you think is responsible?" Amanda asked.

Freddy shrugged casually. "Payne was trying to get me to say there was nothing wrong with the truck and that your high-speed chase caused the accident."

"Did you accommodate the deputy by giving the statement he wanted to hear?"

"I had to, because it was the truth. The truck was running properly. But I did tell Payne that Frank had started drinking before noon and that he never let up while he was here. He was popping pills to beat the band, after having his second argument of the day with Ernie and Irene. It's not like that was the first time Frank went on a binge. He does it—did it—all the time."

"Did you overhear the argument?" Amanda questioned.

"While you're under here, you may as well be of some use." Freddy grabbed her hand, then placed the new flexible seal in her palm. "Shove this into the hole and hold it there while I check for gaps."

Amanda did as requested, although globs of sludge dripped onto the sleeve of her blouse. "I asked you a question, Freddy. You didn't answer me."

"Nope, I didn't hear all the specifics of the argument because I was overhauling this car. I could hear three loud voices, but I couldn't catch the gist of the conversation."

Swell, thought Amanda. It was going to take tremendous effort on her part to wheedle the truth from Ernie and Irene. She would start on Irene, she decided. The woman rattled easily. Ernie, however, was another matter. He was a salesman, and he had learned to come up with an impromptu answer for just about everything.

"So . . ." Amanda began. "What were you and Frank arguing about while I was at the car lot yesterday?"

Freddy didn't answer for a moment. He wormed and

squirmed to stick the seal tightly into place. "The usual," he said belatedly. "Frank expected me to be a miracle worker. I told him that repairs on this car would be costly, because seals needed to be replaced, the transmission is shot and the air-conditioner compressor is on its last leg."

"And Frank said . . ." She paused, waiting for him to fill in the blank.

"Frank said what he always said. He couldn't turn a profit on vehicles if I was sticking new automotive parts on them. He said I was to spiffy up the car, repair the faulty parts by rebuilding them as best I could and keep my mouth shut."

"Did you threaten to quit if Frank continued to cheat his customers?"

A guarded expression spread across Freddy's lean face. "What are you trying to do? Get me to say that I was going to quit my job and that was the reason Frank was in such a stew that he drove into the river?"

"All I'm trying to prove is that Frank Lemon worked himself into a state of duress, because of his argument with you, because of his problems with Ernie and Irene. Deputy Payne has personal reasons for wanting to lay the blame at Nick Thorn's feet. But I was in that squad car with Thorn—"

"And Payne says that's against regulations," Freddy cut in, then scooted out from under the car.

Amanda quickly followed suit. "I witnessed Frank's drunken, high-speed weave down the road," she went on determinedly. "I saw Frank defy flashing lights and a siren, saw him increase his speed and ignore stop signs. Frank resisted arrest. Thorn was only trying to pull Frank over before he injured himself or other motorists. Put quite simply, Thorn was doing his job."

"Not to hear Payne tell it," Freddy smirked.

Amanda gnashed her teeth. Before this was over, she and Payne were destined to lock horns. Amanda just hadn't decided when and where to butt heads with Payne-in-the-butt.

"Exactly what statement did you give Payne?" she demanded as she climbed to her feet.

Freddy sighed, clearly impatient with her questions. "If I tell you, will you get out of here so I can get my work done?"

"Yes," she promised.

"I told Payne that the police chief had a couple of run-ins with Frank. Thorn warned Frank that his license would be revoked and that he would be fined heavily if Frank didn't limit his drinking to the times when he wasn't driving."

"Did you tell Payne about the argument you and Frank had over replacing faulty automotive parts?"

"Nope, he didn't ask."

"I suppose Payne didn't ask about Frank's disagreements with Ernie and Irene, either," she muttered.

"Nope. Payne spoke privately with Ernie, then with Irene, but he didn't ask me about them."

Great, thought Amanda. She suspected Ernie and Irene's version of the story covered their asses from any wrongdoing. She was surprised, however, that Payne had the gumption to interview the husband of the woman he was screwing around with. That certainly said a lot about Payne, didn't it?

Amanda wiped her hands on the rag Freddy offered to her and asked, "Off the record, do you think Frank brought this disaster on himself?"

Freddy pulled a cigarette from the pocket of his T-shirt, lit up, then inhaled deeply. He blew out a steady stream of smoke. "In my opinion, Frank was on a collision course with disaster when he climbed into his truck, while heavily intoxicated. He knew Thorn was keeping tabs on him, but he shrugged it off. But that was Frank's style. He always thumbed his nose at risks. It must have been because he served in the war. Maybe he had faced danger so often back then that it no longer fazed him."

"Do you have any idea why Frank was driving by my house last night?"

Freddy shrugged. "Maybe he decided to deliver the truck after I checked it over, washed and polished it. Maybe he picked up the title from the office and decided to do the paperwork himself, since he didn't trust Irene to do it right. I didn't ask what Frank planned for the evening. It's not like we were buddies who prowled around together after work hours, you know."

"Are you the one who painted the big red truck for Frank?" she asked abruptly.

Freddy smiled wryly. "Yeah, I painted it shortly after Frank bought it. He wanted a red truck, and Frank was in the habit of getting exactly what he wanted, when he wanted it."

"What about the state-of-the-art radio equipment?" she fired at him. "Did you install that, too?"

Freddy nodded his shaggy head. "Sure I did. That's my job. I didn't always agree with Frank's policies, but I did the jobs I was paid to do."

Amanda nodded mutely as she spun toward her Toyota.

"Oh, by the way, Hazard, if you aren't going to trade cars soon, you better have your Toyota tuned up," Freddy said as he leaned leisurely against the outside of the workshop. "I'd say your fuel pump is ready to quit you. Bubba Hix, over at Thatcher's Oil and Gas, can take care of it a lot cheaper than a dealership. I wouldn't wait too long, because you could find yourself stranded beside the road. With your wild hairdo, some folks may not be too anxious to give you a lift."

Amanda rolled her eyes as she cranked the engine of her compact car. She preferred to be known for her keen intellect, not her weird 'dos. But such was the fate of an amateur gumshoe who acquired information at a beauty shop.

Since Amanda didn't have time to trade vehicles, what with wedding plans and an investigation to pursue, she decided she'd better have her Toyota repaired PDQ.

As she drove off, Ernie and Irene veered into the lot. Out of pure orneriness, Amanda waved cordially at them, but they made a spectacular display of ignoring her. She knew that would be the case. But then, she wasn't interested in winning a popularity contest with those two-timers. Soon, Ernie would be wishing he hadn't gotten crosswise with Amanda . . .

Her thoughts trailed off when she realized she had neglected to pick up Frank's accounting ledgers. Ah well, it would give her an excuse to return to the used car office, she mused as she put on her blinker and turned into Thatcher's Oil and Gas.

Nick was sweating heavily. He had discarded his shirt to catch a few sun rays while he was unloading the two-by-fours he had picked up at Pronto Lumber Company. When he heard the phone ring, he made a mad dash in the back door of his house. He picked up the call before the answering machine kicked in.

"Thorn here."

"Well, it's a good thing, because I want to talk to you, Nicky!"

Nick inwardly groaned. It was Mom and she sounded upset. "How's everything at the retirement paradise in Texas?" he asked cheerfully.

"Things are fine," Mom snapped irritably. "Dad is playing golf. I, however, just got a call from Velma Hertzog, informing me that your wedding plans were back on again. I've told you time and again that this mixed marriage isn't going to work. Big-city girls and down-home farm boys don't have anything in common."

Nick had heard that comment at least two dozen times.

"When you cross a farm boy with a city girl, who doesn't even have the courtesy and decency to show up for her own wedding shower, you've got trouble with a capital T. And if you let Velma and her dingbat niece decorate for your reception, after the ridiculous decorations they made for the shower, you can bet this wedding will be a total farce!"

"Mom, have you been taking your estrogen?" Nick asked as he ambled down the hall, with the portable phone in hand, searching for a towel to wipe off the beads of sweat.

"Don't try to blame my bad mood on hormone imbalance," she hissed in Nick's ear. "Dad and I drove all the way up from the coast to attend your wedding shower—under protest, I might add. The guest of honor, if she has any honor at all, was a no-show. For heaven's sake, Nicky! You can't possibly be serious about going through nuptial vows with that airhead you've been dating!"

"Hazard is not an airhead," Nick said. "She was unavoidably detained the day of the wedding shower."

"If you're lucky she will also be unavoidably detained the day of your wedding," Mom came back.

"Hazard will be there," he said with perfect assurance.

"Then I can only hope you have the good sense that Dad and I spent years trying to instill in you *not* to show up. We devoted half of our lives to raising you and your brother, to guiding you, hoping you would make the right decisions when you left the nest. Your poor brother went through a nasty divorce because he didn't apply common sense. I had high hopes that you would profit from Richard's blundering mistakes."

And Mom never let Rich hear the end of his unwise decision to marry a woman who bailed out when things got tough, Nick reminded himself. Damn Velma for picking up the phone and blabbing to Mom. Nick had planned to break the news to her in small doses. Mom dealt with situations better when she had ample time to adjust.

"Mom, if you'll give Hazard a chance, you can get to know her and you'll like her as much as I do."

"Like her?" Mom howled. "For heaven's sake, Nicky. We are not discussing an adolescent romance here. We are discussing the fact that you are about to legally bind yourself to a ditzy city slicker who makes it her business to snoop into everybody's finances. You have to wonder about people like that."

Nick couldn't contain his growl of annoyance. "Hazard is an accountant. It's her job to keep her clients' financial business in proper working order. You make her sound like some kind of crook. You don't even know her."

"And whose fault is that, I ask you?" Mom sniffed. "I drove up from Texas and she skipped out on the shower. And anyway, I know enough about this *Hazard*ous person to realize she isn't the right woman for you. You have a nice, respectable job as chief of police in our hometown. You're still young yet. You have plenty of time to find Miss Right."

"I may not have my job for long," Nick told her, if only to get Mom to cease harping on the subject of Hazard. "I've been temporarily relieved of duty, pending an investigation."

"WHAT!" Mom yelped. "I suppose this Hazard woman was somehow involved in the incident."

"She—"

"I knew it! Good Lord, Nicky, don't let that woman ruin your upstanding reputation. Get out while you can. Call Velma Hertzog and tell her the wedding is off."

The phone beeped, indicating a call waiting. Nick leaped at the chance to cut Mom off. "There's another call coming in," he said. "I'll talk to you later."

"But I'm not finished yet—"

"Yes, you are. 'Bye, Mom."

Nick punched the "flash" button. "Thorn here."

"Thorn, it's Hazard. Could you pick me up at Thatcher's service station? I'm having the Toyota's fuel filter replaced. Bubba said he would have to make a run to the city for a filter. He needs to keep the Toyota overnight."

"Sure thing, Hazard. I'll be there in ten minutes."

"And, Thorn?"

"Yeah, Hazard?"

"Try not to go ballistic when you see my hairdo. Remember that it is all in the name of searching for truth and redeeming your reputation as police chief."

Grimacing, Nick replaced the phone. There was no question that Hazard had gone to Beauty Boutique to wheedle information from Vamoose's most noted gossip. As usual, the appointment wrought disaster. And obviously, Velma had appointed herself to handle the wedding arrangements. Damn, Nick and Hazard should have made a pact to book a flight to Las Vegas—and keep everybody out of their marriage plans.

Hurriedly, Nick grabbed a shirt and his keys. He jogged outside to his black, four-wheel-drive truck. Quick as a wink, he sped toward town.

Nick groaned when he saw Hazard standing outside the service station. Her glittering, pink-tinted hair combined with the smears of grease on her face and clothes, indicated she'd had a busy day on the investigative trail. He cautioned himself against making sarcastic remarks that might set a fuse to Hazard's temper. After all, he reminded himself, Hazard was in pursuit of information that would reinstate him as police chief. This was not the time to criticize her unorthodox methods.

"Hi, Hazard," he said as he rolled down the window and came to a stop beside the gas pumps.

Hazard smiled and touched her hair self-consciously as she walked around the front of his truck.

"Hi, Chief!" Thaddeus waved a stubby arm as he lumbered from the station. "I hear the wedding is back on again. Sure glad about that." Thaddeus removed his ball cap, with the Thatcher Gas and Oil logo on it, and smoothed his silver hair into place. "I already bought a new suit for your wedding, and Gertrude got herself a fancy new dress. In two weeks we'll be watching you speak your vows."

"Two weeks?" Nick turned his curious gaze on Hazard as she climbed into the passenger side of his truck.

"Hope that's okay, Thorn. Velma was pressing me to set a date so she could commandeer the arrangements. I didn't have a chance to confirm it with you."

Two weeks, thought Nick. After the ups and down, ins and outs, of an off-again, on-again engagement two weeks seemed like two years. With Mom preaching gloom and doom, and Hazard's mother bending her ear about how Nick wasn't good enough for her precious, high-society daughter, all sorts of things could go wrong in the next fourteen days.

Nothing was going to go wrong, Nick promised himself. He was crazy about Hazard, even if she looked ridiculous with that mop of passion pink glitter stuck to her head and fluorescent fingernails with . . .

Nick squinted, then silently chuckled. She was sporting fingernails with piggy faces. Beverly Hill's handiwork, no doubt.

"I sure was sorry to hear about your suspension, Chief," Thaddeus commiserated. "I'm sure this misunderstanding will be resolved real soon." He propped his elbows on the edge of the open window. "So what are you doing with the spare time on your hands?"

"I'm building an addition onto my house," Nick informed him. "I decided Hazard and I needed a bedroom suite and a den." He glanced at Hazard and grinned. "I also figured Pops would prefer to stay with us rather than hoofing it back to the city. I've got room in my barn to make a workshop for his antiques."

Evidently, Hazard was pleased with the news. She flung her arms around his neck and hugged him tightly. When she retreated, Nick noticed the smudge of oil on the tip of her nose.

"That's mighty nice of you to take in this li'l girl's grandpa," Thaddeus said, smiling in approval. "And who knows? Before long, Pops might be called upon to babysit."

Nick returned Thaddeus' grin. "Yeah, who knows?"

He wouldn't mind hearing the patter of miniature Thorn feet around the house, but since he was currently unemployed, it was best if he didn't get too far ahead of himself.

"You two take care now." Thaddeus pushed himself upright, then hiked up his droopy pants. "And don't worry about that deputy who has replaced you, Chief. When Payne came around asking questions about you I told him that his theory about you causing Frank's accident was a crock of malarkey."

Nick scowled as he drove away. So Payne-in-the-ass was digging for dirt that might soil Nick's reputation, was he? Nick would like to back that manipulative deputy into a dark corner and . . .

"Don't worry about Payne," Amanda said, effectively cutting through Nick's vengeful thoughts. "He is going to have plenty to answer for when I'm through with him."

She gestured a piggy-face-tipped finger toward Last Chance Cafe. "Do you mind if we eat an early supper. I skipped lunch."

"What about Pops? Is he fending for himself tonight?"

Amanda nodded her pink head, and layers of hair

flapped like loose shingles. "Salty Marcum stopped by this afternoon to take Pops out to his farm. They are going to eat junk food and play cards."

"Glad to hear that cantankerous Vietnam vet is beginning to socialize again," Nick said as he veered into the cafe parking lot.

Amanda smiled. "Salty and Pops are good for each other. The two of them can entertain each other while I'm working on your case."

Before Amanda could climb from the truck, Nick snaked out his hand. "Don't mess with Deputy Payne," he cautioned. "I don't trust him farther than I can spit."

"I don't, either. We've got every reason not to. Guess who Payne is fooling around with while he is supposed to be keeping the police beat in Vamoose?"

"I give up. Who?"

Amanda broke into a sly smile that caused the smears of oil to form accentuated lines in her cheeks. "Loraine Niles, that's who."

Nick blinked like a prizefighter who had received a surprise right cross to the jaw. "You're kidding."

"No, and Ernie Niles is messing around with Irene Pratt after business hours. I have it all documented."

"You mean Ms. Cleavage?" Nick choked, referring to Irene. "Did Frank know about it?"

Amanda eased from the cab, then shut the door behind her. "He knew all right. It is my contention that the turmoil in Frank's personal and business life prompted his drinking. I intend to prove that Frank was so distressed that he wasn't functioning logically. He had to know that you would track him down eventually, even if he did escape arrest. It is also my belief that Frank was so stressed out that he became daring and reckless. No matter what Deputy Payne says, I will have documented interviews that contest his accusations that you mishandled the situation.

"But there is no need for you to fret over this investigation. I will have it under control before the wedding."

"Thanks, Hazard. I knew I could count on you," Nick murmured as he held open the door so Hazard could enter Last Chance Cafe.

Five

Nick skidded to a halt inside Last Chance Cafe, when he saw Sam Harjo, the new county commissioner, sitting at one of the booths. All conversation died the instant Nick and Hazard appeared in the doorway. There was no overlooking Hazard, not with her faddish 'do and grimy clothes. With her eye-catching good looks, she could stop traffic, even on her bad days—like today.

Nick watched Harjo take in Hazard's shapely figure in trim-fitting jeans. To Nick's smug pleasure, he saw Harjo wince when he noticed the ring on Hazard's left hand. The glittering diamond was back in place—a visual reminder that Harjo's quest to charm Hazard had met with complications.

"Hi, Harjo," Hazard said as she ambled past the booth.

"Hazard," Harjo said with a slight nod.

After Hazard took a seat in Nick's favorite corner booth, Nick paused beside the commish. "No hard feelings, I hope."

Harjo slid Hazard a covetous glance. Nick couldn't begrudge his worthy rival for the want of Hazard's affection. Nick knew the commish had it bad for Hazard.

"You're a lucky bastard, Lone Ranger," Harjo murmured. "But you better know, here and now, that if you don't treat that woman right, I'll be there to console her."

Nick's black diamond eyes locked with Sam's glittering

gold ones. "Don't think for even a minute that I plan to mess with the good deal I've got."

Harjo sipped his coffee, then grinned devilishly. "You screwed up once already, while Hazard was solving the Dead in the Mud Case. Do it again, and the ring on her finger will be *mine.*"

That went reasonably well, Nick thought as he strolled away. Harjo didn't like being out of the running for Hazard's attention, but at least his code of ethics were a damned sight more honorable than Deputy Payne's.

After Nick and Hazard placed their order for burgers and fries, Harley Boggs strode to their booth, sucking on a toothpick. The crusty oil-field worker nodded a greeting. "I know it is probably too late, but I want to register a complaint about Frank Lemon."

Nick saw Hazard perk up immediately. In her crusade to clear his name, she didn't even give her analytic brain time off for supper.

"What kind of complaint do you have against Frank?" Hazard asked.

Harley eased down on the red vinyl seat, then propped his elbows on the table. "I don't like to be conned," he grumbled, "especially when it costs me hard-earned money. Working oil rigs is dangerous business, and I earn every red-necked cent I make. Frank Lemon set me up with a truck that didn't even make it to the rig south of Pronto. I had to walk back to town."

"Did you air your complaint to Frank?" Hazard wanted to know.

"Damned right I did. I told that SOB that I wanted my money back and he said I bought the truck 'as is' and I was out of luck."

"Frank's mechanic confided that Frank was notorious for saving money by refusing to replace worn parts," Hazard said. "When did you confront Frank?"

"Two days ago." Harley slouched in the seat. "But don't

think I'm the only one who had a beef against Lemon. The customer I met on my way into the office looked mad enough to spit tacks."

"Did you know the irate customer?" Nick questioned.

Harley nodded his bushy blond head. "It was Lester Higgins from down Pronto way. Seems he bought a sports car for his kid. The car blew the engine on the drive home. Talk about furious! Lester was swearing a blue streak when he burst out of the office door. He threatened to extract the price of the car from Frank's chubby hide if he didn't make good. Frank popped one of his pills and told Lester to get lost."

"Did Lester get lost?" Hazard wanted to know.

Harley grinned, exposing his horse-like teeth. "You mean before or after he grabbed his kid's baseball bat from the trunk of his car and bashed in the hood of a nearby Mercury?"

Hazard leaned forward, all ears—and they definitely showed, because of her cropped hairdo. "Did you witness this incident?"

"Yep," Harley confirmed. "Hell, if I had had a bat handy, I would have helped Lester smash a whole row of used cars."

"How did Frank retaliate?" Nick asked.

Harley settled back to pick his teeth. "I thought Frank was going to burst a blood vessel. His face exploded with color when he stalked toward Lester. I let them battle for control of the bat for a couple of minutes before I stepped between them. The way ole Frank was huffing and puffing I was afraid he would have a heart attack before I had my chance to lay into him."

Sliding sideways, Harley hauled himself to his feet. "I gotta get back to my oil rig. I wanted you to know that I'm planning to file a claim against Frank's estate, and so is Lester."

After Harley galumphed away Hazard stared somberly

at Nick. "Sounds as if Frank had several stress-filled days. I plan to write up Harley's account for my report. Just relax, Thorn. I keep telling you that I've got this situation under control."

Nick reckoned she did. Hazard's unfaltering confidence and her persistence, would see her through, as usual. Satisfied that his reputation was in good hands, Nick wolfed down two chili-cheese burgers and fries, then celebrated by treating himself to a chocolate malt.

"What time is it?" Hazard asked abruptly.

Nick glanced at his watch. "Six-fifteen."

Hazard bounded off the seat so quickly that she nearly spilled his chocolate malt. She clutched his hand, hoisting him to his feet.

"Where are we going?" Nick wanted to know.

"To see how many rats we can catch in the same trap," was all she said as she towed him toward his pickup truck.

Amanda slid beneath the wheel, then took Thorn's keys. Clearly, he was suffering from a sudden case of machismo. Although he didn't object to letting her drive his truck, she knew he preferred to be behind the wheel. It was one of those male things that occasionally clouded Thorn's thinking. But to Thorn's credit, he made no comment when Amanda volunteered to drive.

Without explanation Amanda sped around the block, pausing a discreet distance from the gate of Lemon's Used Cars. As she predicted—and Velma confirmed—Irene Pratt drove off in her car. Five minutes later Ernie Niles climbed into a faded gray Ford. Glancing every which way, Ernie stopped to lock the gate, then drove off.

"Are we on surveillance?" Thorn asked.

Amanda pointed toward the car Ernie climbed into. "At precisely 6:15 yesterday, Irene left work. Ernie climbed into a different car than he's driving today. Guess where he stopped after work?"

"Irene's place," Thorn presumed.

"Exactly." Amanda put the truck in gear, then sped off on a road that paralleled the one Ernie had taken. "Romeo follows the same predictable routine. He drives around Irene's house to make sure no one can identify him, then he parks his car-of-the-day and scuttles into the house."

Amanda backed up and turned around after Ernie sneaked inside Irene's house. "Now let me show you what Loraine Niles does while waiting for her cheating hubby to drag his sorry butt home."

She turned her narrowed gaze on Thorn. "And if you ever pull a stunt like this, Thorn, I'm here to tell you that I will take you for everything you're worth."

Thorn graced her with that ultrasexy smile that made his dark eyes twinkle. "Hazard, Hazard, no way in hell will you ever catch me with my pants down anywhere except with you. I'm planning on offering you the forever kind of *I do.*"

When he leaned over and kissed her, the truck swerved and rammed into the curb.

"Cut that out, Thorn. You know I can't think, and drive, when you kiss me like that."

Reeking smug male arrogance—and the strong scent of sweat—Thorn settled back on the seat. "Since you plan to marry me in two weeks, without consulting me first, where do you plan to take me for our honeymoon? Someplace romantic, I hope."

"I thought one of those bed-and-breakfast places that plays out a murder mystery might be fun."

Thorn jerked upright, his massive chest swelling to expose the muscled lines of his pecs beneath his T-shirt. "No, Hazard. Absolutely, positively not. I'm planning to be married only once and I refuse to spend my one and only honeymoon sniffing out clues at a whodunit-hotel. No, no, no!"

"Geez, Thorn, don't get so huffy. It was a joke."

"Well, it wasn't funny," Thorn said, and scowled.

Amanda turned onto the country road, then accelerated. Silence filled the cab of the truck.

"The Bahamas. We're going to take a cruise to the Bahamas," Thorn said assertively. "I'll call the travel agency in Pronto, first thing in the morning."

"Are you sure you can afford that kind of extravagance when you're out of a job?"

Thorn frowned darkly. "Since you're my accountant, you know better than anyone that I've got a nest egg stashed away that well affords a new addition on my farmhouse and a honeymoon aboard a luxury cruise ship—"

His voice dried up when Amanda topped the hill and gestured toward the squad car that sat in Loraine Niles' driveway. Amanda applied the brakes, then reached for her purse. Quickly, she documented the date and time of Deputy Payne's visit to Loraine.

"We will not be playing musical beds during our marriage, Hazard," Thorn said as he stared down the hill. "I don't care if everybody else's morals stink to high heaven. You and I are going to be loyal and true blue . . . Damn, back up the truck! Here comes the GI-Joe cop. He doesn't need to know we're tracking him."

Amanda put the truck in reverse and sped backward until she could turn around at a pasture gate. Gravel scattered as she mashed on the accelerator and buzzed off.

"Ten to one, Deputy Payne plans to drive by Irene's house to shadow Ernie," Amanda predicted. "He'll probably have Loraine take Ernie to divorce court on the grounds of adultery. Then he'll marry the divorcée and help her spend all daddy's money."

"And I'll hang that conniving cop out to dry," Thorn vowed.

"I'll be there with you to air his dirty laundry," Amanda promised as she made tracks. "Payne is going down!"

Amanda smiled inwardly as she poured herself a cup of morning coffee. The past two nights had been her idea of heaven. She had driven to Thorn's brick farm home for a quiet evening of relaxation. She had approved of the addition Thorn was building onto the house, though she had several reservations about Thorn doing most of the carpentry himself.

When she suggested that he call Buzz Sawyer, the local carpenter, to assist him, Thorn had gotten huffy—another of those male things, she supposed. Thorn had assured her that he was a jack-of-all-trades who could handle a hammer and studs. Yet, to make her happy, Thorn had given Buzz Sawyer a buzz on the phone and asked for assistance.

Amanda knew the building project would keep Thorn occupied while she investigated the Lemon case. With the housing project, and hay to swath and bale, Thorn could keep busy.

Absently, Amanda leaned down to pet the devoted Border collie that sprawled at her feet. After interviewing several customers who had confronted Frank Lemon about sour car deals, Amanda realized why Thorn had warned her away from purchasing a vehicle from Frank. Furthermore, Freddy Lassiter had confirmed that Frank's vehicles weren't always up to snuff.

Thus far, no one Amanda interviewed had kind words for the man she and Thorn found dead in the driver's seat of the wrecked Chevy truck. Frank had made more enemies than friends during his twelve years as a car dealer.

Amanda frowned, wondering what line of business Frank had been in before he opened his car lot. She would have to remember to ask Frank's wife.

The phone jingled, waking Bruno from his nap. Amanda strode off to answer the call.

" 'Manda? This is Cleatus Watts."

"Have you had time to check Frank's pickup?"

"Sure have. Did it early this morning."

There was a pause. Amanda assumed Cleatus was taking a long draw on his cigarette.

"Did you find anything out of the ordinary?" she asked.

"Sure did."

Amanda wondered if Cleatus would ever learn to speak in complete sentences. Probably not. He seemed to be a man a few words—brief and to the point.

"Come by the shop," Cleatus requested. "Got something I want to show you."

"I'll be there in a few minutes. Thanks, Cleatus."

"No problem, 'Manda."

Amanda replaced the phone but it rang instantly. "Hazard's house."

"Hi, doll."

"Hi, Mother. How's Daddy?"

"Aren't you going to ask about me?" Mother said in a wounded tone.

"You sound fine, so I didn't think there was any need to ask," she said, then sipped her coffee.

"Well, I'm not fine. I'm worried sick about you, way out in that rinky-dink town. I met a nice, respectable young man at the country club last night, and I set up a blind date for you."

"You what?" Amanda gasped in disbelief. Mother hadn't pulled that stunt in years.

"Don't yell, doll. I have sensitive ears, you know. Anyway, Carl Plum is taking you to dinner at the club, then you're going to the Civic Center to watch the Broadway show."

"No," Amanda said sternly, "I'm not."

"Yes, you are," came the direct order from Hazard

headquarters. "Carl is a Rhodes scholar who has his doctorate in electrical engineering. He runs one of those multi-million dollar computer companies in the city. He's stinking rich, doll, and he is exactly the kind of man you need, the kind you can't find out there in the boondocks."

"Sorry, Mother, but Thorn and I kissed and made up. We're getting married in less than two weeks, so it would be inappropriate for me to accept a date with your Plum." Amanda braced herself for Mother's inevitable howl of dismay.

"Less than two weeks!" Mother wailed. "That bumpkin of a cop isn't good enough for you, doll. He will never be good enough for you! Besides that, you will be condemned to a life with a snide, interfering mother-in-law. I've met Thorn's mom, you haven't. Believe me, you aren't going to like her. She thinks city girls are incompetent. Can you imagine that? The woman is a hick, and proud of it. She talks with a twangy drawl and has an accent that is a cross between southern Okie and slow-talking Texan."

"Pops managed to survive with you as a daughter-in-law," Amanda mumbled.

"What was that?" Mother demanded, as only Mother could.

"Nothing, Mother. Give my love to Daddy. I've got to run by and pick up Pops. He stayed all night with his new friend."

"Good gad, it sounds as if the old buzzard is going through his second childhood. Since when did he start sleeping over?"

"Since he decided to play poker all night, get drunk out of his gourd and watch girlie movies on the VCR," Amanda said, for effect.

Sure enough, Mother overreacted. She was still yammering one hundred miles a minute when Amanda interrupted with a hasty good-bye, then hung up the phone.

Before she made it out the front door—with Bruno at her heels—the phone jingled again. Amanda let the answering machine pick up. As anticipated, her long-winded Mother was calling back to spout a few aspersions about this ill-fated marriage to the hick cop from nowhereville.

Smiling, Amanda walked away. She didn't want C. Plum, Ph.D., she wanted that sexy country cop with cocoa-brown eyes and a smile that could make women swoon. Now, all Amanda had to do was clear Thorn's name and see him reinstated as chief of police—before Mother got wind of Thorn's present state of unemployment. No need to give her more ammunition to blast away at Thorn.

" 'Morning," Cecil greeted as Amanda strode toward the auto body shop.

Amanda smiled at the Watts brothers who were standing outside their business establishments on Main Street. Cleatus Watts, who owned and operated the mechanic shop, did major engine overhauls and shared the duties of the tow truck service, waved, spit tobacco juice and flashed Amanda a toothy grin.

"Glad to hear you and Thorn patched things up." Cleatus sipped his steaming coffee. "I like the new commish, but I've gotten used to the idea of you and Thorn as a couple, ya know?"

It still amazed Amanda that Vamoose kept such close tabs on her personal life. She supposed that's what happened to a high profile CPA and chief of police. In small-town America, citizens were considered extended family and you kept up with everybody's business, should someone need advice or a helping hand.

Life in Vamoose was a far cry from growing up in the big city. In this rural community, you waved as you passed another driver or pedestrian—whether it was a close friend or nodding acquaintance. Anything less was considered rude.

In this instance, Cecil and Cleatus Watts were here to help Amanda solve her curiosity about the truck Frank Lemon wrecked when he departed from this world to take his place in that gigantic used car lot in the sky . . .

And damn it, there were moments when Amanda had the twitchy feeling that Frank had help getting where he'd gone.

Shaking off the instinctive suspicion that assailed her every now and then, Amanda ambled toward the red truck. "What did you come up with when you gave the pickup a thorough going over?"

Cleatus, dressed in a clean pair of faded blue jeans, followed in her wake. Cecil, dressed identically to his brother—except for the frayed holes caused by drops of battery acid—was one step behind.

"Me an' Cleatus have been inside and out of this truck," Cecil told her in his slow drawl. "We put the truck on the lift to get a better look, didn't we, Cleat?"

"Yep." Cleatus nodded his dark head toward the truck that was suspended six feet off the ground. "See this?" He gestured toward the section of metal on the rear body panel of the passenger side. A gray substance, resembling hard paste, was smeared over what appeared to be a welded seam. Amanda frowned, bemused. Since she didn't know diddlysquat about automotive craftsmanship, she had no idea what she was looking at.

"This is significant?" she asked.

Cecil and Cleatus nodded, but Cleatus spoke. "Indicates the truck has been wrecked before. The original quarter panel, splash shield and door panel have been replaced. And here—" He pointed to the area of metal near the gas tank. "A dent was beaten out and a hole was drilled to pull the metal into shape. The hole was concealed with body filler."

Amanda silently fumed. Frank had never said a peep about Big Red being dented, cut and pasted back together with new parts!

"And check this out, 'Manda," Cecil insisted as he moseyed toward the front portion near the passenger door.

"Same thing, second verse," Cleatus chimed in, pointing a stubby finger at the solidified goo. "I'd say Frank had a few run-ins to trees, fence posts or other vehicles."

Amanda muttered under her breath. Frank Lemon had outright lied to her. The proof was staring back at her.

"There's more," Cecil added as he strode over to flip the switch to the hydraulic lift.

When the truck settled back onto the concrete, Cleatus pulled open the passenger door. "See these bucket seats, 'Manda?"

She stared at the shiny metal braces and bolts that Cleatus indicated.

"Not standard equipment, either. Looks like the truck was customized, not factory-issued. Hell—heck, Big Red is made up of bits and pieces. Even the back seat of this extended cab was a replacement. You can tell by the shiny new bolts and steel attachment plates."

Amanda suddenly recalled a comment Velma and Gertrude had made about Frank's overnight business trips. Amanda had wondered if Frank might be seeing someone on the sly. But maybe not. Frank must have been hauling parts in the U-Haul truck that he rented from Thatcher Oil and Gas.

All the seemingly insignificant facts Amanda had gathered began to whirl around her mind and float into place. She remembered Thorn telling her about the burned vehicle he had investigated while she was on vacation. According to Thorn, parts had been stripped before the vehicle was set afire.

Amanda wheeled toward her Toyota. She needed to speak with Frank's widow to learn what business Frank had been in before he opened the dealership in Vamoose. There had to be a connection.

"Thanks for your time and trouble," Amanda called over her shoulder.

"If this helps get the chief back on duty, we're happy to help," Cleatus said, then lit his cigarette.

"Not high on that Deputy Payne," Cecil put in. "Got a sneaky look about him, if you ask me."

Amanda silently agreed as she whizzed down the street to her office, her brain whirling like the spin cycle of a washing machine. She stopped outside her office, massaged her head, then fished into her purse to retrieve Tylenol to battle the headache she expected to have very shortly.

Something screwy is going on here, came that intuitive voice of reason. *Don't overlook a single comment, Hazard, or you'll miss something important.*

Amanda inhaled a deep, controlled breath of country morning air and told herself not to become impatient. She had to complete her fact-finding mission. She couldn't leap to ill-founded conclusions in a case that had changed from clearing Thorn's name to what might be a clever scam—instigated by Vamoose's used car dealer.

Having regained her composure, Amanda entered the office to find Jenny Long at her desk, taking a phone message.

"Hi, boss," Jenny greeted. "I made strudel and coffee."

Jenny, whose noted culinary skills had earned her blue ribbons at the county fair, gestured toward the top of the file cabinet. Amanda's stomach growled. Eagerly, she strode forward to slice off a piece of cinnamon strudel.

"I just took a call from Imagene Lemon," Jenny reported. "She wants to know if you'll handle the accounts for the estate taxes."

"I will be glad to," Amanda mumbled as the fluffy strudel melted in her mouth, sending her starved taste buds into delighted riot.

"That's what I figured you would say, so I told Ima not to worry about a thing. You would get right on it."

It was the perfect excuse to pay Ima Lemon a house call, Amanda decided.

"Oh, and Thorn called a while ago," Jenny said. "He wants to know if you want him to leave space for one of those whirlpool tubs in the new bathroom he's building onto his house."

Amanda could easily envision herself sprawled in a spacious whirlpool bath, soaking her aching muscles and sipping on a strawberry daiquiri. Thorn was going all out, wasn't he? She grinned around her mouthful of strudel. She could well imagine what Thorn had in mind for that roomy tub. The titillating thought put her on a slow burn. Willfully, Amanda tamped down the warm sensations.

First things first, Amanda lectured herself. She had to save Thorn's name and his job, before they tripped the light fantastic in their whirlpool tub.

"Call Thorn back and tell him to go for the tub."

Jenny grinned as she picked up the phone. "I thought you'd say that, too. Told him so, but he wanted the go-ahead from you, lucky woman."

Dear, sweet, considerate Thorn, Amanda thought to herself. Since they had become reengaged, Thorn had been doing everything right, and he was well on his way to becoming the model husband.

Shaking herself loose from her lapse of sentimentality, Amanda opened the file cabinet to retrieve Thatcher's Oil and Gas account. Noticing the fuel expenses, Amanda recalled seeing the excessive fuel bills charged to Lemon's account. Who, she wondered, was responsible for buying so many gallons of gas. Was it Frank? Or Ernie?

If Frank was driving a rented U-Haul truck around the state, gathering spare car parts that came from only God knew where, then he could have been in a racketeering business that no one suspected.

And what about Frank's comment that indicated Irene Pratt fouled up registration forms and titles?. Hmm . . . Amanda made a mental note to check into that.

While Jenny spoke to Thorn, Amanda plunked down at her desk to peruse the stack of receipts from the U-Haul franchise. She could see a pattern forming, as she thumbed through the receipts. Frank had signed up to rent the U-Haul for a month at a time. Was he collecting car parts, then making a pick-up when he had a truckload stashed from sight? And who was Frank dealing with? Was he also having conflict with his unknown business associate?

No wonder the man popped blood pressure pills like they were going out of style. He was wheeling and dealing in more ways than simply the selling used cars on his lot.

"Hey, boss, Thorn wants to know if you want to come over for supper tonight. He's planning to throw some steaks on the barbecue grill."

Strudel and steak, all in the same day? Amanda's taste buds were going wild. "Sure thing. Tell Thorn I'll be there by seven."

Jenny relayed the message while Amanda mentally calculated the amount of money Frank Lemon spent on his mysterious trips with the U-Haul truck. The mileage on the truck indicated Frank made several long drives, as well as short ones.

Grabbing a notepad, Amanda jotted down a memo to check Frank's phone bills—both personal and professional. He had to be calling someone to arrange pick-ups and deliveries.

"Jenny, call Ima Lemon and tell her that I'm on my way to see her," Amanda requested. "Then—"

The jingling phone interrupted. Jenny took the call, then handed the phone to Amanda.

"Hazard here."

"Hi, hon." Snap, pop. "Sorry to bother you, but one of my clients was telling me about a dress she made for her daughter. When I told her you and Thorn were back together, she offered to let you use the dress. I saw it. It's sensational. It's gorgeous." Crackle, chomp. "Betty June Delroy is a fabulous seamstress and she is going to alter the dress to fit you. Can't beat a deal like that, hon," she added excitedly.

"Besides, it's a white dress, with all the lace and frills you need. It is absolutely perfect for the theme I've chosen for your wedding."

"I was thinking of something sedate and subtle—in beige," Amanda said.

"Beige? No way, hon. This is Thorn's first wedding. We have to do this up right. Beige would clash with the decorations Bev and I are planning for your reception. You just gotta wear white. That's all there is to it."

"Velma, about the reception and decorations. I—"

"I know you don't have time for all these details," Velma cut in. "That's why Bev and I volunteered to help you out. We've already contacted the florist in Pronto and Maggie Whittlemeyer is making the wedding cake and groom's cake. As Bev says, it'll be radical!"

Amanda grimaced. *Radical* was not the effect she wanted for her wedding.

"Velma, I think—"

"Gotta run, hon. I'm giving Ruby Linstrohm a perm. It's time to pour on the setting solution. I'll give Betty June the go-ahead on the dress. You're gonna look like a fairy-tale princess and Nicky will be your Prince Charming."

On that enthusiastic note, Velma hung up. Amanda stared at the phone. The wedding plans were mushrooming out of control. Velma would probably hire some student from the high school journalism class to snap photos with an instamatic camera at the wedding. Great. The marriage ceremony would be a travesty, just as Mother predicted.

Well, what's in a ceremony? Amanda tried to console herself. It was the meaningful relationship and long-lasting marriage that were most important. No matter what Velma and Bev cooked up, Amanda would consider the time and effort her friends dedicated to her and ignore this feeling of impending disaster.

Amanda scooped up Frank's accounts from the service station file, then replaced the folder in alphabetical order. Tucking the information she wanted to double-check in her purse, she strode off.

"Hold down the fort, Jenny. I'll be gone most of the day."

"Sure thing, boss." Jenny beamed at her. "Now that I'm taking Accounting II at the vo-tech, I'm getting the hang of these complicated tax forms. Before long, you'll be able to put me on automatic pilot and I can fly everything from 1099s to Schedule Ds, Es and Fs."

Amanda walked outside, knowing her business was in competent hands. She glanced toward the gigantic sign that read: Lemon's Used Cars, then stared skyward. "Frank, if you're up there in the Great Beyond, I want you to know that I'm disappointed in you. I'd say you were up to no good while you were down here. And I plan to find out just how *bad* no good was for you."

Six

Amanda drove past the outskirts of Vamoose, then veered onto the gravel road that led to Ima Lemon's home. Nice spread, Amanda thought as she followed the line of cedar trees that led to a spacious, two-story brick home. A sea of tulips waved their delicate heads in the spring breeze. Colorful pansies formed a border along the brick patio that led to the front door. The house had "expensive" written all over it. Apparently, Frank's sideline business boasted profit, in addition to his used car lot.

Pausing on the driveway, Amanda stared into the window of the Caddy that had Ima's name on the personalized license plate. Amanda peered at the radio. Sure enough, there was an empty compartment that an equalizer once filled. Now Amanda knew for certain where Frank had gotten his state-of-the-art radio system.

A few moments after Amanda knocked on the front door of the house, a teary-eyed Loraine Niles appeared with a tissue in hand. Odd, thought Amanda, Frank's only child hadn't seemed too bereaved when she was waving to Deputy Payne, while sunbathing in her string bikini.

Anyone who could turn tears on and off like a faucet didn't receive high ratings in Amanda's book. This strawberry blonde seemed entirely too pretentious to Amanda.

"Come in," Loraine said, then sniffed. "Mama is expecting you."

Amanda offered a generic apology to Loraine. There was no telling what Deputy Payne had told his secret lover, but this was not the time to enter into a debate about whether Thorn was at fault in Frank Lemon's traffic accident.

The dry-eyed Ima Lemon glanced up from the leather sofa in her sprawling, expensively furnished den. Ima was dressed in a raw silk suit. Not one hair was out of place on her head, indicating she had made a recent visit to the beauty shop.

Amanda smiled in greeting, then appraised the big screen TV and CD unit that sat on the oak entertainment center. The paneled room was so large that it accommodated two sofas, a reclining loveseat, and three overstuffed chairs—and didn't look the least bit crowded. If Amanda and Pops were sharing this room she would have to yell at him to be heard across the wide distance.

"Sit down, Amanda," Ima requested. "I want to get this business of filing estate taxes rolling. I would also like for you to take over the accounts at the dealership. Frank had been dissatisfied with his secretary for months, and I know he would prefer to have the files in your competent hands."

Amanda knew Frank would, too, because he had told her so while convincing her to buy that red extended-cab pickup that had been welded together like pieces of a jigsaw puzzle!

"Mama?" Loraine inserted. "I need to leave. Will you be okay?"

Amanda silently smirked at the mock concern etched on Loraine's peaches-and-cream face. Unless Amanda missed her guess, Loraine was planning a high-noon tryst with lover-boy Payne.

"Run along, dear. I'll be fine," Ima insisted.

Amanda noted the speed with which Loraine gathered her purse, then hightailed it from the house. Amanda promised to pay her a visit at a later date. They needed to have a long talk.

"Now then." Ima folded her hands on her lap and stared directly at Amanda. "I know that you and Officer Thorn were involved in the incident that led to Frank's death, but you come highly recommended to me by everyone I have consulted about finding an honest, conscientious CPA. I am not planning to file charges against Officer Thorn, because Deputy Payne has assured me that his report will document Thorn's lack of professionalism in the incident."

Amanda felt her fingers curling into fists. Payne-in-the-butt was planning to take Thorn down in a quagmire of scandal, but it wasn't going to happen. Amanda would save the day—she hoped.

And furthermore, Amanda would not sit here and let Payne's influence over Ima go uncontested. If ever Thorn needed to be criticized—and he did occasionally—Amanda felt it her personal responsibility to do it. Let anybody else besmirch Thorn's good name and Amanda came immediately to his defense.

"Despite what Payne told you—or didn't tell you, because it is to his personal and professional advantage—Officer Thorn was not responsible for the accident. I know, because I was there. We both did everything humanly possible to prevent the mishap."

When Ima opened her mouth to interject a comment, Amanda flung up her hand—which was now devoid of the piggy faces Bev had painted on her nails. "I know you are grieving your loss, and it's natural to want to place blame. But denial of the truth will benefit no one. It can only hurt an innocent man."

Ima frowned. "What are you saying?"

Amanda met Ima's gaze head-on. "I'm saying that Frank made the crucial mistake of driving while heavily intoxicated. The medical examiner is aware of that. When

I spoke to him yesterday, he informed me that your husband had taken more than the prescribed doses of blood pressure medication. The combination hampered his mental and physical capabilities. He was a threat to himself and to anyone who happened onto him while he was driving recklessly."

Amanda noted that Ima winced when liquor and medication were mentioned. "Deputy Payne never said anything to me about that."

Now why wasn't Amanda surprised?

"I don't know what got into Frank," Ima confided quietly. "He never used to drink, except back in his younger days. His father was an alcoholic, and Frank witnessed, firsthand, how a man could deteriorate from the abuse. Frank's brother had the same problem for a few years, but he finally got himself in hand."

"Did Floyd Lemon have the problem while you were married to him?" Amanda dared to ask the Lemon widow.

Ima's eyes popped behind her Gucci-framed glasses. Amanda smiled slightly, refusing to be taken in by Ima's sophisticated demeanor until she knew if it was real or pretended. According to Velma, the Lemon family was lousy with screwballs. Ima should know all about that, since she married both Lemon brothers.

Amanda expected Ima to snap back in response to the question, but the widow settled back on the leather sofa and nodded. "Yes, Floyd had a drinking problem while I was married to him. He changed personalities, and not for the better, when he drank."

"Were Frank and Floyd close during those years?"

"Yes, they were." Ima frowned, bemused. "Why do you ask?"

Amanda shrugged a satin-clad shoulder. "Just curious. Were they also in business together?"

Imagene nodded, then settled into a more relaxed position on the sofa.

Amanda wondered if Floyd's drinking bouts had sent Ima running into Frank's arms for consolation, which led to a scandalous affair.

Did she dare ask? *Dare,* Amanda reminded herself, was her middle name.

"Is that how Floyd dealt with the fact that you and Frank were having an aff—?"

"Yes," Ima cut in, snapping like a disturbed Chihuahua. "All right, yes it was. We may as well get this over with before we cover our business dealings. But, just as you insisted that I needed to know the whole story about Frank's drinking and Thorn's attempt to get my husband off the road, I want you to know how it was with Frank and me."

Ima held her head high, her shoulders squared. "Yes, Frank and I had something going, but you don't know the procession of events involved. Until you do, you will never understand. The fact is that Frank and I realized our mistake a few months after the double wedding ceremony took place.

"Frank was in the army while I was dating Floyd. My sister started dating Frank when he came home from Nam. When I announced my plans to marry Floyd, my sister didn't want to be left out. I believe she was more in love with the idea of planning a wedding than she was with Frank."

That, Amanda mused, could be a rationalization rather than an observation. After all, Ima was heavily involved in this double triangle.

"As for Frank, he just wanted to settle down and get on with life after the hell of war." Ima stared intently at Amanda. "And for the record, it was Floyd who lured my sister away from Frank first. The consolation Frank and I found in each other turned to deep, long-lasting affection."

"And then along came Loraine," Amanda murmured, but not unkindly.

Ima nodded, then flicked a speck of lint from her sleeve. She stared at the air over Amanda's pink-tinted head. "Yes, then along came Loraine. Floyd and I ended our farce of a marriage and corrected the mistake we all made by marrying the wrong brothers and sisters.

"I'm sure the local gossips had a field day with us, even if they didn't get their stories straight. But all of us ended up where we wanted to be," Ima insisted.

A tear slid from Ima's eyes, smearing her mascara. Amanda knew it was a sincere tear, not the crocodile kind that Loraine conjured up at her convenience. No matter what else, Amanda could tell that Ima was passionate about the subject of her husband. Amanda hoped that Frank hadn't betrayed Ima's trust and affection, though the man had obviously been involved in shady dealings.

Frank Lemon better have done something right, Amanda thought to herself. Otherwise, he wouldn't be gazing down from the Great Car Lot in the Sky. He would be staring *up* from that smoldering Salvage Yard in Hell.

"I'm sorry if I upset you." Amanda reached out to pat Ima's clenched fist. "I am not here to judge, but rather to gather facts. And you can rest assured that I will be very conscientious while preparing your accounts for the estate tax forms."

Ima muffled a sniff as she nodded. "I know you will. That's why I called you." She scooped up the stack of folders on the coffee table, then presented them to Amanda. "If there are discrepancies in the dealership accounts I expect you to point them out to me." Her expression became very solemn. "I don't want you to conceal facts from me, no matter how unpleasant they might be. If my son-in-law has been—"

When Ima's voice dried up, Amanda stared at the look of resolve that claimed the older woman's features.

"Just do what you have to do, Amanda," Ima told her.

Amanda was pretty certain that Ima was subtly implying that if Ernie Niles was guilty of unethical conduct in the dealership that he was to be punished for it. So, Amanda mused, Ernie was not Ima's prime pick of a son-in-law. Ima obviously knew about Ernie's affair with Irene Pratt. But was Ima aware of Loraine's affair with Deputy Payne-in-the-butt?

Damn it, didn't anybody stay together anymore? Amanda wondered. Well, she and Thorn sure as hell would. If he ever strayed . . . Amanda discarded that thought immediately. She would not give Thorn any reason to betray her the way her first husband had. This marriage was going to be long-lived—or she'd strangle Thorn!

"Everything you need should be in those files," Ima continued. "If not, call me."

Amanda clutched the stack of folders to her chest and stood up. "If you don't mind my asking, what business partnership were Frank and Floyd involved in during their younger years?"

Ima reached over to pick up her coffee cup. "Lemon Auto Repair and Body Shop," she said. "The Watts brothers bought the business when the partnership broke up."

Amanda wasn't surprised to hear that. She had the sneaking suspicion that Frank knew a great deal about mixing and matching car parts. She wondered if his brother, Floyd, could have been in on the scam.

"One more question before I go," Amanda said. "What is Floyd doing now?"

"He is a jobber who travels to auto and salvage auctions in the tri-state area to pick up vehicles at bargain prices."

Uh-oh, thought Amanda. Could it be that Frank and Floyd had actually gone back in business together, making money on the side—and not necessarily in a legitimate manner?

Pensively, Amanda strolled to her car. Ima's information

about her first marriage was in direct contradiction to the tale Velma had told. Amanda didn't know if Ima had lied to hide her shame, or if Velma hadn't gotten the facts straight. After all, Amanda reminded herself, Velma often dealt in hearsay.

Amanda paused to glance at the well-manicured lawn. In the distance she saw a small, shabby cottage that cried out for a fresh coat of paint. There were no vehicles parked near the compact house to suggest that anyone lived there.

Her gaze swung back to the recently mowed lawn. Did the gardener and/or hired man live in the cottage? The small house appeared to be sitting on the corner of Lemon property, and looked as if it had once been a mother-in-law house to accommodate Frank or Ima's elderly parent.

Amanda placed the folders in the back seat, then switched on the ignition. She intended to swing by Lemon's Used Cars to have a word with Freddy, even if Ernie ordered her off the premises—again.

She cruised off, mulling over her conversation with Ima. According to the widow, Frank had been a model husband, loved and respected. But it seemed there was another side to Frank that Ima was unaware of—or chose to ignore. As for this swapping of husbands and wives among family, Amanda didn't know what to make of it. All she had was Ima's version of the story. No doubt, Floyd and Sally Jean had their personal versions.

Amanda marched into the garage at Lemon's Used Cars. When she spotted Freddy, doubled over a Mercury Cougar, she headed straight toward him.

"Why didn't you tell me that Frank had you replace the rear body quarter and door panel on the red truck? That truck I almost purchased was nothing but welded parts covered by body filler and paint."

Freddy grinned at Amanda's militant stance. "Good to

see you, too, Hazard. Its sounds like you had the fuel filter replaced on your Toyota."

Amanda was not to be swayed by Freddy's casual conversation. "You knew that red truck was bit-and-pieced together, and you said nothing to me about it," she huffed.

Freddy laid aside his tools, then braced his hands on the side of the car. "I told you before, Hazard, I just work here. When I called Frank on his decision to hide the fact that the red truck had been wrecked and put back together he jumped down my throat. He rammed it into a tree about three months ago, while he was driving drunk. He didn't want his wife, or anyone else, to know what happened."

So, Frank had been into keeping secrets from his wife, Amanda mused. Undoubtedly, Frank had kept Ima in the dark about a lot of things.

"How many times have you replaced parts on cars for Frank?" Amanda questioned.

"Lots of times . . ."

When Freddy stared past her, Amanda pivoted to see Ernie storming toward her.

"I ordered Freddy not to talk to you," Ernie snapped. "Don't make me call Deputy Payne to get a restraining order against you."

Undaunted by the threat, Amanda ambled toward Ernie. "How many times have you filled your vehicle with fuel from the gas tank beside the workshop?" she asked abruptly.

Ernie blinked, startled, then puffed up with indignation. "Never."

Amanda smirked at him. "If you're going to lie to me about that, when I have seen the excessive fuel bill and I know perfectly well that you have filled up for your personal use, then I can only assume that you are accustomed to lying when it is to your benefit. Don't forget that I am Uncle Sam's eyes and ears, Ernie. Just try to deduct all your personal fuel for business purposes and see how fast the IRS auditors contact you."

"Are you threatening me?" Ernie hissed through clamped teeth.

"Nope, just doing my job as an honest, conscientious CPA," she said, as she sauntered toward her car. "Ima put me in charge of the personal and business accounts, so I'll be keeping close tabs on your activities. Have a nice day!"

Smiling devilishly, Amanda watched Ernie whirl around and stamp back to the office. Ernie thought she was giving him fits now? Well, he hadn't seen nothin' yet!

Amanda checked her watch, then documented the surveillance she was keeping on Deputy Payne. Regular as clockwork, the sneaky cop was paying one of his two daily visits to Loraine.

A few minutes later, Amanda drove off, knowing that Payne's predictability would become his downfall. That horny deputy would soon be wishing he had never tangled with Amanda!

She wasn't due at Thorn's for supper for another two hours, so she cruised the back roads of Vamoose, pondering what she had learned from Ima Lemon and Freddy Lassiter. Although her foremost concern was seeing Thorn redeemed, she had the edgy feeling that, in the distraction of the upcoming wedding, and having Pops underfoot, she had neglected to pursue an important clue . . .

The tilted steering wheel . . .

The thought struck her like a thunderbolt, making her sit upright in the car seat. Previously, she'd had suspicions about the reason why Frank hadn't tilted the steering wheel upward. If Cecil and Cleatus Watts hadn't touched it while checking the wrecked truck, who had? Surely

Frank would not have left the steering wheel in an uncomfortable position while driving.

Amanda glanced up to see that she had veered down the same gravel road Frank had taken during his high-speed escape attempt. It seemed her subconscious was hard at work while she was lollygagging.

Resolutely, Amanda concentrated on the piles of gravel that still showed evidence of Frank's four-wheel-drive truck swerving across the road. Fishtails and skid marks were everywhere.

When Amanda turned onto the highway leading to Whatsit River Bridge she stared at the highway, then glanced in the rearview mirror. Since no one was coming, she veered around the mound of sand that served as a natural guard rail, then she parked her car.

Shedding her pantyhose and pumps, she cautiously sidestepped down the sharp incline that was strewn with broken beer bottles and pebbles. Astutely, she surveyed the clumps of weeds and underbrush—part of which had been smashed flat when Frank's truck plowed into the river.

Watching where she stepped, Amanda canvassed the scene of the accident. She didn't know what she was looking for; she only hoped she would know what it was when she found it.

If she applied the theory that Frank had not raised the steering wheel, because he wasn't actually driving his truck, all sorts of possibilities leaped to mind. Amanda couldn't possibly have identified Frank as the driver behind the wheel the night of the high-speed chase, she realized. She had only *assumed* that it was he. The bright headlights in the darkness had prevented her from identifying Frank's silhouette.

If her suspicions were correct, some person or persons unknown could have transported Frank down the road, then leaped from the moving truck as it bounced over the sand dune to nose-dive into the river.

Amanda strode off to check for footprints that might indicate foul play. For thirty minutes she circled the area near the flattened weeds.

And then she saw it—the telltale sign of footprints leading away from the weeds. Footprints circled a clump of willow trees and skirted the vine-choked barbed wire fence that separated the river from a nearby wheat field.

Amanda's shoulders slumped in disappointment. There was no way she could follow a trail through rows of waist-high wheat. Whoever had been scampering around in the sand had wisely taken an escape route through the wheat.

Wheeling around, Amanda retraced her steps, then squatted down to study an array of smudged footprints that indicated that the wearer of the shoes had left in a flaming rush.

Pushing a clump of weeds out of her way, Amanda stared at the prints. If she was guessing—and she definitely was—the tracks in the sand appeared to have been made by tennis shoes that might fit a woman's feet. Size eight, maybe? Amanda stuck her size seven-and-a-half foot in the print. Eight-and-a-half, she concluded.

Rising, Amanda circled to appraise another shoe print. She predicted it was of the male variety. This particular shoe print had deep imprints like the ones found on athletic shoes worn by basketball players.

Wonderful, thought Amanda. Now all she had to do was figure out which basketball player—and his girlfriend—might have reason to make a wild drive down the country roads, then deliberately veer off toward Whatsit River and make a daring leap into the weeds while the truck, carrying Frank's unconscious body, plowed into the water.

Again, Amanda recalled Thorn telling her about the car that had been stripped, burned and left in a ditch in a remote section of the county. Had Frank, while drinking heavily, passed out in his idling truck? Had teenage hoodlums taken advantage of the situation and attempted to steal the truck with Frank in it?

She hadn't checked Frank's wallet to see if perhaps money was missing, she reminded herself. Could he have initially been the victim of a robbery?

Could it have been mere coincidence that the truck had cruised past Amanda's house? If the car thieves—say, a man and woman—spotted Thorn's squad car, they might have run scared. They would have every reason to ditch the truck with Frank in it before Thorn caught up with them.

Jeepers, the possibilities were endless . . .

Except that Amanda's conjectures had one major glitch, she realized as she retraced her steps to survey the passel of male and female prints that lay in disarray. If two individuals had leaped from the truck as it plowed toward the river, wouldn't she have seen the dome light flick on when the door opened?

Amanda had had a clear view of the truck while it bounced over the sand dunes. To her recollection, the cab light had not flicked on—not even for a few seconds. How could car thieves make their daredevil jumps without Amanda, or Thorn, noticing the light?

Or maybe the car wreck was connected to Frank's underhanded dealings that involved picking up auto parts and vehicles and transporting them in the U-Haul truck, she thought to herself. A mysterious partner may have decided to terminate the business relationship and ensure that Frank didn't object—or retaliate.

Damn, this investigation was getting more confusing by the hour.

Okay, she thought as she tiptoed around the jagged pieces of glass and returned to her car. What if Frank was *not* behind the wheel, but rather slumped on the seat, and someone *else* was driving? That someone else could have tilted the steering wheel downward to suit his or her size and driving preference.

Amanda plopped down on the seat of her car to brush the sand from her feet, then she slipped on her pumps. She had reached a conclusion, one that would most certainly have Thorn howling in disbelief. She was not looking forward to presenting her theory to him.

She backed around the sand dunes and headed for Thorn's farmhouse. Should she spring her latest theory on him over steak, or wait until time for dessert?

Either way, Amanda knew Thorn was going to balk. He absolutely hated it when Amanda insisted that what appeared to be an accident was really a cleverly staged murder.

Seven

Nick stuck his head under the shower to wash away the sweat and sawdust. His muscles ached from climbing up and down the ladder and handling a Skilsaw. But he had made great progress during the day. The concrete block foundation he'd set in place now supported the floor joists and plywood decking.

Buzz Sawyer, the local carpenter, had arrived to offer advice and provide extra muscle to erect the south wall of the new addition.

Nick prayed for a calm evening. The stud wall was braced with only two angled two-by-fours. A strong wind might send the wall crashing down in a pile of broken timber.

Nick doused his head with shampoo, then rinsed. He had left the outdoor barbecue grill smoldering with coals, popped two potatoes in the oven to bake and set store-bought, ready-made salad on the table. He intended to have the sirloin steaks cooking over the mesquite coals by the time Hazard arrived.

Smiling in anticipation of an enjoyable evening, Nick dried off. He thrust his legs into his underwear and blue jeans, then grabbed a clean shirt.

He could get used to the idea of staying on the farm instead of cruising the police beat. He could raise more cattle, plant more alfalfa hay and wheat. He could become a full-time farmer who had time to mend broken fences and repair machinery—instead of hastily patching stretches of barbed wire because he was always short on time.

Yeah, he could do that, but the cop in him would play hell with his conscience. Nick was used to providing police protection for the citizens in the town where he'd grown up.

"Hell, Thorn, who do you think you're kidding? You've been a cop so long that you wouldn't know what to do with yourself if you gave up the beat."

Of course, if Hazard didn't come up with information that exonerated him from wrongdoing in the Lemon case, he would be forced into early retirement. But Hazard was as tenacious as a pit bulldog. She would have a counter for every accusation Deputy Payne pulled out of thin air.

Hell's bells, Nick had followed procedure while chasing Frank Lemon. Any competent cop knew that. Frank Lemon had been warned—twice—that, if Nick caught him drinking while he was behind the wheel, his ass was grass. Knowing that, Frank had blazed off in a cloud of dust, trying to outrun the souped-up engine in Nick's squad car. Frank was the one who made a critical error in judgment, because his mental and physical faculties were saturated with Jack Daniel's whiskey.

Frank should have pulled over the moment he saw Nick's flashing lights and heard the siren . . .

The phone jingled. Nick groaned. That better not be Hazard calling to cancel the romantic, candlelight dinner he had arranged. Nick wanted to set a precedent of dining with Hazard, of sharing an hour of peace and quiet during their hectic days.

Nick snatched up the phone when it blared at him for the third time. "You better be here in fifteen minutes or the steaks will be ruined."

"Chief?"

Nick blinked in surprise when Deputy Benny Sykes' voice came down the line. "Benny?"

"I didn't know I was invited to supper. Heck, I didn't know that you knew I was back from vacation."

"I thought you were Hazard."

"Hazard? Did the two of you get back together? Hot damn, Chief. I knew you could win her back from Harjo. How did you do it?"

Nick grinned rakishly. "Good ole sex appeal, Benny."

Benny chuckled. "Sex appeal, right. I guess all the other eligible females in Vamoose, who have a weakness for a man in a uniform, are all mine now."

"Go get 'em, tiger," Nick purred. "By the way, it's nice to know you're back in town."

"That's why I called. What's this business about misconduct? Payne said you ran Frank Lemon off the road and caused him to splash down in the river. The man has pages of notes from interviews with folks from town. He claims you had it in for Lemon and didn't follow regulations on the chase and capture."

Nick gnashed his teeth. "Payne wants my job, any way he can get it."

"He's an officer of the law, sworn to uphold justice," Benny hooted. "There is nothing in the code book and regulation manual that says: by hook or crook. Hell, that stuff is left for vice squads who have to make up their own rules while walking both sides of the law to catch creeps."

Nick knew all about that separate, unwritten set of rules that applied to undercover cops. He had served his time in the trenches of OKCPD, ridding the streets of Oklahoma's capital city of narcotics dealers and drug pushers.

"When I reported for duty, Deputy Payne gave me orders to get a second set of statements from Ernie Niles and Irene Pratt at the used car lot," Benny continued. "For some strange reason I'm supposed to verify that Frank's state of mind, the day he died, was no different than any other day in the life of a working stiff . . . Sorry, stiff isn't a good expression to use, considering Frank's condition."

"Damn that Payne-in-the-ass," Nick muttered resentfully.

"So what is going on here, Chief?" Benny wanted to know. "What is Payne's angle?"

Nick glanced out the bedroom window to see smoke rolling from the grill. He needed to turn and baste. Otherwise, those expensive steaks were going to be charred black.

"Hold on a sec, Benny. Let me pick up the portable phone."

"10-4, Chief."

Nick strode down the hall to grab the portable phone, then hurried back to the bedroom to hang up the extension. The sound of crunching gravel indicated that Hazard had arrived.

"I'll have to call you back later, Benny. Hazard is here. Where can I reach you?"

"I'll call you when I take a Code 7 at Last Chance Cafe. But don't you worry. Now that I'm back in town, I'll straighten out this mess. I'm not about to have that deputy barking orders at me like a drill sergeant. Geez, which branch of the military service did he serve in anyway?"

"Soldier of fortune is my guess," Nick grunted as he whizzed out the kitchen door to save the steaks from cremation.

"Soldier of fortune, right," Benny repeated. "Over and out, Chief."

Nick set aside the phone and lifted the grill lid. Smoke and steam billowed like a thundercloud. Fire leaped up to singe the hair on his hand as he flipped over the steaks. Another minute and he would have had a full-fledged fire.

Nick sprinkled water on the coals, listened to them hiss and sputter, then adjusted the damper. He had saved the entree for the romantic dinner—barely.

"Yoo-hoo, Thorn! Where are you?" Hazard called out.

Scooping up the phone, Nick leaped onto the porch and sailed into the kitchen where Hazard was filling a glass of water from the tap.

"Nice to have you here, Hazard," he said, as he snaked out his arm, took the glass of water from her hand and set it on the counter. With chivalrous flair, he bent Hazard over backward and delivered a kiss to rival the coals flaming in the outdoor grill.

When Nick set Hazard back to her feet, she wobbled noticeably. "Wow, Thorn. You've turned into a regular Casanova, haven't you?"

Nick wiggled his eyebrows suggestively. "Wait until you see what I turn into at midnight, Cinderella."

"The proverbial pumpkin?" she asked. "I hope not." She stared at him consideringly. "What put you in such a playful mood?"

"Thoughts of you," he said, smoothly, suavely.

"Come here, you big stud—"

The phone blared at the most inopportune moment. Nick cursed Alexander Graham Bell soundly. "Thorn's hell, the tormented speaking."

Chomp, crack. "Nicky? It's Velma. Are you okay?"

"Fine. Hold on, Velma." Nick covered the mouthpiece, then gestured toward the smoking grill. "Do me a favor, Haz. Bring in the steak. Dinner is ready."

While Hazard scooped up a plate and strode outside, Nick braced the phone against his shoulder and lit the candles on the table. "What's up, doll face?"

"Nicky, you rascal. You sure know how to charm the lady folk." Crackle, pop, pop. "I just called to tell you that I'm doing my part to keep down talk about Deputy Payne's ridiculous accusations."

Nick inwardly groaned. Apparently, the whole town was buzzing with news of his temporary suspension.

"Nobody believes you were at fault in the Lemon incident." Crack, snap. "Well, except for members of the immediate family. Loraine Niles has a full head of steam going. 'Course she has always been full of hot air and a few water vapor molecules, ya know. She always did think she was hot stuff, as my niece would say."

Nick wondered if Velma knew that Loraine and Payne were thick as thieves. Hopefully not. Hazard was saving that tidbit of information as her ace in the hole.

"Now, about the wedding," Velma went on—and on. "Amanda put me in charge, ya know. I've already taken care of getting your tux."

"My tux?" Nick repeated stupidly.

Nick had plans of dressing in his country best—Western dress coat, slacks and Mercedes boots.

"Bev is going to pick up your tux when she makes the run to the city for beauty supplies tomorrow. All the rest of the arrangements are under control. I wanted to let you know so you wouldn't fret about your wedding while this dumb investigation is hanging over your handsome head."

"Thanks, Velma, you're a peach."

She giggled and popped her gum. "Ain't I though, sugar? Gotta run, Nicky. I'm picking up the punch bowl and paper goods for the reception. The shop on the west side of the city closes in an hour." Pop, pop. "Oh, and I've made the arrangements for your bachelor party, too. I just flagged down Benny Sykes. He wants to have the shindig at Hitching Post Tavern. 'Bye."

Nick stared at the phone, feeling like a survivor of an F5 tornado. Velma was buzzing around, arranging his life for him, and Nick had been sucked up in the vortex of the whirlwind.

"What did Velma want?" Hazard asked as she set the steaks on the table.

"Do you think it's a good idea to let Velma commandeer our wedding?"

"Not particularly. But if you can figure out a way to stop her, let me know. When she noticed I was wearing the ring, she grabbed the bull by the horns and took off running."

"We should fly to Vegas and make this quick and painless for ourselves," Nick said as he gallantly pulled out a chair for Hazard.

"We should," she agreed. "But with Deputy Payne-in-the-butt breathing down your neck, leaving the state isn't advisable."

Willfully, Nick cast aside the albatross around his neck—namely Payne—and dived into his meal. Although Hazard made all the right noises about the tasty supper Nick had prepared, he could tell she had something on her mind.

"Okay, Haz, out with it."

She stared blankly at him. "Out with what?"

"Whatever is bothering you. It's not the wedding, is it?"

Hazard shook her head. Pink glitter trickled onto her shoulders like dandruff. "I was thinking about that burned car you found while I was on vacation. Could you fill me in on the details?"

Nick beetled his thick brows. How had Hazard gone from sirloin steak to charred cars? He supposed that in Hazard's mind it made sense. She was an accountant, after all. Facts and figures were her bread and butter.

"There's not much to tell," he said. "Benny Sykes radioed me to say that he had a 503, a stolen vehicle, on a remote country road."

"What kind of car was it?"

"A Grand Prix. The bucket seats, radio, license plate, bumpers, grill assembly and the entire engine had been stripped. The vehicle had been doused with gasoline and set aflame."

"Any reports of a missing Grand Prix in Vamoose County?"

Nick swallowed his mouthful of baked potato before he spoke. "Nope. I checked. But just before you came home, I got word of an auto theft in Grady County that matched our sketchy description—"

The phone rang. Nick got up to answer it. Hazard cleared the table.

"Thorn here."

"It's me again, Chief," Benny said. "Guess you heard that Velma and I are planning your bachelor party. I talked to the owner of Hitching Post Tavern. He has agreed to close the bar to the public, free of charge. Now, what's the scoop on this Payne character?"

"The SOB wants my job—permanently. I expect he is planning to bring in one of his pals to replace you, so watch where you step."

"Replace me? Replace *me!*" Benny yelped. "Hell, Chief, this police beat is my life. I'm happy where I am!"

"Then don't cross Payne," Nick advised his deputy. "Find out what you can about Frank Lemon and report back to me."

"Report to you, right," Benny repeated, flustered. "I'll ask a few questions while I'm here at Last Chance Cafe. I'm also going to check the In-and-Out book to see where Payne transferred from. No ex-soldier of fortune is going to waltz into Vamoose and take over our turf without a fight!"

Nick hung up the phone, took a deep breath, then forced himself to discard all thoughts of Payne. He had planned a romantic evening with Hazard. The phone calls were damned distracting.

After switching on the mood music on the stereo, Nick turned off the lights in the living room. This, he told himself, was going to be one of those hot, steamy nights to die for. The future of his career in law enforcement was being put on hold for the evening.

Grinning roguishly, Nick unbuttoned his chambray shirt and struck what he hoped to be an ultraseductive pose on the couch. Then he waited for Hazard to join him.

Amanda stuffed the plates in the dishwasher and spiffed up Thorn's kitchen—soon to be *their* kitchen. Of course she would have to make a few changes when she moved in. The items in the cabinets would have to be alphabetized. Thorn's haphazard habit of stuffing food in cabinets without methodical orderliness would drive her crazy.

When the kitchen was spotless, Amanda turned off the light. It was time to announce her suspicions about the Lemon case. She had to get this over with . . .

Amanda skidded to a halt when she rounded the corner of the dining room. Thorn's shirt hung open, exposing the broad expanse of his hairy chest.

"Thorn," she said, drawing herself up to businesslike stature. "We have to talk."

Thorn laid his head against the back of the couch and groaned aloud. "Damn it, Haz, don't spoil what I imagined to be the perfect romantic evening."

"Button your shirt, Thorn," she ordered brusquely. "I can't think straight while I'm staring at your gorgeous male chest. Entirely too distracting. There is only one thing that can take precedence over getting my hands on your muscled body. If this wasn't important, I wouldn't insist."

Reluctantly, Thorn fastened his shirt. "Okay, Haz, what's so damned important here?" he wanted to know.

Amanda strode up in front of him and blurted out, "I

don't think Frank Lemon died by accident. I think he was murdered."

She could see the look of disbelief spreading across his rugged features, even in the scant light. His disbelief was closely followed by the flattening of his eyebrows—a mannerism that testified to his mounting irritation. She waited, knowing he was going to explode. He always exploded when she cried *murder,* while he maintained *accident.*

"Damn it to hell, Hazard!" His deep, baritone voice ricocheted off the walls, overriding the sound of George Strait crooning a country ballad. "How could anybody in her right mind leap to such a ridiculous conclusion? You and I were at the scene of that accident. We saw Frank whiz down the gravel road, we saw him lose control of his truck, sail over the sand dunes, then plunge headlong into the river. Dead men don't drive trucks, Hazard. The only one who went off the deep end here is you!"

Amanda told herself to keep her cool. She and Thorn would work through this like two rational, mature adults—just as soon as he stopped behaving like a wool-brained idiot!

"Here's the scenario, Thorn," Amanda said, struggling to maintain quiet tones as she sank down in the chair across from him. "Frank Lemon was either dead or unconscious, when we saw his pickup truck drive past my house."

"Oh, sure," he said, and snorted. "Frank drove in his sleep—eternal or otherwise. Right, Hazard. Sure, I'll buy that. Makes perfect sense to me."

Again, Amanda ignored his sarcasm. "I don't think Frank was driving. We didn't actually *see* him that night, now did we? We *saw* the bright, blinding headlights of a red pickup weaving down the road. We noticed the silhouette of a driver behind the wheel. We gave chase, still under the assumption that Frank Lemon, whom you repeatedly told not to drink and drive, had defied your warning.

"If you recall, you said to me—and I quote: What the hell's wrong with Frank? He knows that I know where he lives."

Thorn frowned pensively.

Now that Amanda had Thorn entertaining the possibility of foul play, she strategically continued. "At no time during our high-speed chase, through a cloud of dust, could we positively identify Frank Lemon. For all we know, Santa Claus could have been driving that truck. Santa could have weaved all over the road, pretending to be driving drunk, in order to leave us with the exact assumption we were operating under. We *presumed* that it was Frank Lemon, *expected* it to be Frank Lemon because we recognized the truck. But it could have been a clever illusion."

She stared, long and hard, at Thorn. "If you were on the witness stand in a court of law and I, the attorney, asked you if you could positively ID Lemon, what would you say?"

Thorn squirmed, then muttered under his breath. "I would have to say no, but—"

"No buts, Thorn," she interrupted in her most authoritative voice. "Answer the direct question. Yes or no."

"No," he said, and scowled.

Amanda swallowed down her triumphant smile. This was not the time to gloat. Thorn hated it when she gloated. She didn't want to irritate him just now, not when she had him thinking logically. She wanted him to pay close attention.

"Given the excessive speed of the truck, and the alcohol content level the medical examiner found in Frank's blood—"

Thorn elevated a dark brow.

"Yes," she answered his unspoken question. "I called

the coroner and wheedled the information from him on your behalf. I told him that you asked me to make the call because you were extremely busy at the moment."

Thorn groaned, but he kept his trap shut.

"Given the alcohol content level, and the overdose of blood pressure pills, is it not possible that Frank could have—should have—passed out while driving at excessive speed in the loose gravel, long before he approached my house? Isn't it possible that he could have—and probably would have—wrapped the truck around a fence post long before he reached Whatsit River Bridge?"

"But he didn't," Thorn pointed out.

"But it is possible that he *could have,* and probably *should have,"* she repeated emphatically. "According to the coroner's report, Frank could have passed out hours earlier," Amanda continued.

Thorn slumped, then stretched his long, muscled legs out in front of him. "Yes," he mumbled. "I expected Frank to veer off into the ditch long before he ever turned back onto the highway near the bridge."

"And isn't it also possible that whoever was driving the truck purposely veered over the sand dunes, then leaped to safety before the truck soared into the river?"

Thorn didn't respond immediately. He simply stared at her as if she were some strange and curious creature who had beamed down from the mother ship. "Damn, Haz, how do you come up with this stuff? What clue sent you wandering off into this scenario?"

Amanda stared him squarely in the eye. "I think Frank Lemon was murdered, because the steering wheel was tilted to the 'down' position."

And then it came, that look of astonishment and blatant cynicism. "Good grief, you must have stayed up all night to come up with that one!"

Amanda valiantly held her temper. She told herself that she couldn't fault Thorn for being skeptical. After all, it had taken her several days of intense investigation to arrive at her conclusion. Since Thorn had the disadvantage of operating with a male brain, she had to give him ample time to adjust to the possibility that this case was a cleverly arranged murder, not a freak accident.

"The steering wheel was tilted to the wrong angle?" Thorn repeated dubiously.

Amanda nodded. "When I was at the used car lot, I had to tilt the steering wheel of the red truck *down.* Frank kept it up to accommodate his paunchy belly. When he slid into my Toyota to take it for a test spin he tilted the wheel *up* so he could sit comfortably on the seat.

"I checked the red truck that is impounded at Watts's Automotive Shop. The steering wheel is in the 'down' position and Cecil and Cleatus insist that they haven't altered it."

"So it definitely wasn't Santa Claus," Thorn said thoughtfully.

Amanda frowned, baffled. "What?"

"You said Santa could have been driving the truck, not Frank. But if it was Santa, with his rounded belly that shakes like a bowl full of jelly, then the steering wheel should have been in the 'up' position."

Amanda glared at Thorn's teasing smile. "Okay, so Santa Claus was a bad example."

"So, you think it might have been the Easter Bunny then?" Thorn put in, still smirking. "No, that can't be right. E. Bunny would have run the risk of breaking his colored eggs when he hopped from the speeding truck."

"Enough of your wisecracks, Thorn. This is serious business. Anyone could have been driving that truck and Frank could have been sprawled, unconscious, on the seat. Now, if you will stop being a smart ass I'll continue."

"Do go on," Thorn said with exaggerated politeness.

Once again, Amanda warned herself not to lose her temper. She was determined to convince Thorn that her theory was logical, possible. "The real driver of the truck, and possibly an accomplice, leaped into the tall weeds and scampered through the grove of willow trees, then fled through a wheat field while we were trying to rescue Frank. We were too preoccupied to notice that the perps had skulked away."

Amanda could tell that Thorn was contemplating the possibility.

"If what you are saying is true, and I'm only agreeing with this for the sake of argument," he was quick to stipulate, "we should have seen the interior cab lights flick on when the doors opened. How do you account for the fact that we didn't see any lights, Hazard?"

Amanda winced. "That has me stumped momentarily."

"Our ingenious perps didn't leap out the window?" he asked.

"The windows were rolled up," Amanda mumbled.

"Swell," Thorn grunted. "I suppose your wild conjectures are an attempt to disprove Payne's theory that I caused Frank's accident. If he was murdered, then I'm not at fault, right?"

"It would certainly be in your favor if you were actually chasing perps who had taken possession of Frank's truck while he was unconscious, perps who leaped, undetected, to safety before Frank drowned in the river."

Thorn dropped his head into his hands. "God, Haz, if you're going to cry murder, you have to have motive."

"I'm working on that."

"You also have to have opportunity and malicious intent."

"Give me a break, Thorn. I just landed on this theory an hour ago. I found the prints of a man and woman's tennis shoes in the sand, then I drove out to your place."

"Prints in the sand?" Thorn repeated warily. "How do you know someone wasn't there before, or after, Frank's wreck? It could have been two kids necking, you know.

Teenagers tramp down to the dunes, build campfires, fish, drink and kiss all the time."

"But these tracks led uphill, through the barbed-wire fence and into the wheat field," Amanda insisted.

"God, I should have known better than to give you the green light on this case. You've gone off on such a wild tangent of speculation that the sheriff will laugh himself silly over this one."

Fuming, Amanda bolted to her feet. "I'm going home, Thorn. After you figure out that I'm doing everything humanly possible to salvage your professional reputation and prove that you are the exceptional cop that I believe you are, you can call and apologize for behaving like a hare-brained ass!"

"Hazard, wait a minute—"

Amanda didn't wait, she didn't look back. She was not going to stand around while Thorn poked fun at her. And furthermore, she was not taking the risk of letting Thorn's sarcasm get the better of her—at which point she would lambaste him and set off *his* temper. She was not—repeat *not,* with great emphasis—going to give him the chance to take back her engagement ring again. They were going to be married in less than a week and they were not going to call off this wedding again!

She would marry him, *then* she would give him the hell he so richly deserved!

"Hazard, I apologize. You were right," Thorn murmured in that low, seductive voice that made Amanda's answering machine sizzle with static. "I should have been more receptive to your theory, should have been more appreciative of the time and effort you have exerted in my behalf. I promised myself that, this time around, I wasn't going to do, or say, anything that might give Sam Harjo the chance to take my place with you."

There was a long, noticeable pause.

"You aren't with him now, are you? God, I hope I didn't drive you back to him."

Another pause.

"Even when I'm at my obnoxious best, I'm still crazy about you, Hazard. You know that, don't you?"

Amanda pushed "stop," "rewind," "play," then listened to the message for the third time. Smiling, she reset the answering machine and strode down the hall, with Bruno at her heels.

"Good boy, Thorn, you're learning," she said as she pulled on her nightshirt and went to bed.

Eight

While Pops was in his workshop in the barn, gluing and sanding his antique treasures, Amanda wrote out the thank-you notes for the wedding shower gifts. When the envelopes were sealed and stamped, she set them aside to prepare lunch for Pops. Leaving his tuna salad sandwich wrapped in cellophane, and a note of explanation by his paper plate, Amanda strode outside.

She was running out of time to solve the Lemon case. Her first order of business was to check Frank's truck again. She needed to know if the dome light in the cab was functioning properly. Keeping her fingers crossed that she could prove opportunity to commit murder, Amanda drove to Watts's Auto Mechanic Shop.

To her relief and satisfaction, the dome light did *not* flick on when she opened the driver's door. Feeling more confident by the minute, Amanda strode around to the passenger side to open the door. Nothing. Not even the slightest flicker of the overhead light.

When Amanda saw Cecil step from the garage she motioned to him. "Could you do me another favor, Cecil? It will only take a sec."

"Will it help get rid of that annoying Payne and get Thorn back on patrol?"

Amanda nodded her head. The last of the glitter, which

hadn't come out during her daily shampoos, fluttered onto the shoulder of her red, Western-cut blouse.

"Well, then, I'd be glad to oblige," Cecil drawled.

Amanda hurried back to the driver's seat, then gestured toward the underside of the instrument panel. "I want you to check the electrical wiring and see if the fuse to the dome light has burned out."

Cecil contorted his long, lean body on the floor and stuck his head beneath the dashboard. Using a penlight, he checked the wiring and fuses.

"What's up, bro?" Cleatus called as he ambled from his shop.

"Bring me a fuse, will ya, Cleat?"

Cleatus reversed direction. In less than a minute he returned with a miniature fuse. When Cecil replaced it, the light flicked on instantly.

Amanda frowned. She couldn't swear the dome light had been working properly when she took her test drive, because it had been daylight and she hadn't paid close attention. She had been intent on testing the wipers, automatic windows, brakes and blinkers. The dome light had escaped her notice.

"So, Cecil," she asked, turning the burned fuse over in her hand. "Were the electrical connections making good contact?"

Cecil lifted his head. "Everything seems to be fine, except for that fuse."

Amanda wondered if the bad fuse had been purposely tampered with to prevent the dome light from coming on at a crucial moment.

"Anything else, 'Manda?" Cecil asked as he unfolded himself from the floorboard.

She glanced at Cecil, then at Cleatus. "You are absolutely, positively certain that this truck was previously damaged and repaired? Certain that the radio is not factory-issued?"

The Watts brothers nodded simultaneously, then said in unison, "Absolutely, positively."

"I'll testify in court if that will get the chief back on his police beat," Cecil insisted. "I'll—"

His voice trailed off when Deputy Payne pulled into the lot. The Watts brothers ambled back to their respective shops, leaving Amanda to deal with the annoying cop.

When Payne climbed from the car Amanda smirked. The deputy flexed a few muscles as he shut the door, then struck a pose against the side of the car. He crossed his feet at the ankles, his arms over his chest.

Amanda was not the least bit impressed. In her opinion, Payne should have selected a shirt two sizes larger than the one he wore. The fabric stretched tightly across his broad chest. His breeches could have been larger, too, she noted with disgust. The tight pants called attention to the gender-specific equipment beneath his fly.

The deputy, no doubt, liked to strut his stuff. And Loraine Niles, shallow, superficial, self-absorbed flirt that she was, got her kicks by tumbling around in bed with GI Joe Payne.

"Still supporting your lost cause, Ms. Hazard?" Payne asked.

Engage in battle or retreat? she asked herself. *Cut this cocky creep down several notches or let him wallow a little longer in his pigsty of conceit?*

Amanda thought it over and decided to let the peacock baste for a few more days before she cooked his goose.

"Cat got your tongue, honey?" he taunted when she didn't rise to his baiting.

Oh yes, she was really going to let this big, muscled ox have it, when the time was ripe.

"You better move along if you don't have business to conduct with the Watts brothers," he said, flinging his wrist to shoo her away, as if she were a pesky gnat. "I'd hate to have to arrest you for loitering. It would be bad for your image."

Amanda visualized herself doubling her fist and connecting with Payne's goading smile—right before she kicked him squarely in the crotch. Admirably though, she didn't throw a single punch.

"Before I go, I'm curious to know if you occasionally wear sneakers instead of those clunky combat boots."

Payne stared at her warily. "Why do you want to know?"

Amanda shrugged but didn't reply. She climbed into her car and drove off. When she glanced in the rearview mirror, she could see Payne snickering, as if he were sharing some private joke with himself. The jerk!

"Kiss your cocky ass good-bye, Payne," she muttered into the rearview mirror. "You're going down—big time."

Amanda turned into Lemon's Used Cars, then glanced toward the shop. Freddy Lassiter was working on another vehicle. The car he'd repaired the previous day was sitting on the lot, shining like a new penny. Ernie Niles was nowhere to be seen.

"Is Ernie around?" Amanda called to Freddy.

"He just took off on a test drive with a customer. He should be back in ten or fifteen minutes."

Good, thought Amanda. It would give her the chance to grill Irene without Ernie rushing in to defend his lover.

Amanda ambled into the office to see Irene pecking at the computer keyboard with her index fingers. Geez, it must take the woman hours to handle a simple transaction.

"May I help—" Irene's artificial smile faded when she realized who had entered the office.

"You again," Irene muttered. "Ernie told you not to come back."

"Did he? I must not have heard him," Amanda said.

"I'm surprised you're still here. Frank told me he planned to fire you."

Irene smiled nastily, then flung Amanda's words back in her face. "Did he? I must not have heard him. And anyway, I have worked here for over a year and he never once complained. Frank and I got along just fine."

Amanda was reasonably certain that Irene had been coached by lover-boy Niles. The secretary sounded like a recording. Push her button and she gave all the right responses.

"Did you and Ernie leave here with Frank the night he died?" Amanda fired the question at Irene, hoping to throw her off guard. Sure enough, it worked.

Irene's fake lashes fluttered like twin butterflies. When she frowned, the thick coat of makeup formed defined creases on her forehead. "No, we didn't. Why?"

"When was the last time you were in the health club, working on your artificial tan?"

Irene did a double take. "Why do you want to know that?"

"Just answer the question," Amanda insisted. "When? How many times a week?"

"Yesterday at lunch. Two times a week," Irene replied.

"How often does Ernie work out?"

"Twice, but wh—?"

"Does he shoot hoops at the gym?"

"Well, yes—"

"Where were you the night Frank died?" Amanda grilled the secretary.

"At home."

"Alone?"

Irene tilted her chin to a defiant angle. "Ernie was there."

Amanda gnashed her teeth. Clearly, Irene had been coached for that question, too. "So . . . you're saying that Ernie is your alibi and vice versa."

"Alibi? Why would I need an alibi?" Irene asked with pretended innocence.

Amanda didn't think that playing the dumb blonde was completely an act, not in Irene's case. The secretary was a few cherries short of a fruit pie.

"It is my opinion that Frank was murdered, or at the very least, unconscious, before the truck was purposely driven into the river."

"Don't be ridiculous. I didn't kill him," Irene blurted out.

"Did I say you did, Irene?"

"Y-You—" Irene gasped and sputtered, obviously rattled by too many rapid-fire questions. Amanda stared longingly at the bottom drawer of the desk that held Irene's personal belongings. She was itching to know if a pair of tennis shoes, used to work out at the gym—and to run through the sand beside the river—were stashed in the drawer.

Her gaze darted to Ernie's desk, wondering if he, too, kept his work-out clothes in the bottom drawer.

"Unless you have business pertaining to the dealership, I want you to leave," Irene said.

Amanda was ready and waiting for that remark. "I do have business here. Frank asked me to take control of his accounting ledgers. Ima also gave me the personal files to settle Frank's estate."

When Irene's mouth dropped open, Amanda took advantage of the silence. "I assume the ledgers are in the file cabinets," she said, as she aimed herself toward the far corner of the office.

Irene scurried from her seat and planted herself in front of the file cabinet. "You can't have the files without Ernie's permission."

"I don't need Ernie's permission. He doesn't own this dealership. Ima Lemon does. She gave me permission to do whatever I need to do to finalize the estate. If you don't believe me, then give her a call to verify."

"Well, well, look who's back. It's the walking plague," Ernie smirked as he strode inside, his hands stuffed in the pockets of his trendy slacks. "It's Vamoose's most noted pest. You do insist on pushing your luck, don't you, Hazard?"

"She wants the business accounts," Irene said in a rush.

Ernie's dark brows formed a continuous line across his narrow forehead. "No."

"I told you that Ima gave me permission," Amanda reminded him. "If you have objections then take them up with her."

Ernie muttered under his breath. As best as Amanda could make out, by reading his lips, what he said about her wasn't very nice.

Still, Irene didn't move and Ernie didn't back down.

"Don't make me go get Thorn to file a court order," Amanda threatened.

"Thorn?" Ernie scoffed. "Your fiancé isn't in any position to get an order. According to Deputy Payne, Thorn is as good as fired for misconduct."

"Don't bet on it, Ernie," she retaliated. "This case has gone from an accident to probable homicide. Considering your two arguments with your father-in-law the day of his death, and considering the affair he knew you were having with Irene, you have more than enough motive to be a suspect."

With extreme satisfaction Amanda watched the color seep from Ernie's features. Then he got all defensive and assumed a hostile stance.

"Take the damned files and get the hell out!" he roared, eyes snapping.

"I also want the registration forms compiled from the past month," she requested.

"No!"

"Why not? Afaid I can tell at a glance that Irene's typing skills are substandard, that she botched up and that Frank did indeed intend to fire her?"

Amanda glanced out the window to see Leon Pike approaching. She smiled wryly. "Uh-oh, Ernie, looks like Leon is returning to complain about that sedan you sold him. You better pacify him before he calls the Better Business Bureau."

Ernie wheeled toward the door. "Irene, give Hazard the files." He glared at Amanda. "Then I want you out of here."

She flashed him a sunny smile to counter his thunderous frown. "Hey, no problem, Ern."

When the door banged shut, Irene turned her back to dig through the file cabinet like a dog unearthing a bone. While Irene was intent on her task, Amanda discreetly reached down to slide open the top desk drawer. As expected, a stack of registration forms—plus several copies that had been typed incorrectly and set aside—sat beyond her fingertips. She scooped up the forms, and another item—which she predicted would be tremendously helpful in her pursuit of truth and justice—appeared. She tucked them in her purse.

Irene never noticed what Amanda was doing, for she was grabbing manila folders as fast as she could—without breaking off her acrylic fingernails.

"There, you've got what you want," Irene snapped hatefully. "Now get out of here."

Amanda stepped outside to see Ernie patting Leon on the back, assuring the senior citizen that Freddy Lassiter would repair the faulty ignition switch as soon as possible.

"I'll give you a ride home, Leon," Amanda volunteered as she ambled toward her Toyota.

Leon smiled gratefully. Ernie glared pitchforks at her.

Amanda helped Leon into her car, and the old man muttered to himself half the way home.

"I never should have bought that dad-blasted car from the Lemon lot," he grumbled. "It's definitely a lemon."

"I'm sure Freddy will fix you up," Amanda consoled him. "Freddy seems to be a competent mechanic."

"Yeah, well, maybe he is, but I'll never trust Ernie Niles again, I can tell you that!"

Amanda wasn't planning on trusting Ernie, either. Ernie and Irene were her Number One suspects. Unfortunately, the trail was more than a week old, and she was going to have to do some fancy footwork if she was going to prove her theory of murder. She wanted Ernie and Irene to get nervous and edgy, wanted them to become careless.

When Ernie returned to the office, Irene was wringing her hands nervously.

"What are we going to do about that Hazard woman?" she asked.

Ernie hurried over to give her a comforting hug. "I'll take care of her. Don't worry about it."

"How can I not worry?" Irene whimpered. "She's going to shut us down, I just know it."

"You've got to relax," Ernie murmured. "If you let Hazard get to you—"

Ernie backed away when the door whined open. Freddy Lassiter appeared, holding the faulty ignition in his grimy hand. His disapproving gaze bounced back and forth between Ernie and Irene. "The sedan will be ready by closing time. Are you going to charge Leon for the parts and labor?"

"No," Ernie insisted. "With that Hazard woman snooping around, I'm not giving her any ammunition to use against me."

Freddy shrugged nonchalantly. "Whatever you say. Just call Leon and tell him to pick up his sedan at six o'clock," he said before he turned and walked away.

* * *

After Amanda dropped Leon off, she reminded herself not to narrow down her list of suspects too hastily. She had yet to interview Floyd and Sally Jean Lemon. Floyd, after all, had been in business with his brother, before selling out to Cecil and Cleatus Watts. Floyd, Amanda reminded herself, had previously been married to Frank's widow. And since Floyd was a jobber who purchased cars at salvage and auto auctions, then sold them to used car dealerships for profit, he could very well be involved in whatever illegitimate activities had forced Frank to drive off on overnight trips in the U-Haul truck.

Pensively, Amanda drove past Ima Lemon's acreage, then turned south to see another spacious brick home. A bright yellow mailbox, with the name Lemon printed in bold black letters, sat by the driveway. Amanda pulled in, noting that several late model cars and short-bed pickups were loaded on a trailer. A tall, lean man was strapping down the vehicles.

This, Amanda presumed, was Floyd Lemon. He was in better physical condition than Frank, and Floyd could have easily slid beneath a steering wheel tilted to the "down" position. And furthermore, Floyd was aware of his brother's drinking problem, because Floyd was known to have had the same problem in his younger days. Floyd was also aware of his brother's high blood pressure, Amanda speculated.

In Amanda's opinion, Floyd could easily have dissolved excessive amounts of medication in Frank's whiskey and waited for him to pass out.

Waving cordially, Amanda slid off the car seat. "Floyd Lemon, I presume?"

"Who wants to know—" Floyd's voice evaporated when he realized who had arrived. "Oh hell, it's the circling vulture of doom. Somebody dies around here and you swoop down."

There were times, like now, that Amanda sincerely wished that her reputation as a gumshoe didn't precede her everywhere. Floyd had taken an antagonist's stance—hands on hips, chin tilted upward.

"Okay, Floyd, we can do this the easy way or the hard way. Your choice."

"Do what?" he snapped. "What do you want to hear me say? That I haven't shed tears over my departed brother? Fine, I'll say it. Frank got himself in deep shit. He tried to take me down with him, but I have already been there and done that with him. I played stupid once in my life. That was enough."

Whew! Floyd was in a flaming rush to get his frustration—or was it guilt?—out in the open. It sounded to Amanda as if he wanted to spill his guts to her. It sounded as if he had been *waiting* for her to show up so he could get his confession off his chest.

"You are claiming that you were *not* involved in Frank's scam of heisting cars, chopping them up and putting them back together with unidentifiable parts?" Amanda asked point-blank.

Floyd's eyes widened in surprise. "How'd you figure that out so fast?"

He had confirmed her speculations about Frank. This business about stripped cars being left to burn in remote areas of the county, mysterious overnight trips in U-Haul trucks and pieces of cars being replaced on vehicles on Frank's lot had settled neatly into place in Amanda's mind. The thought had crossed her mind at four o'clock that morning and she had been operating on that theory ever since.

"So you're telling me that you disapproved of the illegal racket? Is that why you broke up the partnership with Frank years ago and sold out to the Watts brothers?"

Floyd studied her warily. Amanda wondered if Floyd was watching where he stepped—mentally. He was willing to let it be known that there was no love lost between him and his brother, but there was a limit to how much he was willing to incriminate himself.

"Is that why you sold out?" Amanda repeated.

"Yeah." Floyd spun around to fasten another nylon belt to the underside of the powder-blue Ford Taurus that sat on the trailer.

"Did Frank threaten to ruin you if you didn't help him with his latest scam?" Amanda quizzed him.

Obviously, Floyd was getting irritated. His face turned the color of raw hamburger.

"Yeah," Floyd bit off.

"And you made a counterthreat—?"

"Floyd, is there a problem here?" a third voice asked.

Amanda pivoted on her boot heels to see a younger, more petite version of Ima Lemon standing on the front porch amid pots of geraniums. Amanda stared thoughtfully at the running shoes that Sally Jean wore, then zeroed in on the black Nikes that encased Floyd's large feet.

Uh-oh, thought Amanda. If she didn't watch her step, she could end up in a world of hurt. No one knew where she was—not her secretary, not Pops, not Thorn. Her body could be left in the tall weeds that clogged the ditch of an isolated country road for days—weeks maybe.

"You're asking for trouble, Hazard," Floyd warned as he snapped the belt into place with a decisive click. "Sally Jean and I have things to do and places to go. I'd hate to dent that tin can you call a car when I pull out of the driveway."

It was then that Amanda noticed the scrape on Floyd's elbow—a scrape that looked about a week old. A scab crusted the injury, and Amanda wondered if the older man, who wasn't as agile as he used to be, might have banged his arm as he leaped from a moving truck that was headed for the river.

"Lock the door of the house, Sally Jean," Floyd ordered. "We need to hit the road."

Amanda glanced at Sally Jean, whose gaze was bouncing back and forth between her husband and the unwanted guest.

Amanda cut her losses and left.

Sally Jean Lemon stared at the cloud of dust that Amanda kicked up as she drove off. "Something is going to have to be done about that woman," she mused aloud.

Floyd double-checked the security belts that were attached to the trailer load of cars. "Just follow me out of town, Sally Jean," he requested.

"I'm not riding in the truck with you?" she asked, surprised.

Floyd shook his head grimly. "You need to drive the car."

Casting a worried glance toward the Toyota that blazed over the hill, Sally Jean locked the front door, then climbed into her car and followed her husband.

Amanda stopped by her office and met Jenny Long on her way out the door.

"I think you have your days and nights mixed up, boss," Jenny teased.

"This investigation to clear Thorn's name has my schedule screwed up," Amanda replied.

Jenny peered at the stack of files clamped under Amanda's arm. "Need any help with that stuff?"

Amanda shook her head. "No, it's the accounts from Lemon's Used Cars."

"Poor Ima," Jenny murmured. "She must be at a total

loss as to what to do with the car lot. I'm sure she's relieved to have you in charge of the finances." With a wave and a smile, Jenny strode off.

Amanda shouldered her way through the office door and dumped the files on her desk. She needed to make preparations for her wedding, but with this case hanging over her head, she had to keep her mind on her first priority—reinstating Thorn as police chief. All of Vamoose was counting on her to exonerate Thorn. No one liked having GI Joe Payne lording over them.

Amanda opened the Lemon folder and started to work, tired though she was. For an hour she focused on the listings of cars sold, the transfer of titles and registration numbers.

When one particular make and model of car caught her attention, Amanda reached for the carbon-copy registration form she had confiscated from Irene's desk and compared registration numbers. She wondered if the state department of motor vehicles paid the slightest attention to vehicle ID numbers. Obviously not, she decided, because several title numbers were reversed.

Amanda stuck her finger between the louvers of the mini-blinds to stare at the car lot. Then she checked her watch. In a few minutes, Ernie and Irene would be making their nightly departures. She waited to see which vehicle Ernie would select for his rendezvous.

Shortly thereafter, Irene sped off. Following his customary procedure, Ernie slid beneath the wheel of a black compact car—Amanda was too far away to determine the make and model. She was also knee deep in registration forms and she didn't have time to follow Ernie to double-check his destination.

Hurriedly, Amanda picked up the phone to call Janie-Ethel, the police dispatcher.

"Vamoose P.D."

"Janie-Ethel, it's Amanda Hazard."

"Congratulations," the dispatcher said. "I hear you and the chief patched things up. Wish he was back on duty, too. I'll be glad when Payne—"

"Thanks," Amanda cut in hurriedly. She didn't have time for a lengthy chitchat about Payne's annoying qualities. "I need to contact Deputy Sykes PDQ. Is he on duty this evening?"

"Sure thing. Want me to relay a message to him?"

"Yes, ask him to swing by Irene Pratt's house to see if there is a black car in the driveway. If there is, ask him to call my office to confirm the time."

"Black car?" Janie-Ethel repeated curiously.

"Right."

"At Irene Pratt's?"

"Right," Amanda said hastily. "I'll be waiting for Benny's call."

Amanda hung up and focused on the second file in the stack. Five minutes later it dawned on her that she had yet to come across many original car titles. When she did, Frank Lemon's name was on them. She failed to see how Frank could possibly have paid for that long list of new vehicles, especially when he ran a *used* car lot.

Quickly, Amanda reached for the bank statements Ima Lemon had given her. Although Frank had borrowed a considerable amount of money from Vamoose Bank, the price of the automobiles exceeded the loan contract.

Amanda plucked up the list of title transfers and scrutinized it carefully. After cross-referencing the information, her suspicions were confirmed.

Frank Lemon had definitely dealt in stolen vehicles.

"Shame on you, Frank," Amanda murmured as she grabbed a pencil and placed check marks beside several title transfers.

It was obvious that Frank had been acquiring stolen cars—and parts stripped from stolen vehicles. No doubt, he had used the U-Haul truck to transport automotive parts to his shop. By the time the cars were pieced back together, painted, and the registration numbers altered, the vehicles were practically impossible to trace—unless you were the accountant in charge of the personal and business accounts . . .

The thought sent Amanda rifling through the phone bills for the business accounts. She noticed that one phone number appeared more than a dozen times. Very interesting . . .

The phone blared and Amanda nearly leaped out of her skin, so deep in concentration was she.

"Hazard's Accounting. Hazard here."

"It's Deputy Sykes," said Benny. "I got the Code 2 and took a cruise past Irene's."

"Did you confirm the vehicle?" Amanda asked.

"Confirmed. Do you want a 10-23 for the 11-54?"

Amanda frowned. Benny's police code jargon was like a foreign language that she couldn't translate. "Would you mind putting that in layman's terms."

"Sure thing," Benny accommodated. "Do you want me to stand by and tail the suspicious vehicle?"

"No, I would like for you to 10-23 an 11-54 at another location," she requested. "Check to see if Deputy Payne happens to be at Loraine Niles' home."

"What!" Benny said loudly.

"I plan to nail that GI Joe Payne with conduct unbecoming a law enforcement officer, so I want you to keep it under your hat, Benny."

"Right, under my hat. But Payne is 10-70D," Benny came back.

"What's that?"

"He's off duty."

"He wasn't two days ago when I tailed him to Loraine's," Amanda insisted. "I'm planning to hold these little trysts over his cocky head, should he refuse to back down from his charges that Thorn mishandled the Lemon case. Help me out here, Benny."

"10-4, Amanda."

Amanda replaced the receiver, then looked out the window to see that darkness had settled over Vamoose. She was itching to give the office at the car dealership a thorough check. There was very little traffic moving through Vamoose. The lights from the baseball field beamed in the darkness, indicating that the high school team was playing.

Leaving the file open to the phone number that cropped up with suspicious regularity, Amanda dug into her purse to retrieve the key she had swiped from Irene's top drawer, along with the carbon copies of registration forms. Amanda hoped she had latched onto the spare office key, because she wanted to search the place without having someone hovering over her.

Amanda stepped outside, then scampered across the open area between her office and the post office. Following an inconspicuous path, she glided between the metal pipes of the fence surrounding the car lot. The colorful banners snapped and popped overheard as she sneaked, unseen, from one car to another in order to reach the metal office.

When she twisted the key in the lock, the door creaked open and Amanda quickly shut it behind her. After opening the mini-blinds just enough to illuminate the office, she tiptoed toward Irene's desk. The bottom drawer came open without a hitch. Amanda squatted down to survey the contents. She plucked up a pair of spandex shorts and a skimpy sports bra that Irene apparently wore when she worked out at the health club. A pair of white tennis shoes, stacked one on top of the other, sat at the bottom of the drawer.

Amanda stuck her hand into the drawer, brushing her

fingertips over the metal surface. Particles of sand clung to her fingertips.

Very interesting, Amanda mused as she closed the bottom drawer.

Twisting around, she headed for Ernie's desk. She expected to find high-dollar sneakers in Ernie's drawer. Instead, she scooped up several packages of condoms. "Wonder what he needs those for?" she asked herself, then smirked.

Pensively, Amanda surveyed the dark office. While she was here, she might as well look through Frank's desk. Who knew what she might turn up?

Amanda grumbled when she opened the top drawer of Frank's desk and found nothing but rubber bands, paper clips, thumbtacks and . . . license tag stickers . . . ?

Amanda frowned, bemused. Had Frank stuck stickers on license plates of the stolen vehicles in his lot, leaving the impression that previous owners had registered the vehicle and renewed their tags?

Disillusioned by the depths to which Frank Lemon had sunk to make an illegal buck, Amanda opened the bottom drawer. Her eyes widened when she pulled out several bills of sale that had Floyd Lemon's name scrawled on them.

She distinctly remembered hearing Floyd say that he had played stupid once and that had been enough.

Apparently, Floyd had not been entirely honest with her. And damn it! Those cars and trucks Floyd had hauled off earlier this evening could have been stolen! He was hiding the evidence in plain sight and Amanda hadn't realized it.

Chastising herself for allowing evidence that could link Floyd and Frank in car theft, Amanda tucked two bills of sale in her pocket, then inched toward the unisex restroom. And there, stashed in a small closet, were Ernie's spare sports jacket, a T-shirt, nylon shorts . . . and a pair of expensive sneakers.

Amanda plucked up the shoes, shook them, and watched particles of sand fall to the floor. When she set the shoes down, she noticed the shoes weren't sitting together like a matched pair. The toes pointed out. Automatically, she arranged the shoes so that the left one was on the left and the right one was on the right—in natural order.

Her fetish for organization prompted her to match up the shoes correctly. She simply could not tolerate disorderliness.

Slipping quietly from the restroom, Amanda skulked to the office door. She needed to make her getaway before the high school baseball game ended and streams of cars poured from the park. She didn't wanted to be spotted, especially not by Deputy Payne!

Trotting in a doubled-over position, Amanda scuttled from one used car to another, then hightailed it back to her accounting office.

Nine

When Amanda returned to her office, the answering machine winked at her. She walked over to punch "play."

"Amanda, it's Benny. Deputy Payne's car pulled out of Loraine's driveway ten minutes before the black Chevy I saw at Irene Pratt's house pulled in. It was Ernie Niles!"

"I know that, Benny," she said to the answering machine.

There was a short pause. "If you need anything else, let me know. I'll be on duty tomorrow night, but I'm taking off early Friday evening so I can put up the decorations for the chief's bachelor party at Hitching Post Tavern."

The answering machine beeped, then Thorn's rich, baritone voice wafted across the office. "Where the hell are you, Hazard? I called the house and Pops said you hadn't come home yet. Now I'm calling your office and you aren't answering. Are you working late? Pick up, Hazard."

There was an impatient pause, in which Amanda heard Thorn breathing into the phone.

"Well fine," he mumbled. "I just hope that little disagreement we had the other night didn't send you running to H—"

Amanda smiled when Thorn's voice dried up. Thorn started to say Harjo, then bit back the name. She hadn't seen Sam Harjo for three weeks, except for that chance meeting at the cafe. She had, however, noticed Harjo driving past her farm once, but he hadn't stopped. Sam Harjo was a good, decent man. If Amanda hadn't been so stuck on Thorn, Harjo might have turned her head. Of course, it didn't hurt Thorn to keep fighting for what he had already won, she reckoned.

"Call me when you get this message, Haz," Thorn added belatedly.

Amanda was quick to note that he had reverted to that sultry voice. The man could be unbelievably seductive when the mood suited him.

Refusing to be distracted, Amanda plunked down at her desk. While she was rifling through Frank Lemon's financial records, she jotted down the necessary information that Jenny Long would need to type on the forms for Frank's estate taxes, then she made a note for Jenny to call a real estate appraiser to place a value on Frank's home and car dealership.

Yawning, Amanda picked up the phone to call the number that was listed repeatedly on Frank's business phone bill. She blinked, startled, when a woman's soft voice came down the line.

"Is Nick there?" Amanda asked, for lack of much else to say.

"No, this is the Williams residence. You must have the wrong number."

Amanda replaced the receiver. No, she thought to herself, she hadn't dialed the wrong number. But Frank had—too many times for the call to be a mistake. Amanda had the sneaking suspicion that Frank was a hypocrite. He didn't want Ernie Niles two-timing Loraine, but Frank could very well have arranged his own rendezvous during his overnight "business" trips.

Hurriedly, Amanda matched the dates of the phone calls with the dates of the business trips and expense receipts for fuel. Sure enough, there appeared to be a correlation.

Amanda shook her head in disgust. Apparently, Frank

had fooled around with the Williams lady while on his overnight trips. Damn that silver-tongued scoundrel. He had been tomcatting around while his wife waited trustingly for his return.

Muttering under her breath, Amanda gathered her files and locked up her office. The lights at the baseball diamond had long since been shut off and the town had all but shut down for the night. Amanda punched the Indiglo button on her Timex watch. It was 10:30.

Distracted by a zillion thoughts that centered around Frank Lemon's illegal activities and indiscretions, Amanda hung a left onto the gravel road toward her rented farmhouse.

She was singing along with Oklahoma's own country star, Garth Brooks, on the radio when bright headlights reflected in her rearview mirror. She switched the mirror to "night" position, but she couldn't do much about the glaring light that reflected in her side mirror. Damn, her eyes were sensitive, after poring over those financial ledgers. Those blinding headlights behind her weren't doing a thing for the queen-size headache that accompanied her home from the office . . .

Amanda's head whiplashed when the speeding car banged into her rear bumper, causing the lightweight Toyota to skid in loose gravel.

Cursing mightily, Amanda clenched her hands around the steering wheel as the unidentified vehicle shoved her toward the ditch. She braced herself, then stamped on the brakes with both feet. The vehicle behind her slammed into her rear bumper again.

Amanda heard wheels screech. Gravel pelted her car as the unidentified vehicle revved up to give her another forceful shove toward the ditch. Teeth gritted, she spun the steering wheel, but all she accomplished was aiming herself toward the ditch on the opposite side of the road.

The overpowering momentum of the car behind her sent

her plunging into the ditch. Amanda prayed for all she was worth when the Toyota bounced and tilted, as if it were about to flip over. She screamed bloody murder when her headlights flared against the corner fence post that was directly in her path.

Amanda stamped on the brake, but it was too late. The sound of crunched metal exploded around her the instant before she expected to feel her chest slam into the steering wheel. Luckily, the air bag popped open like a parachute to cushion the blow.

Pinned in the seat, with the front end of her car crunched against the unyielding fence post, Amanda glanced back to see the bright headlights retreating like a monster slinking into the darkness.

Hard as she tried, she couldn't ID the car that had run her off the road. All she could see was those damned headlights.

Amanda stayed where she was for several minutes, listening to the fractured radiator hiss, sputter and gurgle. No way was she going to attempt to back from the ditch and give the driver of the hit-and-run vehicle the chance to attack again. Better to let the driver think she had been knocked unconscious.

Amanda opened the door—slightly, then reached down to press her index finger on the button that triggered the dome light. She managed to climb from her car, cloaked in darkness, then she retrieved the accounting files without alerting her attacker that she was making her escape. No way did she want to be seen hiking off on foot while that maniac was close enough to the scene of the wreck to turn her into road kill!

When Amanda saw headlights coming toward her again, fear threatened to cloud her thinking. Willfully, she got herself in hand. She had found herself in scary scrapes several times during investigations, she reminded herself. There was always someone trying to discourage her from digging for facts. By now, she should be accustomed to these unnerving attempts to warn her away.

Should be, but wasn't.

Amanda inhaled several deep breaths, then ducked down in the Johnson grass when a vehicle approached.

"Oh God!" Nick yelped when he spotted the Toyota that was wrapped around the fence post. While steam roiled from the damaged radiator Nick stamped on his brake and skidded to a halt.

In the time it took to blink, he bounded from his truck and dashed toward the wrecked car.

"Hazard!" he yelled. "Hazard!"

Frantic, he yanked open the door, expecting to see his fiancée sprawled on the seat, blood gushing from multiple head wounds.

Hazard wasn't there.

Damn, if she hadn't been wearing her seat belt, she might have been ejected from the car. She could be lying in the wheat field—dead or dying. It could take several crucial minutes to locate her.

Nick wheeled around, then stopped short when he saw a trim silhouette rising from the grass.

"Boy, Thorn, am I glad to see you."

Nick jogged over to Hazard to examine her for injuries. There was a goose egg on her forehead and a dazed look in her eyes. Otherwise, she seemed to be in reasonably good condition.

"What the hell happened?" he wanted to know.

"Somebody ran me off the road," she said, in between quick snatches of breath.

Clearly, Hazard was rattled, though she was doing her damnedest to remain calm and collected.

"Did you get an ID?" he asked as he shepherded her toward his truck.

"No, all I could see was blinding headlights," she said shakily. "Then *wham.* I was crashing into that corner fence post that is as big around as a telephone pole."

"Where the hell have you been all evening?" Nick asked as he swung her into his arms and set her in the cab of his truck.

"Not where you think."

Nick slumped in relief. He had to admit that he had spent the past two days fretting over whether or not Sam Harjo had decided to make one last-ditch effort to win Hazard over before the wedding. Not that Nick blamed him; he would have resorted to the same tactic if the situation were reversed.

The dome light beamed down on Hazard's peaked face. "I was searching for evidence and filling out tax forms for the Lemon estate," she informed him.

Nick studied her for a long moment. "Are you sure you're okay? Do you want me to take you home before I pull your car from the ditch?"

The question appeared to be too complex for Hazard's dazed mind to handle. She stared blankly at him, as if trying to process his words.

Nick slid beneath the wheel. "I better take you home, Haz. You look a little rattled."

"I'm fine," she insisted, in a wobbly voice.

But she didn't object when Nick sped down the road to her house.

Three-legged Pete put up a fuss when Nick stepped from the truck. The dog piped down when Nick assisted Amanda across the lawn. Bruno barked his head off from inside the house when they strode across the porch and didn't calm down until Amanda staggered inside.

Pops had long since gone to bed, Nick decided as he switched on the lamp in the living room. The dishes had been put away, and the TV was off. Hank the tomcat was napping on the couch.

"Sit down, Haz," Nick ordered. "I'll get you something to drink."

Obediently, Hazard sank down on the LA-Z-Boy recliner. She was staring blankly at the wall when Nick returned with ice water and Tylenol.

"Just leave the Toyota where it is for the night," she mumbled.

"Done." Nick plunked down on the couch beside the lounging tomcat. "Who did you upset today that might have decided to retaliate?"

Amanda blinked, then glanced in his general direction. "Everybody who was involved in Frank Lemon's personal and profession life, is all."

"I suggest you back off, Hazard. Somebody out there doesn't want you snooping around."

"I don't have time to back off."

Nick studied Hazard astutely. The color was returning to her face and the expression in her eyes was no longer disoriented. Hazard was beginning to function normally, after her brush with disaster.

"If it's okay with you, I prefer to keep you alive until the wedding," he said. "We'll sort all this out after—"

"No," Hazard cut in. "You're going to stand at the altar with your reputation intact. I want this case resolved before I walk down the aisle, Thorn."

"Now, Hazard—"

"Don't *Now, Hazard* me, Thorn," she interrupted. "I've found proof that Frank Lemon was placing stolen cars on his lot and tampering with registration forms and car titles. I think his brother, his son-in-law and his secretary are involved in this scam. The fact is that you were not only pursuing a speeding driver the night Frank wound up dead in the driver's seat, but you were chasing a racketeer who was stealing vehicles, stripping car parts and falsifying registrations and titles."

"Geez, Hazard, if you have that kind of evidence, then

we can take the information to the sheriff, first thing in the morning."

Hazard gave her head a shake. "I want Frank's killer, too," she insisted. "If I turn the evidence over to the sheriff and let him begin his investigation, the murder trail will be several weeks old."

"I'm not sure there actually was a murder," Nick said.

Her head snapped up. "Don't start on that again, Thorn. I'm convinced Frank had help driving into the river. While I was searching the office at the used car lot tonight—"

"Damn, Haz, you B-and-Eed the dealership?" he croaked.

"Not exactly, I had a key."

Nick groaned. "I'm not sure I want to know how you got your mitts on that."

"Probably not," she said, then plowed ever onward. "I found tennis shoes, both men's and women's, with river sand sprinkled nearby. Those shoes might be connected to the wreck at the river.

"I also found some contracts with Floyd's name on them. They were in Frank's desk drawer. I think Floyd might have been helping Frank transport stolen cars to the lot. I won't be the least bit surprised to discover that Frank's gang of hoodlums were responsible for chop-shopping and burning the car you found while I was on vacation."

"Geez, Hazard, you've had a busy day. Makes mine seem like a day off."

"What did you do while I was investigating the case?"

"I built the interior walls for the room addition. Buzz Sawyer came by to help me nail the rafters in place." Nick smiled, then winked. "I also found time to make the travel arrangements for our honeymoon. We're Bahama bound, Hazard. Next week we'll be basking in the tropical sun and enjoying some much-needed R and R."

Nick's expression grew serious. "For that reason I would appreciate it if you would keep a low profile for the next couple of days. If you wind up dead, I'm not going to have a damn bit of fun on our honeymoon."

Rising to his feet Nick hoisted Hazard from the recliner, then ushered her down the hall. "Get some sleep and don't worry about your Toyota. I'll pull it from the ditch first thing in the morning. Then we'll pick up the results of our blood tests and get the marriage license from the courthouse."

Hazard plopped onto her bed and Nick knelt to pull off her pumps. By the time he unbuttoned her blouse and tossed it aside, Hazard's arms had glided up his chest to loop around his neck.

Nick might not be a genius, but he was sure as hell smart enough to recognize an overnight invitation when he saw one. He grinned in eager anticipation.

"You know, Thorn, I really like your bedside manner."

Nick stretched out beside her. "How 'bout my *in*-bed manners?" he growled playfully.

"Even better."

Nick took it from there . . .

Amanda awoke long after the sun came up. Her head was pounding and the muscles in her neck and shoulders screamed when she propped up on her elbow. Thorn was up and gone.

After a good soaking to ease her achy muscles, she grabbed a clean pair of jeans and dressed hurriedly, then strolled into the kitchen to fix breakfast . . .

Amanda screeched to a halt when she saw the ham and cheese sandwich awaiting her. She glanced at her watch. Good heavens, it was 11:30!

A note from Pops sat beside her plate.

> Hope you're feeling better, Half Pint. I helped Thorn tow the wrecked car into the driveway. Thorn said he would be back at 12:30 to pick you up. I'll be

gone most of the day. Salty Marcum and I are driving into the city.

Pops

While Amanda was eating, the phone jingled. Chasing a bite of sandwich with Diet Coke, Amanda hurried to pick it up.

Chomp, crack. "Hi, hon. I set up your pre-wedding appointment for two o'clock this afternoon. Betty June Delroy altered your dress and it's ready to go," Velma reported. "This is so exciting! I can hardly wait until tomorrow night. The whole town will be at the ceremony."

Great, thought Amanda. Her wedding was less than thirty-six hours away and she still hadn't solved the Lemon case.

"Be at the salon at precisely two o'clock, hon." Crackle, snap. "Bev and I want to have plenty of time to get your wedding 'do absolutely perfect!"

The phone went dead. Amanda set the receiver in the cradle. She had only taken two steps toward the kitchen when the phone screamed at her again.

"Hazard's three-ring circus, ringmaster speaking."

"So you really are going through with this, are you?" Mother harumphed into the phone.

Damn, Amanda wished she hadn't slept so late. She and Thorn might have been at the courthouse when Mother's call came down the wire.

"This ceremony is going to be a catastrophe," Mother said, and snorted. "I can't believe you're letting that nobody of a beautician and her redneck niece handle all the arrangements!"

"I'm sure Velma and Bev are doing a bang-up job," Amanda said in their defense.

"Bang-up job?" Mother hooted. "Have you seen the wedding invitations?"

"No, actually I've been pretty busy."

"Well, you should see them. The invitations look like cheap flyers for a countrified auction. They have been hand printed and run through a copy machine. They are an embarrassment to the Hazard name!"

"I'm sure you're exaggerating, Mother."

"I most certainly am not! I never exaggerate!"

"I'm sorry to cut you off, but I have things to do and I'm working on a short time clock," Amanda said.

"Working on the day before your wedding? You should be taking charge of this fiasco, doll. Or better yet, let me do it," Mother yakety-yakked. "I don't want to be the laughingstock of the country club and—"

"Oops, there's someone at the door," Amanda interrupted. "Gotta run, Mother."

"But—"

" 'Bye."

Amanda replaced the phone the instant before the doorbell rang. Damn, she had things to do, several places to go and people to see during these last few hours of her wedding count down.

Grabbing her purse, Amanda whizzed toward the door to find Thorn waiting on the porch. "Hi, Thorn. Let's be quick about taking care of the license. I have a hair appointment at two o'clock."

Amanda saw Thorn wince at the thought of her subjecting herself to another of Velma's cosmetic catastrophes, but he wisely kept his mouth shut. Together, they climbed into his truck and headed for the courthouse.

With Bruno at her heels, Amanda strode toward her jalopy truck to keep her appointment at Velma's Beauty

Boutique. Thorn had driven off to take the marriage license home with him for safekeeping.

As Amanda started the old clunker truck, she glanced at the wrecked remains of her Toyota. The vehicle was salvage-yard bound, she decided, only worth the total of parts that could be removed. She needed to call her insurance agent and report the mishap.

When she put the truck in gear, Bruno stared up at her with his big, sad eyes. "Sorry, boy, you better stay home. After my beauty appointment I need to scout out those shoe prints by the river again. I can't have you messing up the evidence."

Bruno stood there, silently begging her to let him ride along. Obviously, she had left her faithful bodyguard behind too many times in the past two weeks. Bruno was feeling neglected.

Amanda leaned over to open the passenger door. "Okay, you big lug, get in, but don't whine when you have to wait for me in the truck."

Bruno bounded onto the mat and plunked down. Amanda could almost swear the dog was smiling in satisfaction as she drove off.

"Here comes the bride," Beverly Hill singsonged as Amanda strode into the beauty parlor.

The place was packed. Heads, in various stages of the hair-care process, turned in synchronized rhythm as Amanda sank into The Chair.

After several rounds of "congratulations on the upcoming wedding" and "you're lucky to catch that hunk of a cop," the crowd settled beneath the row of humming hair dryers.

"Like, this is so exciting!" Bev enthused as she wrapped her meaty fists around the manicure tray. "By this time tomorrow, we'll be making our last-minute preparations for the wedding of the decade. Wow, like this is so awesome! I can't wait for you to see the dress I bought for the occasion, Amanda."

Amanda couldn't wait to see it, either. Bev's taste in clothes ran to the "radical" side.

"Gee, hon, I'm so nervous"—snap, pop—"that my hands are shaking." Velma lumbered toward The Chair. "I hope I don't whack off a chunk of hair from the wrong place. I'm just planning to blend in a few choppy areas." Crack, smack. "I want this 'do to be perfect.

"Ready or not, here we go," Velma said as she scooped up her scissors.

Amanda was never ready for Velma's creations, but she couldn't let the beautician know that. She wouldn't hurt Velma's feelings for the world.

"I've got all the arrangements made for Nicky's bachelor party." Crackle, crackle. "The guys are gonna have a grand time. Benny is over there right now, putting up the decorations."

Amanda clamped her hands around the arms of the chair when Velma ran a hurried brush through her hair. "I know Thorn is excited about the party."

Actually, she knew nothing of the kind. The last time they had discussed the bachelor bash, Thorn commented that he'd just as soon jump ship in the middle of shark-infested waters.

When Velma had Amanda's hair brushed and standing on end she swooped down with her scissors to snip off the uneven strands. "Just wait 'til you see the wedding and groom cakes tomorrow night." Snip, pop. "The decorator is working around the clock to get everything just right. My friend Maggie, from church, runs a cake decorating service from her home. Maggie Whittlemeyer designs the most amazing cakes you have ever seen."

"Like, no kidding," Bev chimed in as she pried Amanda's right hand loose from the arm of The Chair.

"My girlfriend from high school used the Southwest art theme for her wedding reception. Maggie made a coyote cake that sat upright on its haunches like it was howling at the moon. It was a hoot! Maggie even had a cassette tape of a howling coyote to play during the reception."

Amanda inwardly groaned. Mother would be howling if her darling daughter had a coyote cake at her wedding.

"What do the cakes look like?" Amanda questioned.

Snip, whack. "Can't tell ya, hon. It would ruin the surprise."

"I don't like surprises."

"Well, you'll love this one, trust me."

Amanda winced.

Snip, snip. "I even got Billy Jane Baxter, our local country music star, to bring the Horse Shoe Band to perform at your wedding dance."

"Wedding dance? I didn't know I was having one."

"Like, sure you are," Bev said as she buffed Amanda's nails. "It was kind of short notice, but Billie Jane said she wouldn't miss the wingding. She tried to get Garth Brooks and Vince Gil to come along, but they're booked solid."

The Oklahoma-grown Garth Brooks and Vince Gil performing at her wedding? Now there was a thrill Amanda would agree to. Instead, Billy Jane, with her twangy, nasally voice, would be yodeling her heart out, blinding guests when the lights reflected off the gaudy silver and turquoise jewelry she was fond of wearing.

"Billy Jane even volunteered to play the organ and sing for the ceremony," Velma put in. "She said she was glad to help out her accountant, since you do such a terrific job of keeping her business finances in great shape."

"This must be a country-style wedding then," Amanda presumed.

"You never know." Velma's plump face creased in a

wry grin. "Just because Billy Jane Baxter and the Horse Shoe Band are performing doesn't mean it's countrified."

Whatever the theme of the wedding, Mother was going to have a cow, Amanda predicted. Mother had visions of a wedding on the grand scale. Of course, Thorn's mom would prefer country style—which was the only thing she *did* approve of. She certainly didn't approve of Amanda!

"Irene Pratt isn't coming to the wedding," Velma said as she clipped and shaped Amanda's cropped hairstyle. "I don't know what set Irene off, but when she was here this morning to have her dark roots bleached, she said she wouldn't come if we paid her." Crackle, snap. "She must be envious because she's dating you-know-who and he can't propose because you-know-why."

Amanda knew the real reason she was on Irene Pratt's shit list, but she kept her trap shut.

Delores Grimes stuck her head out from under the dryer. "I don't think Ernie Niles will attend the wedding, either. When I stopped in yesterday to look for a car for my daughter, he nearly bit my head off when I mentioned the wedding. Whew, talk about being in a sour mood! He just finished talking to his uncle-in-law—"

"You mean Floyd Lemon was at the car dealership?" Amanda broke in.

"Yeah, and Sally Jean was with him," Delores continued as she recoiled a droopy hair roller. "I don't know what Ernie and Floyd were discussing, but they were glaring at each other. Floyd shoved some papers in Ernie's face, shook them at him, then stalked off."

Hmm, thought Amanda. Could it be that those bills of sale that she had seen in the office building were forgeries? Had Frank Lemon signed them for Floyd? Or was Floyd irritated because damaging evidence had been left in plain sight?

"I don't know what got into Floyd but he stormed into

the garage while Freddy Lassiter was working on a car and he started yanking automotive parts off the shelves."

Amanda frowned curiously. "Did Freddy object?"

"Nope, he just looked at Floyd as if he'd gone bonkers. But what does Freddy care? He just draws wages while the Lemons and Ernie Niles feud like the Hatfields and McCoys."

"What kind of auto parts did Floyd swipe from the garage?" Amanda asked.

Delores shrugged her thick shoulders. "I'm not an authority on vehicles. I just wanted to get something for my daughter that was dependable and reasonably priced. The only thing I recognized was a chrome bumper and a box that had 'filter' stamped on it."

Now, why would Floyd need spare car parts—unless he knew he might bang up his car when he smashed into Amanda's Toyota, in hopes of warning her away from this case . . .

Amanda's thoughts trailed off when she glanced in the mirror. Velma had trimmed her bangs so short that it looked like she had a bowl on her forehead. Holy haircut!

"Wow, radical, Aunt Velma," Bev said, glancing up from her work. "After you get the Prussian purple and glitter tint soaked in, this is really going to be a perfect 'do and a perfect match for Amanda's signature colors."

Oh God, Amanda thought sickly. No veil in the world could conceal this disaster.

Amanda sat upright in The Chair, staring at her hideous reflection while Velma waddled over to retrieve the hair color mixture.

"Don't leave that stuff on for more than two minutes," Amanda insisted. "You know how porous my hair is."

Chomp, crackle. "No can do, hon. Gotta let it set for fifteen minutes to get the right shade of purple. Bev and I know because we tested it on her toy poodle's tail."

Oh, God. Prussian purple hair tint splattered on

Amanda, forcing her to close her eyes. She sat there like a statue while Bev polished her nails and Velma coated hair color on every strand. The crowd of onlookers "oohed" and "ahed" while Velma tugged on the tinted tendrils, making them stand at attention.

Smacking her gum, Velma herded Amanda to the dryer. "Just sit tight while I comb out Delores's hair, hon. I'll get right back to you in a jiffy."

The smell of hair dye circled inside the dryer, making Amanda feel nauseous. Visions of a disastrous wedding contributed to her queasiness. She never should have allowed Velma and Bev free rein over the ceremony. But it was that or let Mother run the show.

Amanda had picked the lesser of two evils, and she had to live with it.

When Delores stood up, Velma galumphed over to lift the dryer from Amanda's head, then checked her watch. "Perfect timing, hon. We've got a match," she called to Bev.

"Good. Like, I can't wait to see Amanda's 'do after you rinse and blow dry. This is s-ooo cool!"

"My head is burning up," Amanda said, plucking at the strands of hair. "Are you sure you didn't leave this stuff on too long?"

"No, it'll be fine . . . Oh dear," Velma wheezed as she touched the red patches of Amanda's scalp. "I forgot about your allergic reaction to that herbal hair conditioner. Quick, Bev! Help me rinse Amanda's hair before it gets so brittle that it breaks off!"

Amanda panicked. She had horrible visions of being bald at her wedding. When Bev and Velma shoved her head under the cold water faucet, every patron in the parlor rushed forward to view the cosmetic calamity.

"Oh, my," Velma mumbled.

Amanda was pretty certain that when a beautician said "Oh, my," you were in serious trouble.

"Bev, get me some of that neutralizing solution PDQ," Velma ordered.

A foul-smelling mixture dripped into Amanda's ears while the beauticians held her facedown in the sink. She could hear the gasps and groans of bystanders over the gurgle of running water.

"Now what, Aunt Velma?"

"I don't know. I've only seen an allergic reaction of this magnitude once in my professional career."

Oh, Lord! Amanda was assailed by the overwhelming urge to crawl into the sink drain—and stay there.

Velma massaged Amanda's head vigorously. "Bring me some of that hypo-allergenic conditioner, Bev."

Time ticked by at a slug's pace, and the patrons waited with bated breath. Finally, Velma allowed Amanda to raise her head from the sink.

"Now don't freak out," Bev cooed. "It always looks worse when it's wet."

Amanda tried, unsuccessfully, to swallow her shocked shriek. Her hair had fallen out in patches. Bright lavender globs stuck out at a forty-five degree angle from her head. When Velma tried to run a comb through the brittle strands, more hair broke off!

"Oh my God!" Amanda wheezed.

"Sit down, hon." Pop, pop, pop. "Dang it. Bev's poodle came out looking fine when we made our tests. I can't imagine what the heck happened."

"Oh God, oh God, oh God," Amanda chanted, trying to keep from hyperventilating.

Thorn loved to run his fingers through her hair. And now her hair would fall out like molting chicken feathers when he touched it. She looked like a mutated freak, an alien from a galaxy far, far away.

"You better not watch, hon," Velma advised as she spun The Chair away from the mirror. "I'll fix this mess, trust me."

Amanda was never going to trust Velma again for as long as she lived.

For several anxious moments Amanda sat there, stunned to the bone, imagining Thorn's reaction. Mother's reaction. Amanda wondered if she would be the first bride in recorded history to appear at church with a brown paper sack over her head.

"Okay, okay. This is going to be okay," Velma repeated. "I'll just spray it down good and you'll have to sleep with a hairnet tonight, hon. Better yet, we'll put one on you now to make sure that . . . um . . . no hair falls out of place."

Amanda inhaled a deep breath the moment before Velma grabbed the hair spray. A fog filled the salon and patrons rushed over to open the door and windows. Amanda could hear the ozone layer sputtering as pollutants floated skyward.

"There now, all done." Crack, chomp. "Not too bad, all things considered."

As The Chair spun toward the mirror, Amanda prepared herself for the absolute worst—which is exactly what she encountered. Even Dennis Rodman of the Chicago Bulls wouldn't appear at mid-court with a 'do like this!

"We'll just slip this hairnet on your head and you'll be finished. Don't try to comb your hair between now and time for the wedding. Let me do it before the wedding."

Amanda knew she didn't dare touch her hair. Each strand looked like a loose tooth on the verge of falling out. Never in her worst nightmare had she expected to look this hideous at her wedding!

"No charge, hon," Velma said, forcing a smile.

Amanda staggered outside. When she glanced down to retrieve her keys from her purse, she noticed her hands. On each Prussian-purple-colored fingernail Bev had painted a letter in black. Put them all together and they spelled M-A-N-D-Y T-H-O-R-N.

Amanda's shoulders slumped. She had no dignity left for her wedding. If Thorn called off the ceremony she wouldn't blame him.

When Bruno bounded up on all fours and barked at her, Amanda blinked. Her devoted bodyguard couldn't pick up her scent, because the stench of glitter, dye and hair spray hovered around her like a bad case of B.O.

"It's okay, Bruno," she called to the dog that had slapped his front paws on the dashboard and bared his teeth in warning. "See, it says right here, Mandy soon-to-be Thorn." She held up her hands, displaying the letters printed on her nails.

Still, Bruno wasn't convinced that he knew her.

"Bruno, sit," Amanda said in her most commanding voice.

The dog cocked his head, then sank down on the seat.

"Good boy." Amanda slid onto the seat of her clunker truck, then reached out cautiously to pat Bruno's head.

The dog sniffed her sleeve, then sank down on his side of the truck. God, how Amanda hoped Thorn wouldn't react the same way!

Ten

After Amanda's traumatic experience at Velma's Beauty Boutique, she drove home to retrieve her Bad Hair Day hat, then headed for the river to take another look at the shoe prints she had seen a few days earlier.

Pensively, Amanda sank down to stare at the prints in the sand. She hadn't figured out what subconscious need to reexamine the prints was calling her back to the crime scene, but here she was, wondering what she had overlooked.

The odd arrangements of the tennis shoe prints indicated the individuals were hopping around on one foot. Amanda frowned, wondering if the perps had twisted a knee or ankle during their leap from the truck. That would explain the skimble-skamble sets of prints that were scattered on the sandy hill.

Yet, Amanda didn't notice her prime suspects limping noticeably. Except for Ernie Niles, who always walked as if he had corncob stuck up his butt. However, that did not mean that her suspects hadn't tried to conceal an injury from her, she reminded herself. It had taken her more than a week to realize this was a case of murder, not an accident.

After Amanda gave the prints a thorough going over, she ambled back to her gas-guzzling truck. She recalled seeing the scrape on Floyd Lemon's arm and wondered if he might have injured himself during the incident.

She also wondered if the car she had seen parked in Floyd and Sally Jean's driveway might have been the same one that had run her into the ditch.

On impulse, Amanda drove out to Floyd's secluded home. To her disappointment, neither the truck-trailer rig nor the car was anywhere to be seen.

Amanda scowled. She knew that if the car had been damaged, Floyd, the former auto body repairman and mechanic, would cover the evidence of the hit-and-run. And for all Amanda knew, Floyd might even trade off his car to prevent Amanda from appraising the damage. Floyd was certainly in a position to make a quick trade—if he needed to.

The sound of an approaching vehicle prompted Amanda to spin around. Bruno barked his head off inside the jalopy truck, as Floyd and Sally Jean Lemon pulled into their driveway. Amanda noticed immediately that Sally Jean was not driving the same car. Very interesting.

"Did you have the sudden urge to trade vehicles, Floyd?" she fired the question in place of a greeting.

"Yeah, so?" Floyd grunted as he climbed from his truck. "Is there a law against that, Hazard?"

"Depends on why you felt the need for the change." She eyed Floyd intently. "You didn't happen to damage your car last night, did you?"

"Nope." Floyd said without batting an eyelash. "I happened onto a honey of a deal that I couldn't turn down at the auction."

I'll bet, thought Amanda. She stared pointedly at the scrape on Floyd's elbow. "How did you hurt your arm?"

"He got hung up while unfastening the belts that secure the vehicles on the towing trailer," Sally Jean answered for her husband.

Amanda glanced down at the woman's puffy ankles. Thick ankles—or a recent sprain?

"What are you looking at?" Sally Jean demanded.

"Do you have weak ankles?"

Sally Jean blinked. "Why do you want to know?"

"No reason." Amanda gestured toward Sally Jean's low-cut running shoes. "But if you do have ankle problems you should keep in mind that hi-tops offer extra support."

Sally Jean eyed her warily. "Why this sudden interest in our scrapes and sprains?"

Sprains? Amanda hadn't said anything about sprains.

"I'm just being neighborly." Amanda gave the Lemons a sugary smile, then gestured toward the new car. "Nice wheels, but I didn't see anything wrong with the wheels you were driving yesterday . . . unless the car was stolen property and you didn't want me to trace your 'hot' car from the fake bills of sales that I found in Frank's office desk. Is that why you were so peeved at Ernie? Because he didn't dispose of those incriminating papers with your name on them?"

Amanda noted that Floyd didn't confirm or deny her conjectures. He just glanced at his wife, who was staring apprehensively at Amanda.

Amanda wanted the Lemons to know that she had grave suspicions about their involvement in the theft ring. She hoped she had made Floyd and Sally Jean nervous enough to become careless. She needed a break in this case, because time was running out. After all, she couldn't conduct a long-distance investigation from the Bahamas.

Amanda made a spectacular display of strolling around the Lemons' new car. She halted directly behind the Buick Park Avenue to jot down the license tag number.

Without saying another word, she climbed into the bucket-of-rust truck and drove off.

* * *

"That woman makes me nervous," Sally Jean muttered.

Floyd stared after the old truck. "Yeah, me, too," was all he said before he pulled the receipts of his transaction from his pocket to give them a thorough check.

Amanda made a quick stop at Lemon's Used Cars to let her presence be known. Ernie and Irene watched, in hostile silence, while Amanda ambled around the car lot, under the pretense of searching for a replacement for her Toyota.

"Now what are you doing?" Ernie demanded as he followed her around the row of pickups.

Amanda was pleased to note that Ernie had given up his attempt to order her off the premises. He must have realized that she was not to be denied.

"I still need another vehicle."

"Fine, pick out the one you like and take it for a test drive."

Amanda was quick to note that Ernie didn't ask what had happened to her Toyota. Chances were that he already knew about the hit-and-run incident.

While Ernie kept his distance, Amanda pretended to survey the selection of trucks, looking for a car that might have been dented during the hit-and-run. She doubted that Ernie was foolish enough to leave the vehicle in question on the lot, but who knew when a suspect might become careless.

Her gaze darted discreetly toward Freddy Lassiter's workshop. In the shadows of the garage, she could see a dark-colored car. Could it be the one that slammed into her?

"Maybe I'll look at cars instead of trucks," she said breezily. "I might like to test drive one of the many cars you drive when you're sneaking over to do the horizontal hoochie-koochie with Irene."

Ernie's face exploded with color. "You've been spying on me!" he hissed.

"Sure have," she said. "I can tell you precisely what time you left work, which vehicle you were driving, and what time you arrived at Irene's house."

"That's invasion of privacy," he said.

"No, it isn't," she contradicted. "Now, if I had bugged Irene's house—and I'm not saying whether I did or didn't—then *that* would be invasion of privacy. If I taped your conversations and presented them to your wife—"

"You didn't!" he snarled. "Damn you, Hazard. You better watch your step. If you mess with me, I'll—"

"You'll what? Run me into a ditch? Tamper with my brakes and cause another fatal wreck? Or do you plan to use the same tactic on me that you used on Frank?"

Ernie slammed his mouth shut, then opened it again. "Be very careful, Hazard, that tomorrow, the day of your wedding, doesn't become the day of your funeral."

"Are you threatening me?" she challenged.

Irene came rushing from the metal office building. Obviously, she had been eavesdropping on the conversation.

Amanda watched the secretary scurry up behind Ernie. She noted that Irene shuffled her feet. Was she trying to conceal an injured knee or ankle?

"You have no right to interfere in our personal lives," Irene muttered.

"Personal lives?" Amanda scoffed. "Excuse me, Irene, but you and Ernie aren't supposed to be sharing a personal life. Ernie is a married man."

Irene clamped her lips shut and glanced at Ernie. Amanda couldn't be sure, but she suspected Irene occasionally harped on the subject of a divorce. But no way in hell was Ernie going to walk away from the financial nest egg he was squatting on. He was probably stalling, claiming that he wanted to wait until the *appropriate time* to get a divorce, making all the right noises to keep Irene on the leash. Amanda was willing to bet on it.

And Irene, schmuck that she was, allowed herself to fall for Ernie's empty promises.

Ernie's arm shot toward the gate of the car lot. "I want you to leave. I'm not selling you a vehicle or listening to you lambaste us for another minute, Hazard. Just go away and leave us alone!"

Amanda slung her purse strap over her shoulder and strode toward the garage where Freddy was doubled over the car he was working on, his head stuck somewhere under the raised hood.

Freddy raised his head to watch Ernie and Irene storm back to the office, then glanced at Amanda and chuckled. "You really have those two going," he said, as he reached for the rag in his hip pocket. "You're got them whispering to each other, afraid someone might overhear what they're saying."

"I don't suppose you've overheard anything that would help me with this investigation," Amanda said.

Freddy shook his tousled head. "No, but I walked into the office last night while Ernie and Irene were in a clinch. They're always stealing kisses and gropes when they think no one is looking."

"What happened to the black Chevy Ernie was driving when he left the dealership last night?" Amanda quizzed him.

Freddy shrugged, then reached for a wrench. "I don't know which car he was driving, because I clocked out before Ernie and Irene left."

Amanda's shoulders slumped in disappointment. "Do you ever work overtime and leave after Ernie and Irene do?"

"You seem to be under the impression that I have more prestige than I do," Freddy said as he bent forward to repair the broken heater hose that was attached to the engine. "I don't have a gate key. I just work here and draw my wages."

Amanda's gaze swung around the shop to see paint sprayers, toolboxes, grilles from cars, and various auto parts propped against the walls. She would love to take a closer look at the garage, to determine what else Frank had stashed in here while he was running his auto theft racket.

Of course, if she started snooping around, Ernie would be out here in a flash to run her off the lot.

Frustrated, Amanda turned on her heels and ambled to her jalopy truck. Time was running short and her evidence for this case wasn't strong enough to present her report to the sheriff. Tonight, she was going to have to sit herself down and think things through so she could offer something to the sheriff, something that would prompt him to check into this incident himself, rather than leaving GI Joe Payne in charge!

Nick put away his carpentry tools, then stepped back to appraise the new addition to his home. He had worked nonstop the past two weeks. With Buzz Sawyer's assistance, the vinyl siding had been installed on the new rooms. Of course, he had yet to nail up Sheetrock or install fixtures in the new bathroom, but at least a drenching rain wouldn't warp the flooring and stud-wall partitions.

The insulation had been stapled into place, and Nick itched all over from handling it. He needed a long, soaking shower.

Satisfied with his hard day's work, he ambled into the house—in time to catch the incoming phone call.

"Nicky, it's Mom."

Nick sighed. "Hi, Mom. Where are you?"

"We're in the city, visiting with your brother," Mom said in a clipped voice that indicated she was none too happy to be in Oklahoma for the upcoming wedding. "I don't suppose you have come to your senses and broken off this doomed wedding."

"No, Mom, the wedding is still on for tomorrow."

Nick heard Mom's theatrical sigh of disappointment.

"Well, fine. Dad and I are staying all night at Rich's place, then we'll drive out to Vamoose tomorrow afternoon."

"Good, now can I talk to Rich?" Nick requested.

"Why?"

"Last-minute preparations, Mom," he said evasively.

"Yo, bro," Rich said cheerfully. "What's-a-matter? Getting the pre-wedding jitters?"

"No, I just wanted to remind you of the bachelor's party at Hitching Post Tavern tonight. You're coming, aren't you?"

"Sure thing. Wouldn't miss it. Soon as I get Mom and Dad settled in, I'll be on my way."

"Do you have a Western suit to wear to tomorrow's ceremony?"

Rich snickered. "No, I thought I'd wear my silk boxer shorts and give the crowd a thrill."

"You might as well," Mom piped up, while listening on the extension. "It will be the only entertaining moment at this disastrous wedding."

"Mom . . ." Nick said warningly. "Hang up the phone."

"Why? Do you plan to say something that you're afraid for me to hear? Such as, you know you're making the biggest mistake of your life and you don't know how to bow out gracefully?"

Nick gnashed his teeth. "Never mind, Rich, I'll talk to you later."

"Okie-dokie, little brother. I'll be there with my bells on."

"Wait a minute, Nicky, I'm not finished with you—"

" 'Bye, Mom," Nick said, then hung up before Mom started yammering in his ear.

Hurriedly, Nick headed for the shower. If Mom wanted to add her two cents' worth—again—then she could deal with his answering machine.

He sighed appreciatively as warm water trickled over his head and shoulders, rinsing away the itchy particles of insulation. Ah, the reviving effects of the shower were just what the doctor ordered . . .

Nick yelped, startled, when an unidentified hand slid over his bare derrière. He wheeled around, assuming his martial arts stance. He blinked in disbelief when he recognized Hazard who was wearing a black stocking cap, black windbreaker pants and matching jacket. Smudges of black mascara covered her cheeks, forehead and chin.

"What the hell are you doing? Auditioning for a part in Rambo XII?" he scowled at her.

"Nice to see you, too, Thorn," she said. "You do look good in your birthday suit."

While she looked her fill, Nick shut off the shower, then grabbed a towel. "What are you up to, Haz?"

"Some good old-fashioned cloak and dagger stuff," she told him as she took the towel from his hand to dry his back. "I thought you might like to join in the fun."

Nick snatched away the towel, "I'm going to my bachelor party, remember?"

"The party isn't until eight o'clock," she reminded him. "We can do some snooping between now and then."

"No," he said firmly. "And you aren't going snooping, either. If we get picked up, we'll spend the eve of our wedding in the slammer. Deputy Payne would have a heyday with that."

"This is important, Thorn," she insisted as she followed him down the hall so he could dress. "We aren't going to get caught."

"Famous last words, Haz. That's what all criminals think."

Before Nick could select a respectable shirt and jeans to wear to the bachelor party, Hazard laid a black sweatshirt and sweatpants on his bed.

"Put these on," she ordered. "The vows state you're going to marry me for better or worse. You have got to help me out here. After all, I'm doing this to salvage your good name and upstanding reputation."

Hazard peered at him with a placating look in her luminous eyes, then flashed one of her knock-'em-dead smiles. "Please, Thorn?"

He caved in immediately—he always caved in where Hazard was concerned. "All right, damn it, I'll go, if only to keep you out of trouble. But I'm calling the shots."

Hurriedly, Nick dressed in the clothes Hazard laid out for him. Then she pulled a tube of mascara from her pocket and rubbed it on his face.

Smiling, she stepped back to appraise her handiwork. "The caped crusaders," she said. "The dynamic duo. Lone Ranger and Tonto, Batman and—"

"Cut it out, Hazard," Nick grumbled as he sank down on the edge of the bed to don his tennis shoes. "Where the hell are we going?"

"To Lemon's Used Cars," she told him as she led the way down the hall.

"What are we looking for?"

Hazard shrugged. "I'm not sure, but my guess is that Frank stashed the spare parts that he removed from stolen cars in the shop. I'm also curious to know if the bent grille of the car that Ernie drove last night is stashed in a corner of the garage."

"Are we doing a B-and-E?" Thorn asked warily.

Hazard held open the front door for him and then smiled as she dangled the key from her colorfully painted fingertips. "Just happen to have a key. It's the master key to the workshop and office."

"The one you stole from Irene Pratt's desk?" he muttered. She nodded. "When we get married, I want you to promise that you'll quit bending the laws I'm sworn to uphold."

"Yeah, whatever," she said as she closed the door behind her.

Nick scanned the brightly lit area around the car dealership. A steady flow of traffic cruised down Main Street. The Friday night crowd of teenagers were parading through town, and Deputy Payne was parked near Thatcher's Oil and Gas so they wouldn't cause a disturbance or exceed the speed limit.

Hazard parked her jalopy truck behind her office, then crouched down to skulk through the weeds that lined the fence row.

"Hurry up, Thorn," she whispered.

Nick muttered under his breath. If he got caught, there was no way in hell he would get his job back. Why had he agreed to Hazard's scheme? He must have had a momentary lapse of sanity.

"Gimme the key, Haz," he murmured as he went to his knees beside the garage.

Hazard handed over the master key.

Scanning the area, Nick unlocked the door, then pushed Hazard ahead of him into the shop.

"See there? A piece of cake," she whispered.

"We just got here," he grumbled. "Save the piece-of-cake bit until we're back at my house."

Fishing the penlight from her pocket, Hazard scanned the workshop. Her attention focused on a stack of license plates in a cluttered corner.

"See that, Thorn? I'll bet those plates were removed

from stolen cars and are waiting to be switched after the 'hot' cars have cooled off."

She shined her light on a stack of hubcaps. "What do you want to bet those caps have been switched out, too?"

Nick took the flashlight in hand and shone it on the car in the garage. "Is that the vehicle that followed you last night?"

Hazard shrugged. "I can't tell, but it doesn't look like the one I saw in here this afternoon."

"This looks to be a dead end, Hazard," Nick murmured. "Let's get the hell out of here before we get caught."

"Give me a few more minutes to look around," Hazard requested as she skulked over to scrape the paint off the car that was sitting in the middle of the garage.

Nick glanced down at his watch. "If we don't hurry up, I'll be late for my own party. Come on, damn it."

"Keep your pants on, Thorn. I'll be there in a minute," she said from the far side of the shop.

An unidentified object clattered to the concrete floor.

"Sh-sh!" Nick hissed.

"Oops, I tripped over a spare steering wheel," Hazard whispered back.

Several moments later, Hazard approached. "Well, damn."

"What's wrong? Didn't you find a signed confession of guilt lying around?"

"No need to be snide, Thorn," she said, and scowled.

Nick rose slowly from his crouch to stare out the window. The teenagers who had been cruising Main Street, had congregated in the parking lot at Last Chance Cafe.

"The coast is clear. Run for it, Hazard."

In silence, Nick and Hazard skulked outside and then locked the door. When Deputy Payne drove past, Nick grabbed Hazard's hand and dragged her down in the weeds beside him.

"Belly crawl," he murmured in her ear. "Payne-in-the-ass is pulling up to the gate of the car lot."

Slithering like snakes, Nick and Hazard made their way to the jalopy truck. Once inside, Nick breathed a huge sigh of relief.

"I think you should turn your findings over to the sheriff," he insisted, and not for the first time. "Let the sheriff follow up this investigation while we're on our honeymoon."

"I still have twenty-four hours," she protested as she cranked the engine. The old truck coughed, sputtered, then hummed.

Nick didn't press the issue again, until Hazard turned into his driveway fifteen minutes later. "Tell me you are going straight home and that you'll stay there. Tell me you'll write up your report and take it to the sheriff, first thing in the morning. I won't be able to enjoy my bachelor party if I'm worrying about whose house, or place of business, you're breaking and entering while I'm at Hitching Post Tavern."

"Okay, Thorn, consider yourself told," she said without glancing in his direction.

Nick cupped his hand around her grimy chin, forcing her to stare him squarely in the eye. "You're going home? Yes or no?"

"That's what you wanted me to tell you and that's what I told you. Geez, Thorn. What do you want? A statement signed in my own blood?"

"What I want is for you to be alive, and in one piece, tomorrow night when I meet you at the altar."

"I said I would be there and I will be," she promised.

When Hazard drove off, Nick stared after the clunker truck. He had the unmistakable feeling that Hazard had told him what he wanted to hear just to shut him up.

Ten minutes later Nick had showered, changed and strolled into the living room. His brother was sprawled on the sofa, thumbing through the latest issue of *Sports Illustrated.*

Rich looked up when Nick appeared. "Ready to go, bro?" He frowned when he noticed a black smudge on the underside of Nick's jaw. "What have you been doing?"

"Don't ask," Nick grumbled. "You don't want to know."

Rich grinned broadly. "Sure I do. It has something to do with Hazard, doesn't it? She's up to something, isn't she? She's always up to something. So, what unauthorized case is she working now?"

"Mine."

Rich blinked, bemused. "Yours? What the hell does that mean?"

"It means that I have been suspended from duty, because Deputy Joe Payne, from Vamoose Sheriff's Department thinks I mishandled the chase that left Frank Lemon dead in the driver's seat."

Rich's mouth dropped open. "Holy shit!"

"My sentiments exactly. I had to ask Hazard to use her unorthodox methods to investigate. Deputy Payne has his sights set on my job. He wants control of this one-horse town, and his findings will indicate that my misconduct, and deviation from S.O.P.—standard operating procedure—caused the fatality."

"Who the hell is Deputy Payne?" Rich asked.

"Some GI-Joe type who graduated from Vamoose while we were serving our hitch in the armed forces. He likes to throw his weight around and act important," Nick muttered resentfully. "He also has a vested interest in Vamoose, because he has been shacking up with Loraine, Frank Lemon's daughter."

Rich bounded from the couch and strode toward the telephone. "I'll have my coworkers at OSBI run a check on the guy. If he's got so much as one blemish on his record, I'll know by morning.

"Replace you as police chief!" Rich hooted. "Not damned likely. Not if I have anything to say about this, which I sure as hell intend to!"

Rich snatched up the phone and placed the call.

"Did I ever tell you that you're my favorite brother?" Nick asked as he and Rich ambled out the door.

"I'm your only brother."

Nick grinned. "That's what makes you so special."

Broad shoulder to broad shoulder, elbow to elbow, the Thorn brothers walked toward Nick's truck, then headed for the bachelor party.

Eleven

Amanda was greatly relieved now that Thorn had been delivered to his home, none the wiser about her catastrophic hairdo. The black stocking cap concealed all evidence. Thorn wouldn't have to know about her hellish 'do until the wedding. She just hoped the shock of watching her hair fall out while she walked down the aisle, wouldn't kill him while he stood at the altar.

Amanda had no intention of going straight home. She had told the little white lie for Thorn's own good. She didn't want to sour his mood before he attended the bachelor party.

Her mind was buzzing with previous conversations and facts that she had collected for this investigation. Amanda knew she had overlooked a clue that could prompt the pieces of this puzzle to tumble neatly into place. She simply had to keep stirring around, waiting for her thoughts to gel.

On intuitive impulse, Amanda drove to Whatsit River Bridge, then glanced into the darkness where she had seen footprints near the clumps of weeds. Something about those footprints still niggled her. But what! Damned if she could figure it out.

Cutting a sharp right turn, Amanda cruised past Floyd and Sally Jean Lemon's house. Dim light glowed from the window, indicating the couple was at home.

When Amanda drove past Ima Lemon's estate, she noticed Deputy Payne's squad car parked in the driveway, behind Loraine's small sports car. Now that was interesting. Was Loraine visiting her mother . . . and Payne just happened to show up?

Those two really had the hots for each other, thought Amanda. She expected the couple would say their farewells, then drive off to park on some secluded stretch of road. Ernie Niles would be none the wiser, because he presumed his wife was spending the evening with her recently widowed mother.

While Amanda drove around, waiting for Loraine and Payne to have their rendezvous, she noticed a dirt path that led into the pasture behind Frank Lemon's house. Unidentified objects near the base of the pond dam reflected moonlight. What, Amanda wondered, had Frank stashed out of sight in this obscure pasture? Skeletons of cars that he had stripped and chopped to put parts in other vehicles?

Amanda climbed from her jalopy truck to open the gate. A flock of sheep darted in front of her headlights, then scattered. Amanda hurried to shut the gate behind her, before the sheep escaped.

Switching off her headlights, she drove by the light of the moon. Amanda parked near the pond dam and grabbed her flashlight. Sure enough, Frank, and/or Floyd, had stashed the remains of dismantled vehicles in the inconspicuous spot behind the dam. From the road, the area was barely visible. This car graveyard told the tale of theft. Radios, bucket seats, back seats, arm rests, taillights—you name it and it had been stripped from the cars.

Everything Amanda saw pointed to Frank's ring of car thieves. Tags were missing. Engines and transmissions were missing. No doubt, the items had been run through the shop and listed on the financial accounts as purchased items. Frank had been listing stolen parts as part of his inventory, then deducting them as expenses on his tax reports.

Uncle Sam was not going to be pleased!

That sneaky old goat, thought Amanda. There was no telling how many stolen vehicles Frank had sold to unsuspecting Vamoosians. His neighbors and friends had been cheated, and Frank had snickered all the way to the bank.

Scowling, Amanda climbed atop the pond dam to stare toward the brick home—where Deputy Payne was probably asking Ima Lemon all sorts of leading questions to wrap up the investigative report that would cause Thorn to get the ax. Amanda stared down the hill toward the silhouette of the small cottage that sat near the west end of the property. Maybe she should mosey down there and look around. Frank might have stashed more evidence in the shack.

Hiking off on foot, Amanda crossed the pasture. With the silence of a shadow, she inched around the outer wall of the cottage, then halted by the back window. She peeked inside, surprised to see an unmade, twin-sized bed in the corner of the room. Maybe the gardener who kept the Lemon estate well manicured did live here, she mused. Someone obviously did, though he or she didn't appear to be at home.

Amanda eased her hip onto the windowsill, then climbed inside. Flicking on her flashlight, she appraised the room. It was an absolute pit. Several pairs of soiled jeans were strewn around the room. Empty cellophane food wrappers glinted in the light.

Amanda wouldn't be surprised to learn that Deputy Payne had rented this cottage. By living in this secluded area of Vamoose County he would have easy access to Loraine's house, which was only two miles down the road. Why, for all Amanda knew, Payne and Loraine might wallow in their sordid affair—right here in this room!

The distasteful thought sent Amanda striding into the hall. She halted in the cramped living room to survey the broken-down blue sofa, threadbare armchair and small TV.

A regular palace, she thought with a smirk. Yes, indeedy, she hoped she did discover that this was where Payne hung out . . .

When Amanda noticed an electrical cord protruding from the pleated skirting on the couch, she sank to her knees. She reached under the sofa to pull out a state-of-the-art stereo unit that was designed for installation in a vehicle.

Amanda dug a little deeper and came across a cardboard box of magnetic license plates and brackets. Now wouldn't those come in handy if you wanted to steal a car and change tag numbers to befuddle the police?

A thorough search of the kitchen cabinets turned up a box of door handles, taillight reflectors and various sizes of screws and bolts. A stack of magazines displaying cars—and women in skimpy bikinis—was stashed on the shelves, alongside catalogs that listed auto parts for every make and model of car and truck under the sun.

Amanda scanned the magazines and catalogs, looking for the name of the subscriber. Frank Lemon . . .

Bright headlights flashed across the sheets that formed improvised curtains over the windows. Damn, thought Amanda. The last thing she needed was to get caught trespassing. Thorn would throw a ring-tailed hissy.

Amanda careened around the corner of the living room, dashed into the bedroom, then dived to the floor when lights flared against the bare window. Man, that was close. She had very nearly been caught as a silhouette in the headlights!

When she heard a car door slam, she slithered across the floor at record speed.

Of all the rotten luck! she thought. Her heart was

pounding in her chest like a piston. Whoever had arrived was coming through the back door into the kitchen. She would have to wait until the unidentified person was inside the house before she climbed out the window.

Amanda slithered across the bedroom floor, making as little noise as possible, then coiled beneath the window. The moment she heard the creak of kitchen door, she crawled out. After she closed the window—an inch at a time—she took off in a sprint—and cursed mightily when she stepped in a hole. Her ankle gave way and she fell flat on her face in the grass. Although pain streaked up her leg, Amanda levered onto her hands and knees.

She had to gut it out, she told herself. Sprained ankle or no, she had to reach her truck. Grimacing, limping, Amanda made her way across the uneven terrain of the pasture.

The moment she sank down on the seat of her jalopy truck she burst out with a loud "Ouch! Damn, that hurts!"

Amanda started the engine and followed the dirt path to the gate, then limped out to close it behind her. She sped off to check on Deputy Payne, but she had lingered too long. The squad car, and Loraine's sports car, were no longer parked in Ima Lemon's driveway.

Flicking off her headlights to prevent being noticed, Amanda drove past the cottage from which she had barely escaped undetected. From the road, she couldn't see any vehicles parked beside the house. Whoever had arrived had pulled around to the back. Amanda couldn't tell if one or two vehicles were parked near the cottage.

Considering the way her ankle was throbbing, she couldn't risk sneaking back to the shack to identify them. There was nothing else to do but go home and ice down her ankle—and pray that she didn't have to attend her wedding on crutches!

* * *

Nick glanced around the dimly lit tavern that sat on the east edge of Vamoose. Hitching Post Tavern had all the necessary ingredients of a country-style bar. Hat trees, made from old cedar fence posts, were positioned between tables so patrons could hang Stetsons and Resistols—if they were so inclined. Bronzed boots, lariats, sheriff badges polished to a shine, bridles and copies of limited-edition paintings, depicting scenes from the Old West, decorated the rough-hewn cedar walls. A bar, complete with saddles for bar stools, spanned the north wall which was lined with shelves of shot glasses and antique whiskey bottles. A jukebox in the corner was crooning Garth Brooks' song: "I've Got Friends in Low Places."

Balloons and streamers were thumbtacked to the ceiling tiles and plastic tablecloths, with wedding bells and brides and grooms stamped on them, covered every table in the bar.

"Hell, Nick," Rich said, glancing around the packed house. "The entire male population of Vamoose must be here. You're quite the celebrity in our hometown, aren't you?"

When Nick's deputy, Benny Sykes, noticed the guest of honor had arrived, he lifted his Mason jar of beer in toast. "Here, here. The honorable chief of police has arrived."

Everyone raised their Mason jars to Nick.

"Fine catch you made, Chief," someone called out from the corner table.

"You lucky rascal, you!" somebody else chimed in.

"Tomorrow night we'll all be wishing we were you, Chief."

That comment drew snickers from the entire crowd.

Nick scanned the sea of grinning faces and uplifted Mason jars. He saw Sam Harjo sitting in the far corner, his back to the wall. Sam was the only man in the tavern who wasn't grinning good-naturedly. The county commish was guzzling beer—and scowling.

Apparently, Sam Harjo was trying to be a good sport about losing Hazard to Nick. Sam was in attendance, after all. But Nick could tell that he was drowning his disappointment in beer.

Now that Nick's engagement ring was back on Hazard's finger, and preparations for tomorrow's wedding were arranged, Nick sympathized with Sam Harjo. The man had fallen hard and fast for Hazard, while she was investigating the Dead in the Mud Case.

"Have a drink, Chief," Benny Sykes said as he thrust a Mason jar into Nick's hand, then offered a beer to Rich. "Well, what do you think of our decorations?"

Nick nodded approvingly, then sipped his beer. "Nice, but not gaudy, Benny. I appreciate your time and effort."

"Wait until you see the surprise we have cooked up for you," Benny said, then grinned broadly. "This is going to be the bachelor party to end all parties." He grabbed Nick by the elbow, towing him toward the vacant table in the center of the tavern. "You and Rich park your carcasses. I'll bring you some beer nuts and pretzels."

Nick burst out laughing when Cecil and Cleatus Watts, posing as women with long blond wigs, busty chests, tight clothes, high heels—and heavy five-o'clock shadows—sashayed inside. The rowdy crowd guffawed when Cecil and Cleatus pulled Nick and Rich from their chairs to dance the two-step.

Even the somber-faced Sam Harjo chuckled as Nick twirled Cecil around the dance floor.

The Watts brothers made the rounds to dance with other members of the crowd. Even men who rarely set foot on the dance floor, because they were self-conscious about their limited skills, were on their feet, trying to learn to line dance.

Sam Harjo remained in the corner, polishing off another drink.

"Excuse me, Rich, I'm going to mill around," Nick said as he came to his feet.

Sam looked up with bloodshot eyes when Nick halted in front of his table. "Stop by to gloat, did you, Lone Ranger?" he slurred out. "Take a load off and sit down."

Nick straddled the seat and rested his arms on the back of the chair. Silently, he watched Sam drain his Mason jar, then call for another. "I don't want any hard feelings between us, Harjo," Nick said over the blaring music. "I mean that sincerely."

Sam snorted. "Of course you do. You aren't the one on the outside looking in, now are you?"

"If things had worked out differently, I'm sure I would feel the same way you do, Harjo."

Sam stared at Nick for a long, pensive moment. "Just how the hell did you pull it off? I thought I had Hazard thinking seriously about giving me a chance, especially after the stupid stunt you pulled while she was investigating the Mud Case."

Nick shrugged nonchalantly. "All I did was ask her to investigate Frank Lemon's death while I am temporarily suspended."

Understanding dawned on Sam, and he smiled reluctantly. "So that's how you got back in her good graces. You placed unconditional faith in her ability to dig up facts to save your reputation. I suppose you even gave Hazard the go-ahead to use her unorthodox method of following leads from the gossip she picks up at Velma's Beauty Boutique."

Nick nodded and grinned. "Yep. I told Hazard to pull out all the stops and go for it."

"So . . . how is the investigation progressing? Is Hazard about to redeem you?"

"She was doing fine until she got on her murder kick,"

he confided. "Haz thinks somebody set me up. She believes Frank was either dead, or unconscious, before I gave chase in the squad car."

"Interesting theory," Sam murmured.

"Yeah well, personally, I think this murder case is a product of Hazard's active imagination. She lives for this stuff, you know."

Sam slouched back in his chair, then sipped his beer. "Admit it, Lone Ranger, you can't stand it when she turns out to be right. She makes you look bad. That's why she should be marrying me instead of you. I respect her intellect, intuition and hunches."

Nick puffed up defensively. "That's bull, Harjo. You simply cater to Hazard in attempt to gain her notice. You would probably agree that Timothy McVeigh didn't bomb the Murrah Building if she arrived at that conclusion."

Nick wagged his finger in Harjo's face. "Let me tell you something about Hazard that you obviously haven't figured out. She thrives on challenges. Hell, she lives for them. And if she thinks she has a man wrapped around her finger she walks all over him, leads him around on a leash. She's assertive and dominating. You have to stand up to her occasionally, debate her theories. And although I admit she is almost as smart as God, what with her calculative, highly analytical brain that is constantly processing facts, you can't let her think she is right *all* the damned time."

"So *now* you tell me what's the best strategical approach," Sam muttered. "Maybe I should stop by her place tonight and give it one last shot."

"Try it and I'll—"

"You'll what?" Sam cut in. "Try to beat the shit out of me? Now, that would look good on your record, Lone Ranger. You can't go around picking fights with your male rival while Hazard is trying to redeem you."

Nick muttered under his breath. Sam was right, but

that wasn't a deterrent. Nick wanted Sam to keep his distance from Hazard. The commish was too damned good-looking, too damned charming and . . .

"If you ask me," Sam continued, after sipping his beer, "Hazard could be right about this case. From what I've heard around the county, Frank Lemon left a sour taste in lots of people's mouths. That wheeler-dealer car salesman sold several Vamoosians real lemons. And everybody knew you were after him for driving drunk. I can see that a high-speed chase, with you in the squad car, could have been a perfect cover-up for a cleverly staged murder. Maybe I'll go tell Hazard that I agree with her—"

When Sam tried to rise, Nick grabbed his forearm and yanked him back to his seat. "Stay put, Harjo," he ordered in his most authoritative tone. "The only way you are getting out of here is with a designated driver—me."

Sam eyed Nick's jar of beer. "Damn, wouldn't it be a shame if Deputy Payne pulled you over. Wonder if he would unlock you before time to arrive at your wedding. I might have to stand in your stead."

Nick leaned forward, a tight smile on his lips. "No chance in hell, Harjo. Hazard is mine and you better back off!"

Sam slouched in his chair, smiling wryly. "We'll see, Thorn. I still have twenty-four hours left to change her mind."

"Most of which you will spend sleeping off the hellish hangover you're going to have," Nick predicted.

"Dream on, Lone Ranger. I have a no-fail remedy for hangovers," Sam assured him. "I'll be up at the crack of dawn tomorrow, wide-eyed and bushy-tailed."

"You never quit, do you, Harjo?" Nick muttered as he rose to his feet.

"Would you, Lone Ranger?" Sam asked as Nick walked away.

No, Nick thought grudgingly. He didn't suppose he would.

Amanda came through the back door of her house and halted in the utility room to lean heavily on the washing machine. Her ankle was killing her. If she didn't pack it in ice—and quickly—it would be swollen up like a melon.

On her good leg, she hopped into the kitchen to grab a plastic bag and ice. For several minutes, she sat with her foot elevated on the table, letting the ice work its magic. When her ankle was numb, she scooped up the bag and limped to the bathroom to shower.

She held up her leg to let warm water pour over her injured ankle, then scrubbed her face vigorously. After drying off, she sank down on her bed to place the ice pack on her foot. The swelling was minimal, thank goodness. With a little luck, and hot-and-cold packs to reduce swelling, she would be able to walk the following day . . .

The thought made her frown suspiciously, wondering if the suspects in this case had applied the same remedy. Whoever had leaped from the truck and sprained an ankle or knee could have treated the injury just as Amanda had.

After several minutes of numbing her ankle Amanda dressed for bed, then walked gingerly into the kitchen to fetch a drink. She noticed the answering machine winking at her in the dark living room.

Hobbling, she walked over to listen to the message.

"Amanda? This is Freddy Lassiter. I called to tell you that I got a look at the car you asked me about when you were at the lot this afternoon."

Despite her throbbing ankle, Amanda perked up.

"Ernie Niles pulled a black Chevy into the workshop an hour before closing time and asked me to replace the grille and front bumper that was dented up. I don't know if that means anything to you, but I thought you might want to know."

The answering machine beeped again, then Mother's voice wafted across the room. "Hi, doll. Just called to see if you have changed your mind about tomorrow. It's never too late, you know. I talked to Carl Plum at the country club again this evening. He is really anxious to meet you."

"God, Mother," Amanda snorted. "You don't know when to quit, do you?"

"I hope to hear from you in the morning," Mother yammered. "If not, I suppose we're going to have to come out to that podunk town, sit in the church and watch you make the second mistake of your life. But remember, everybody is going to be there, all your uncles, aunts, cousins, niece and nephew, your brother and that lazy wife of his. They'll all be there to watch you mess up your life if you marry that country-hick cop."

Amanda snarled at the answering machine, limped off to fetch a glass of water, then headed to bed to pack her foot in ice. Knowing Mother, she would perceive Amanda's limp down the aisle as some subconscious manifestation that indicated the wedding was a mistake. But by damn, Amanda was not going to favor her injured leg during the bridal processional—even if she had to silently scream in pain every step of the way to the altar!

Two hours into the bachelor bash and Nick was ready to go home. The crowd had become exceptionally rowdy when the bartender switched on the VCR to play "girlie" movies. Whistles and wolf calls rose to a roar. Nick had seen about all the artificially endowed breasts and bare hips that he cared to see for one night. He was almost a married man and his tastes centered exclusively on the feminine charms of one woman.

"Poor bastards," Nick muttered to his brother. "You would think they have no sex lives at all."

Rich chugged his beer and then grinned. "Here's one of the poor bastards who doesn't," he said, tapping himself on the chest. "I've been running my ass ragged, working for the OSBI since my divorce. You think I have time for meaningful relationships? Guess again, bro. If a 'girlie' movie is all you get, then you hoot and howl."

When Rich glanced toward the big-screen TV, then threw back his head and proceeded to howl like a dying coyote. Nick rolled his eyes. "You are pathetic, Richard."

Suddenly, the bartender pulled the plug. The men in the tavern raised their voices in protest. "Calm down, you yahoos." He gestured a stubby finger toward the front door, which opened, as if on cue.

Benny Sykes and Thaddeus Thatcher appeared with an artificial, king-size wedding cake. Nick silently groaned. Hazard would have a conniption if a strip-teaser rose from that cake and planted herself on Nick's lap. Hazard didn't approve of such nonsense. If word got out, she might very well turn to Harjo for consolation—and that lovesick commish would be waiting eagerly.

Nick slid Harjo a glance. Sure enough, the commish was grinning broadly—for the first time all night. Harjo raised his Mason jar, then mouthed: My compliments, Lone Ranger.

Nick sank a little deeper in his chair, waiting for the guillotine to drop on his neck.

Good old-fashioned strip-tease music blared from the jukebox, while Benny and Thaddeus positioned the oversize cake in front of Nick's table.

Nick was dead meat. There wasn't a man in the place who wouldn't prevaricate about the upcoming incident—and make it sound worse than it was. It was one of those things—the boasting and bragging which was indigenous to the male.

Nick promised himself, there and then, to conduct himself with as much dignity as the situation allowed.

"A drum roll please, you rednecks!" Benny called out.

Every man in the tavern pounded his fists on the tabletops and broke out in catcalls. Nick hoped and prayed that one of his male acquaintances had dressed up like a woman and waited to rise from the cake. If that wasn't going to happen, then he hoped Hazard was in on this gag and had agreed to leap out to greet him—dressed respectably, of course. He sure as hell didn't want this raucous crowd to get a gander at Hazard in a skimpy bathing suit! That body of hers was for his eyes only.

The answer to Nick's hopes and prayers was: *Not a chance.* To his dismay, a curvaceous, bleached blonde, wearing next to nothing, rose from the cake. Her synthetically enlarged bosom was concealed—barely—by glittering pasties. The glittery g-string was every bit as skimpy and indecent.

Nick cursed under his breath when the cake lady wiggled and jiggled her way down the tiers to plant herself on his lap.

The crowd went wild!

"To your last taste of freedom, sugar," the cake lady purred.

When she planted a kiss on Nick's lips, and pulled his arms around her waist so she could snuggle up close and personal, the patrons of the taverns rolled in the aisles and hooted in laughter.

Nick glared accusingly at Harjo, whose broad shoulders were shaking in amusement.

Rich, bless his heart, came to Nick's rescue by pulling the cake lady off Nick's lap and plunking her down on his.

"I'm the best man, after all," Rich announced then waggled his eyebrows.

While two dozen men filed past the table to take a close

gander at the cake lady, Nick polished off his beer and stared at the air over Rich's head.

If Hazard found out about this, the shit would hit the fan. Nick swiveled his head around to glower at Harjo, but the corner table was empty. Harjo was up and gone.

Nick bounded to his feet, determined to chase Harjo down, but the crowd of men converged on him, wishing him well in his marriage—if there was one, after Hazard got wind of this incident—and she undoubtedly would.

When a loud rap rattled the door hinges, the cake lady reached inside the artificial cake to retrieve her trench coat. She had covered herself by the time Velma Hertzog appeared in the doorway.

"Okay, fellas." Chomp, pop. "Time to break it up. Your designated drivers are here to haul you home."

Like a general taking command of the field, Velma motioned to her troop of women. Wives and girlfriends of the party-goers filed inside to claim their misbehaving men.

Now this, Nick decided, was something Hazard would approve of. The male party-goers had been granted their play time, but now they were being chauffeured home and tucked into bed. Women were back in control.

"Come on, groom and best man," Velma said as she halted beside the Thorn brothers. "You've got a wedding tomorrow." Snap, crunch. "I intend for you to look sharp by eight o'clock tomorrow night. Nobody, and I mean *nobody,* is going to mess up the wedding of the decade."

Velma grabbed the Thorn brothers by the napes of their shirts and hauled them to their feet.

"Head 'em up and move 'em out, cowgirls!" Velma bugled, then wheeled toward Benny Sykes. "Deputize some of these men who are unattached to help clean this place up."

"Clean up the place, right," Benny repeated as he wobbled off to appoint his work detail.

"And who do I have to thank for this unauthorized cake

prank?" Velma demanded as she guided the Thorn brothers outside.

Nick glanced at Rich who stared close-mouthed at him.

"Not talking, huh?" Crackle, snap. "Well fine then, let me guess." Velma didn't even hesitate. "It must have been Benny, because I put him in charge for the evening. He must have decided to exert a little authority on his own, the naughty boy."

"No, actually it was—"

Velma shoved Nick, headfirst, into the back seat of her car.

"Don't try to defend that deputy of yours, Nicky." Pop, pop. "Now, you just sit there, keep your trap shut, and behave yourself until I get you and your brother home."

"Geez, Velma," Rich groused. "You're treating us like we were misbehaving delinquents."

Velma gave Rich a shove into the car. "That's the way you boys behave without proper feminine guidance. I sincerely hope Amanda doesn't hear about that cake incident." She glared at Nick. "And you better not have kissed that two-bit fleshpot, either!"

Nick sank a little deeper in the seat. He hadn't done the kissing, but who, he wondered, was sober enough to corroborate his plea of innocence? He glanced at Rich who was three sheets to the wind.

"Well damn," Nick said, and scowled.

"Fasten those seat belts, boys." Chomp, chomp. "I don't want Deputy Payne stopping us with one of his lame excuses, then slapping on heavy fines because we aren't buckled up."

Nick did as he was told, wondering if the cake incident, and the kiss he didn't participate in, would provoke Hazard to leave him standing at the altar—much to Mom and Mother's relief, no doubt.

Twelve

Amanda was jostled from sleep by a quiet but steady tapping on the window. Yawning, she crawled from bed to see a brawny silhouette in the darkness. When she realized who had come to pay her a late-night call, she flung open the window.

"Harjo, what are you doing here at this ungodly hour?"

"Came to see you," he slurred out, staggered, then propped himself against the window pane.

Amanda frowned disapprovingly. "You're drunk."

"And you're as gorgeous as ever, Hazard."

"Why are you here?" she wanted to know.

"I came to mourn the greatest love affair that never was." Harjo's bloodshot gaze drifted down her nightshirt, which barely covered her hips.

Amanda wrinkled her nose when Harjo panted at her through the window screen. "Your mouthwash is as strong as Frank Lemon's was. And we all know how he ended up."

"Yeah, and Thorn tells me you think the traffic fatality was a carefully arranged murder. I'm sure there were several people itching to put that guy out of business—permanently. Have you figured out who did it?"

The fact that Harjo believed her theory intensified her affection for him. And furthermore, her tender-hearted tendencies got the better of her as she stared at Clint Eastwood's look-alike. "Come around to the back door and I'll make you some coffee. You look as if you could use it."

"Even if that's all you're going to offer, I'll take it," Harjo mumbled.

When Harjo disappeared around the corner of the house, Amanda stepped into her blue jeans, then strode toward the utility room to unlock the back door. She was greatly relieved to know her tender ankle was functioning better. That was certainly a relief!

Harjo wobbled inside, using the wall for additional support. "Thanks, gorgeous."

Amanda steered him into the kitchen and planted him in a chair, then flicked on Mr. Coffee, which Pops had readied for the following morning. She sank down at the table to peer into Harjo's red-streaked eyes.

"That must have been some bachelor bash," she commented.

Harjo nodded his tousled head. "Beer flowed like tap water."

Amanda was far more intrigued by Harjo's previous comment about Lemon's enemies than hearing a blow-by-blow account of the party. "You spend a lot of time driving the country roads, commish. Have you seen anything that might further my investigation? I'm running out of time and I've narrowed my suspects down to four. Well, five, actually," she amended. "I can't cross out Deputy Payne, because he has a vested interest in this case and I don't trust him."

"Why? Because he takes coffee breaks and lunch breaks at Loraine Niles' country estate?" Harjo smirked. "He's been doing that since he hired on last month with the Vamoose police department to make some extra bucks."

Amanda realized that the new commissioner was a good source of information about the goings-on in obscure sections of the county. Harjo surveyed the road conditions before sending out his crews to repair bridges, add gravel to roads and send out the road-grader brigade.

Intently, she leaned her forearms on the table—Mr. Coffee belched and perked on the counter.

"Did you see Frank and his brother together often?" she asked.

"Occasionally. I drove by one day last month while Frank was helping Floyd load some cars on his trailer. When I drove by an hour later, Frank was taking off in Floyd's truck."

So they were in cahoots . . . Amanda frowned when she remembered seeing Floyd at the car dealership, shaking his fist—which was clamped around copies of bills of sale—in Ernie's face. Had Frank taken advantage of his brother by borrowing his trailer rig, then forging Floyd's name on bills of sale? Had Floyd become so outraged that he confronted Frank while he was drinking and driving around the countryside? Or was Floyd involved up to his eyeballs?

"Two weeks ago, I passed Frank and Ernie standing in the middle of the road near the gate that leads into the pasture behind Frank's house," Harjo continued.

Amanda knew the location well. She had spent a considerable amount of time in that pasture this evening.

When the coffee pot hissed, Amanda retrieved two cups and filled them to the brim.

"Thanks," Harjo murmured as he inhaled the steaming brew. "Frank flagged me down and asked me if I would have my road crew dump some gravel on the dirt path so he wouldn't get stuck in his pasture. The man had nerve, I'll give him that. The county commissioner's office is not authorized to gravel private access roads and he damn well knew it."

From what Amanda had learned about Frank Lemon she wouldn't put anything past him. Although Ima Lemon had nothing but kind words for her departed husband—

was that just a charade played for Amanda's benefit?—no one else had been fond of Frank. Not even his brother, or the ex-wife who was now the double sister-in-law.

It seemed Frank had a nasty habit of using everyone he associated with to his advantage. Willingly, or unknowingly, Frank's associates, and family, were drawn into his scam of stealing, chop-shopping and tampering with registration forms and car titles.

Remembering the radios she had found stashed under the sofa in the cottage, Amanda stared curiously at Harjo. "Do you know who lives in that cottage that sits down the hill from Frank's estate? It doesn't happen to be Deputy Payne, does it?"

Harjo shrugged a muscled shoulder. "I'm not sure. I saw the squad car parked there late one afternoon last week, but I can't say for certain where Payne lives."

Was Payne on the take? Amanda wondered. Had he been stealing hot merchandise for Frank? The man was certainly in the position to get his hands on a few vehicles, using his duties as a law officer to his benefit. Had Frank threatened to expose the deputy's illegal activities if Payne didn't play along with some new scam Frank had cooked up?

Had Payne decided to become the mastermind behind the auto-theft ring by disposing of Frank?

Amanda frowned. If Payne had driven the red truck and leaped into the weeds, he could have left his getaway vehicle near the wheat field, then volunteered to investigate the incident when Amanda placed the call for assistance at the sheriff's department. Payne had opportunity and motive, Amanda thought to herself.

Now, Payne was in the perfect position to shine the light of suspicion on someone other than himself. In essence, that was what Payne was doing now—framing Thorn.

Amanda glanced at her watch. It was late, and she had

dozens of tasks to tend to on the day of her wedding. "How about if I drive you home."

"Good, I'll pick up a few things, throw them in a suitcase, and we can elope."

Amanda shook her head at the expression on Harjo's face. He was trying to be charming and pleading, all in the same moment. The effort was comical, considering how much he had had to drink. "Bring your coffee along with you, Harjo," she said, as she stood up to test her tender ankle.

So far so good. The ankle wasn't throbbing as it had been a few hours earlier.

Harjo frowned as the kitchen light beamed directly on Amanda's head. "Is that a hairnet you're wearing?" He squinted at her. "Your hair looks purplish-pink."

Amanda touched the cosmetic disaster self-consciously. "Another of Velma's experiments gone bad."

Harjo stared intently as her as she guided him toward the back door. "How bad is it, Hazard?"

"The worst ever," she told him.

"Has Thorn seen it yet?"

Amanda grimaced as she scooped up her keys. "Nope, not yet."

"Then I guess that makes the two of you even—almost."

Amanda frowned at the enigmatic comment. "Come again?"

Harjo flashed her an utterly rakish grin as they walked toward the truck. Amanda didn't ask him to translate that smile into words. She was sure Harjo had given a double meaning to her request to repeat his comment.

Leaving Harjo's Chevy Blazer parked in the driveway, Amanda steered her truck down the gravel road that led to Harjo's home near the small community of Adios.

Harjo sipped his coffee while Amanda mulled over the sightings of Frank Lemon with his brother, the private meeting between Frank and Ernie near the pasture gate, and the squad car parked at the cottage. Damn it, how did all these facts fit together? Who *didn't* have motive and opportunity to dispose of Frank Lemon? And why couldn't Amanda get her mind off those scattered footprints she had seen in the sand? Were the tennis shoes Amanda had seen stashed in the bottom drawer, and closet, at the dealership office the ones used to make the leap from Frank's truck and the mad dash uphill after the wreck?

When Amanda stopped in the driveway of Harjo's farm home, he handed her the empty cup. Before she realized what he was about, he pulled her into his arms and planted a steamy kiss on her lips. It was not the playful peck of a friend, but the passionate embrace of a desperate, would-be lover.

Wow! Harjo's kiss packed quite a wallop. Secretly, she had wondered how he would compare to Thorn, but she had never before taken the opportunity to find out.

Eventually—and it was definitely a long breathless moment—Harjo retreated into his own space. He stared into Amanda's eyes. "Now you're even," he said referring to the befuddling comment he made before they left her house. "You need to know that a bombshell blonde popped out of Thorn's cake at the party and planted her skimpily clad bod on his lap to give her rendition of a tonsillectomy. Seems to me that what's good for the groom is good for the bride. And to be perfectly honest, I've been wanting to do that since the first time I met you, Hazard."

Amanda simply sat there like a slug, gaping at him. He slid off the seat, then leaned back inside the cab to flash her a roguish smile and a wink. "If you change your mind about the wedding, I'll be there, ready and waiting to drive you off in the getaway car. 'Night, doll face, sweet dreams. I'll sure as hell be having a few of my own."

And then he was gone, disappearing into the darkness. Amanda blinked, stunned. Mechanically, she put the truck in reverse and backed from the driveway.

Thorn had hauled a shapely female onto his lap, wrapped his arms around her and kissed her senseless, while the woman was wearing little more than a smile?

Why that big lug! Did he think he could have one last fling and show off in front of his male cohorts before the wedding took place? Amanda silently fumed at the prospect of Thorn and the cake lady—and that was using the term *lady* very loosely!—pawing at each other in front of an audience of her friends and clients. How dare he!

Amanda exhausted her repertoire of oaths during the drive home. She had enough on her mind with this frustrating case without being hounded by speculations about where the cake lady was spending the night—and with whom!

Maybe Harjo was right. Maybe she did need a getaway car to rescue her from the drastic mistake Mother kept insisting that she was about to make. It would serve Thorn right if he was left at the altar with all of Vamoose as witness. If Thorn thought the cake lady was such hot stuff, then maybe he should keep her!

Nick leaped straight up in bed when the phone blared at him. He had lain awake half the night, dreading this call.

The phone rang again. Nick stared at the receiver as if it were doused in poison. He did not want to take this call. Reluctantly, he started to pick up after the fourth ring. To his relief, the phone became silent. Reprieve!

A moment later, Nick realized that his brother—who had camped out on the couch—must have answered the phone.

"Damn it to hell," Nick muttered as he swung his legs

over the edge of the bed. This was it. The big kaput. Hazard was calling off the wedding. She was delivering the bad news to Rich. All Velma's plans for a grand wedding and reception were about to be flushed down the toilet.

Grimly, Nick pulled on his jeans, then strode down the hall. Rich was propped on his elbow, speaking quietly into the receiver. His hair was standing straight up, as if he had slept on his head.

"Yeah, okay. I'll tell him," Rich said, glancing up at Nick.

"That was Tom Knapp from OSBI," Rich reported, then frowned when Nick collapsed in the chair. "Are you all right, bro?"

"Yeah, fine. Just swell," he mumbled.

Rich looked at him oddly, then continued. "Tom ran a check on Joe Payne for me. Definitely the GI-Joe type. Payne served in the armed forces for four years, then did a two-year hitch with the special operations troop of Army Rangers."

Nick knew the Rangers were a highly specialized group of individuals who were asked to take on impossible missions in impossible situations.

"Thing is, Payne got the boot after he decided to disobey his CO's orders during one of their tactical crusades in the Middle East. The army politely asked him to resign and he took a job training and commanding troops in Turkey."

"Soldier of fortune, I knew it," Nick murmured.

"Apparently so," Rich replied. "From there, Payne entered the police academy, then hired on the Tulsa force. But it seems he has a weakness for the ladies. He was accused of propositioning a female while he was on duty. Charges were never filed officially. Payne left his position and turned up in Vamoose Sheriff Department a couple of years ago. He has kept a low profile, no blemishes on his record at present."

"I'm sure Payne feels he has been holding down a subordinate position long enough," Nick speculated.

"To borrow an expression from the Old West, Payne came gunning for you, bro," Rich said "He cast his greedy eyes on the position of chief of police in Vamoose, hired on for night duty to get his foot in the door, then he was ready and waiting for the opportunity to make his move."

"Any advice?" Nick asked.

"Yeah, you better hope like hell that Hazard has enough on Payne to send him running with his tail tucked between his legs. He could get your job if he's cunning and shrewd. And from the reports, Payne is exactly that."

When Rich ambled off to shower, Nick raked his hand through his hair and sighed audibly. Definitely dead meat, all the way around, he thought. Hazard would be so pissed about that cake incident that she would pitch her investigative report into the incinerator, then stand aside and watch Nick be permanently dismissed from his duties.

"Hey, Nick, you better spiffy this place up before Mom gets here," Rich called from the shower. "Her nose is already out of joint, because of this wedding of yours. Don't give her anything else to grouse about. If you'll clean up the kitchen, I'll vacuum while you're showering."

Nick heaved himself to his feet to make coffee and pick up the clutter. He may as well keep busy while he waited for the phone call of doom.

Or maybe Hazard decided not to call at all, he mused as he carried dirty dishes to the kitchen. Maybe she thought standing him up at the altar would be more dramatic.

Flat on her back, Amanda stared at the ceiling of her bedroom. She hadn't gotten much sleep after her encounter with Sam Harjo. The man had certainly served up considerable food for thought—all of which she had spent the past several hours chewing on.

Twice, Amanda had reached for the telephone, then reconsidered making the call to Thorn. No, she decided, she would let Thorn stew in his own juice until this evening.

"Hey, Half Pint, up and at 'em," Pops called from the hall. "The coffee is perking and breakfast is on the stove."

Half-heartedly, Amanda crawled from bed. Dressed in her nightshirt and jeans, she padded barefoot to the kitchen, then screeched to a halt when she saw the large gift sitting on the table.

Pops' eyes popped when he noticed her hair. "What in the hell happened to you!" be croaked.

"Velma gave me a wedding 'do," Amanda mumbled. "It's pretty bad."

"Pretty bad, hell!" Pops said, and snorted. "It's the worst yet."

Amanda gestured toward the package on the table, hoping to divert her grandfather's attention from the sensitive subject of her atrocious hairdo. "What's with the package, Pops?"

"Salty and I drove to the city yesterday to pick up your wedding gift." He smiled as he leaned on his aluminum walker. "Salty brought it by while you were still in bed." He gestured to the gift. "Go ahead, open it up."

Amanda peeled off the silver wrapping paper and stared bewilderedly at the box. It was a high-powered state-of-the-art microwave oven with push buttons for frozen food, popcorn, reheat for leftovers and a computerized sensor that prevented overcooking.

"This is much fancier than that radioactive microwave you have that nukes food," Pops explained. "This baby cooks food perfectly. All you have to do is push the right button and the computerized system does the rest."

"Oh, Pops, you're so thoughtful and generous."

Amanda hugged him so tightly that he nearly stumbled over the legs of his walker.

"You like?" Pops asked.

"I love," Amanda said in a choked voice.

"Good, because you'll be doing your own cooking, Half Pint. I've decided to move in with Salty Marcum."

Amanda reared back, blinking like a turn signal. "But you can't! Thorn built an addition onto his house so we would all have our own space."

"One of these days you'll have babies to fill up the spare rooms," Pops replied. "Salty and I are good company for each other. He's trying to recover from losing his teenage daughter in that traffic accident last year, and I'm exceptionally good for his morale. Besides that, I won't have to move back in with your mother. Seeing her at family gatherings—like today, for instance—will be enough. I'm tired of waiting to see which one of us is going to drive the other one crazy first."

The phone jingled. Amanda hurried to take the call, pleased that her ankle wasn't complaining. True, it was slightly swollen, but nothing she couldn't live with.

"Hi, doll. Since you didn't call last night, I suppose that means you're going to marry that country bumpkin," Mother said. "All the family is getting dressed and gathering at my house so we can come to watch this farce. I told everybody to dress down, of course. Don't want to make the hicks from Vamoose look bad."

Amanda gritted her teeth. "How thoughtful of you."

"It's the least I can do."

"You certainly got that right," Amanda muttered, half under her breath.

"Pardon, doll?"

"Nothing, Mother."

"Well, I've got to run. Your daddy forgot to pick up his dress shirt and suit at the cleaners, so I have to do it. Don't know what the poor man would do without me."

Amanda managed to keep her speculations to herself. Daddy wasn't nearly as helpless as Mother liked everyone to think he was.

" 'Bye, doll. And remember, it's never too late to call off this . . . er . . . wedding. I guess we'll be there about seven."

The line went dead. Amanda dropped the receiver in the cradle.

"Well, how is the old biddy?" Pops asked in a tone that indicated he wasn't all that interested.

"Mother is still Mother," Amanda said.

"Damn, I was hoping she'd had a personality transplant. So . . . what time will she and her broom be touching down in Vamoose?"

"Seven o'clock."

Pops pivoted toward the stove. "Let's have breakfast. I don't want to think about your mother's arrival on an empty stomach."

Amanda finished off the hearty breakfast of pancakes and sausage. She was washing dishes when a loud thump reverberated on the front door. Bruno, who had been lounging on his pallet, bounded onto all fours and barked.

"Down, boy, I'll handle this," Amanda said.

Bruno plunked down, his head resting on his oversize paws.

Amanda opened the door to see Velma, decked out in an oversized, Pepto-Bismol-pink sweatshirt, sweatpants, and rollers pinned on her head. The Amazon beautician held up a garment bag.

"Here, hon." Snap, pop. "You forgot to pick up your dress when you were in the salon yesterday." She squinted to appraise the net that confined Amanda's frizzy, purplish-pink hair. "You better take that net off and let me fluff up your 'do."

In Amanda's opinion, there was no salvaging the disastrous 'do, but Velma invited herself inside. Like a physician carrying a medical bag for a house call, Velma fished into her oversize purse to retrieve her comb and hair spray. She motioned for Amanda to take a seat at the kitchen table.

"Hi, Pops," Velma called cheerily.

Pops glanced from Amanda's head to Velma's greeting smile. "You really botched up this time, didn't you?" he said candidly.

Velma looked the other way, clearly uncomfortable. "Well, it happens occasionally."

"I hope the hell that dress in the bag comes with a veil, or my granddaughter will have to wear a sack over her head."

"Don't mind him," Amanda said confidentially. "Pops is always a little cranky in the morning. He just called my mother a witch."

Velma chewed her gum as she stood behind Amanda, styling her hair. "Um . . . is everything still on for tonight?" she asked hesitantly.

Amanda had the unmistakable feeling that she knew why Velma posed the question. The town's most reliable gossip knew about Thorn's wild fling. But Velma, in her eagerness to see her wedding arrangements carried out, was keeping her trap shut.

"Er . . . I couldn't help but notice County Commissioner Harjo's vehicle is parked in your driveway." Her gaze darted toward the hall. "Is he here?"

Amanda grimaced. She had forgotten about Harjo's Chevy Blazer. No doubt, the beautician was making all sorts of sordid speculations.

"Harjo better not be here." Snap, chomp. "Is . . . he—?"

The phone rang again, saving Amanda from responding to Velma's question.

"I'll get it," Pops volunteered. He clomped into the living room on his walker. "Like, *what?* What the hell kind of English are you speaking, lady? Slow down, will you. I can't listen that fast!"

"It must be Bev." Velma scurried into the living room. "Give me the phone, Pops."

Pops dropped the receiver into Velma's meaty hand. "Sounds like an alien from another planet. She speaks gibberish."

While Pops hobbled to his room, Velma talked on the phone. "You're kidding. Well, can't she improvise? No, there isn't time to make another cake. She shouldn't have dropped the first one! Just tell Maggie to make up a batch of frosting and glue the darn thing back together. And make sure you're at the church when the florist arrives, Bev. Oh, and don't forget to turn on the air conditioner. We don't want the icing on the cake to slide off in the heat. One broken cake is enough disaster to deal with!" Chomp, crack, pop!

Amanda silently groaned. Maybe cutting out with Harjo before this carnival of a wedding took place wasn't a bad idea. Mother would be at the church, looking down her high-society nose at the peons of Vamoose. Thorn's mom would be carrying on—and on—about the pitfalls of a "mixed marriage." And from the sound of Velma's phone conversation, the wedding cake, or groom's cake, was in pieces.

The phone rang again, and Velma lumbered off to answer it. "Now what, Bev?" Chomp, crackle. "I don't know how much Ginger Ale to add to the fruit punch mix. Call your mother. Surely she knows. Yes, I'll be over as soon as I finish styling Amanda's hair."

Amanda could hear Bev's voice yammering in Velma's ear, all the way from the living room.

"You haven't delivered it yet?" Velma howled. "Well, get that tux out to Nicky's house, PDQ. If you don't, he'll show up in his Western wear. Leave the punch until later and deliver that tux!"

Velma waddled back to Amanda, shaking her head in dismay. "I'll tell you what, hon, organizing a wedding is more trouble than I thought. But don't you worry about a thing. It's all going to come together . . . I hope."

Amanda sat there, staring at the wall, while Velma tried to salvage what she could of yesterday's cosmetic calamity.

"I know everybody in Vamoose plans to attend this wedding." Snap, chomp. "But I hope Loraine Niles doesn't make good on her threat to show up and accuse Nicky of killing her father. That woman is fond of theatrics."

Amanda closed her eyes. Lord, this evening was gearing up to become a full-scale disaster. She wasn't sure she wanted to be there when fireworks erupted. Mom, Mother, Thorn and the cake lady. Loraine screeching at Thorn. Harjo waiting to whisk her away from it all . . .

"I've heard that you have been asking all sorts of questions about Frank's accident, in hopes of clearing Nicky's name," Velma continued. "Now, Sally Jean and Ima aren't on speaking terms. Ernie walked out on Loraine, who appeared to have been fooling around with Deputy Payne, while she was supposed to be at Ima's house for the evening.

"Ernie claims Loraine has been unfaithful. Imagine that!" Crack, chomp. "Ernie must be trying to file the complaint for a divorce before Loraine beats him to it. Freddy Lassiter said the whole bunch of them showed up at the used car lot to have their feud and he was tired of the whole mess. He up and quit when Ernie chewed him out for not repairing a car fast enough."

Amanda frowned. It sounded as if the Lemons were coming apart at the seams. She wondered if the conversation about the car Freddy was supposed to repair—the one that slammed into her—initiated the argument that prompted Freddy to quit his job. Obviously, Ernie wanted the evidence of thc hit-and-run concealed before Amanda showed up to investigate.

"And Nicky's substitute!" Velma hooted distastefully. "That Payne character is really starting to get on my nerves. I've been zipping around town, making last-minute preparations and that damnfool deputy pulled me over twice! Tried to give me a citation for speeding. He's the one who zips around like a maniac."

Amanda contemplated the comment. So, Payne liked to speed, did he? Maybe he was the type who enjoyed high-speed chases, especially when there was the added element of danger—like an unconscious body in the truck beside him. Somehow the scenario fit that GI-Joe cop. Amanda needed to call Thorn to see if he knew the low-down on Payne. But since she wasn't speaking to Thorn, it would make for an impossible conversation.

"Velma, do me a favor and call Thorn. Ask him if he has anything on Payne's background."

Velma galumphed to the phone and placed the call. Then she glanced back at Amanda. "Are you sure you don't want to speak to Thorn yourself?"

"Vcry sure," Amanda insisted. She didn't want Velma to eavesdrop on the inevitable shouting match.

"Nicky? It's Velma." Snap, crunch. "Amanda wants to know if you know the scoop on Payne?"

There was a slight pause while Thorn spoke.

"Uh-huh? Un-huh. Sure, sure, mum's the word. My lips are zipped. By the way, your tux is en route as we speak. You're going to look sensational."

Amanda waited impatiently for Velma to deliver the information. "Well?"

"Payne is ex-army, ex-special forces, ex-soldier of fortune," Velma reported as she gathered her combs and hair spray. "Seems he was also quite the ladies' man in Tulsa, before signing on with the Vamoose County Sheriff Department."

It was just as Amanda thought. Payne was a thrill-seeker. She wouldn't put anything past that cop who had visions of snatching Thorn's job out from under him. Furthermore, there was no telling how far a special forces commando—who suffered delusions of grandeur—would go to achieve his goals. Frank Lemon could have been nothing more than a convenient target selected to cast suspicion on Thorn. Payne had probably pried information about Frank from his daughter, Loraine. And Loraine, Amanda thought to herself, had gone ape over that wacko commando. Or maybe Loraine appeared to be stuck on Payne so she could have her revenge on her two-timing husband who was banging Irene Pratt.

Jeepers! Peyton Place had nothing on Vamoose!

"I gotta run, hon," Velma said as she lumbered toward the door. "Your flowers will be arriving at the church any minute. I've got to set up for the reception." She paused to stare meaningfully at Amanda. "And for heaven's sake, get Harjo's Blazer out of your driveway!"

When Velma buzzed off, Amanda slumped in her chair. This was not a good day to wrestle with the facts of this complicated investigation—too many distractions. How was she supposed to focus her mind when her life had become a three-ring circus?

What she needed was a hot, relaxing bath and the chance to sort out the facts, to put the events leading to Frank's death in chronological order. Somewhere in this tangled mess of clues and interactions between Frank Lemon and his family and associates, there had to be one tiny piece of evidence that was crying out to be noticed.

Amanda pulled on her shower cap and went to take a bath.

Thirteen

"Yo, Nick! Mom and Dad are here!" Rich called from the living room.

Nick was in such a state of shock that he couldn't reply immediately. He was staring at the tux Beverly Hill had delivered that morning. Nick had been so busy cleaning house and packing for the honeymoon cruise—a cruise he might end up taking by himself—that he hadn't bothered looking at the tux. Now, it was time to dress and drive to church, and the tux was nothing like he expected!

"Nicky!" Mom called impatiently.

"I'll be out in a minute, Mom. Rich, get in here, will you?"

Rich appeared a few moments later. When he saw the tux—costume was more like it—he cackled like a nesting hen. "It looks like Velma is decking you out as Prince Charming," he said between snickers. He pointed to the golden vest and black cummerbund that was draped over a hanger. "God, sweet prince, you're going to be something else."

"She expects me to wear white?" Nick chirped. *"White?"*

"Well, it is your first wedding," Rich reminded him, grinning widely.

"I'll feel like a priss standing at the altar. I can't wear this," he muttered.

"You'll hurt Velma's feelings," Rich countered. "She has gone to considerable effort to arrange your wedding."

"What about *my* feelings?" Nick grumbled.

"You aren't supposed to have any. You're supposed to be the dazed, befuddled groom who stands at the altar with a stupid smile on your lips." Rich grabbed the frilly white shirt, then tossed it to Nick. "Get dressed, pretty boy."

"If I end up looking like a lily-white ass, all for nothing, I'm going to strangle Hazard."

Rich's teasing smile vanished. "Do you think she's a no-show?"

Nick pulled off his T-shirt and plucked up the sissified shirt with its ruffled sleeves. "If Hazard refused to speak to me on the phone, and Velma had to make the call for her, I would say that I'm in deep shit."

"Well, you shouldn't have kissed the lips off the cake lady," Rich razzed him.

"I didn't kiss her, damn it. She kissed *me!*" Nick erupted in bad humor.

"Couldn't prove it by me."

"I know," Nick said, and scowled. "You were too busy staring at the cake lady's *ass*ets."

Rich sauntered from the bedroom, snickering. Nick didn't think the situation was a damned bit funny. He was probably going to end up looking like an absolute fool, while dressed in this Prince Charming costume, standing all by his lonesome at the altar.

This better not be all for nothing! he thought as he stabbed his arms into the gold brocade vest.

After Pops drove off with Salty Marcum to grab a bite at Last Chance Cafe, Amanda sat at the table, nibbling on a sandwich. She had spent the afternoon making the first draft of her investigative report which would be delivered to the sheriff. She had included facts about Frank Lemon's recurring drinking problem and his stressed mental state before his death. She had also added concise information that she had picked up from interviews with Frank's family and acquaintances. She had listed her findings at the pond dam behind Frank's house and noted her suspicions of a theft ring. It was all in the report, ready to be typed up.

Amanda had lambasted Deputy Joe Payne good and hard, because she didn't trust the man's motives and because she was pretty certain he was involved in this murder that he had set up to implicate Thorn.

Pensively, Amanda reread her report. It was driving her crazy, knowing there was some vital clue that she had overlooked, some tidbit of information she hadn't double-checked.

On impulse, Amanda opened the file of business accounts from Lemon's Used Cars. Meticulously, she went through the expense receipts, waiting for something to catch her eye . . . and finally something did.

Amanda plucked up several receipts for meals, noting that Frank had paid for a guest while on his mysterious overnight business trips to Tulsa, Ponca City, Hobart—to name only a few. Hmm. Now, who had gone along with Frank? Was it the Williams woman whose phone number showed up at regular intervals on Lemon's Used Cars' phone bill?

Intently, Amanda rifled through the files to extract every receipt for meals. And sure enough, Frank had never eaten alone. Who had been with him? Damn it, that *someone* had to be the key to this investigation! Was the Williams woman involved in this auto theft ring?

On impulse, Amanda opened Frank's personal financial file to scan the bank accounts one last time. A thousand-dollar withdrawal, dated the day before Frank's death, caught her attention. She wondered if Frank had planned something big, something that had backfired.

Glancing at her watch, Amanda calculated how much time she could spare to stop at her office to type the report before driving to the church. If she gathered up her garment bag, and the suitcase for the honeymoon cruise—provided she didn't bail out at the last minute because she was still pissed at Thorn for pussyfooting around with the cake lady—she could swing by the office, then go to the church. And if she was lucky, some elusive fact might leap at her while she was typing the report.

When the doorbell rang, Amanda groaned at a prospective delay. She answered the door and found Sam Harjo standing on her porch. His head and broad chest were concealed by two dozen red roses.

The dear, considerate man, she thought, staring appreciatively at the flowers.

Harjo peeked around the delicate blossoms and smiled charmingly. "For you, gorgeous," he murmured. "I'm sorry about waking you up in the middle of the night. I'm sorry about leaving my Blazer in your driveway and making you look bad." He stared at her for a long, meaningful moment. "But I'm not sorry about the kiss."

On the wings of that comment, Harjo handed her the flowers, then turned and walked away. "I'll be waiting, Hazard."

Amanda took time to smell the roses and read the card that pleaded with her to elope from the church. Sighing in frustration, she hurried into the bedroom to apply a quick coat of makeup. She scooped up the financial file Ima Lemon had entrusted to her, then stacked it on top of the garment bag Velma had delivered.

At the last minute, Amanda decided to bring along the windbreaker pants she had worn the previous night. Although she didn't have time to wash and dry the windbreaker suit, she could hand-wash it on the cruise ship—*if* she went. Hurriedly, she rolled up the pants and jacket and set them on the stack.

Lord, her bedroom was a mess, she thought, glancing around. She didn't have time to clean it up, not if she intended to type the report before heading to the church.

With an armload of clothes, a suitcase and files, Amanda strode toward the door, thankful that her ankle wasn't aggravating her. Bruno bounded to his feet, ready to accompany her.

"Sorry, boy, but you have to stay here and fight it out with Pete. Pops and Salty will make sure you're fed and watered."

Amanda scurried to her truck and sped away in a cloud of dust.

Much to Amanda's disappointment, the information and clues she had gathered for this case didn't leap from the monitor screen while she typed the report at her office. So much for wishful thinking.

Damn it, she could use a breakthrough! Soon, she would be surrounded by family and guests at church. How was she going to figure out who bumped off Frank Lemon, and why, in the middle of chaos?

Exasperated, Amanda clicked the mouse to print out her report. After the printer coughed out the papers, Amanda stuffed the report in the file with Frank's personal folder, switched off the computer and scampered out the door.

Very soon, she told herself, she was going to have to decide whether to forgive Thorn for dallying with the cake lady, or tell him where he could go—and what he could do with himself when he got there.

Nick paced the sanctuary, then glanced at his watch for the umpteenth time. He might look like Prince Charming, but he felt like the very devil. Where the hell was Hazard? She should have been here by now!

Velma, decked out in yards of Prussian purple chiffon and silk, her dyed red hair clashing with her ensemble, scurried up the aisle to stick passion-pink bows on each row of pews. The oversized bows clashed with the red carpet that Velma and Bev had rolled out fifteen minutes earlier.

"Is she here yet?" Crack, pop.

"No," Nick muttered.

Velma glanced worriedly around the sanctuary. "I was hoping we could take the wedding pictures before the ceremony, but if Amanda is running late, we'll have to do the photo shoot afterward."

Nick inwardly groaned when he saw the "photographer" sink down on the back pew. Josie Wheelwright, Velma's next-door neighbor, was equipped with an instamatic camera and twelve rolls of film. Good grief!

Nervous and frustrated, Nick strode from the sanctuary to the reception hall. He skidded to a halt when he noticed that Velma had dragged out those embarrassing posters of him and Hazard in their pre-adolescent years and thumbtacked them to the wall. There Nick was—in a life-size poster—with his thumb stuck in his mouth, his hair standing up, and a stupid look on his face. Hazard's poster displayed ample amounts of baby fat, and her hair was sticking out from the sides of her head, as if she had her finger stuck in an electrical socket.

Geez, thought Nick. This wasn't going to be the happiest day of his life, it was going to be the most embarrassing—especially if Hazard didn't get her fabulous fanny to the church PDQ!

Grimly, Nick glanced toward the table where the wedding cake sat in all its splendor and glory. The five-tier cake was decorated with pumpkins and little white mice.

Gee whiz! Velma's theme for the wedding was obviously Cinderella and Prince Charming.

Nick groaned aloud.

Hazard's mother would throw a fit when she saw the decorations and the cake . . .

Nick stumbled to a halt in front of the groom's cake. It was shaped like a giant white rat. The cake looked as if it had been broken in several pieces and then patched together with globs of icing. Pipe-cleaner whiskers stuck out the sides of the sharp nose that sat above oversize teeth. Black licorice eyes stared back at him.

Prince Charming? Pumpkins and rats? And where the hell was Cinderella?

"She's here!" Velma trumpeted. "She's coming in the back door."

Velma buzzed into the reception hall to bustle Nick into the sanctuary. "You can't see the bride before the wedding. It's bad luck, Nicky."

When Velma handed Nick into Rich's care, she scuttled off to tend her last-minute duties. Nick breathed a huge sigh of relief, now that Hazard had arrived. Surely that indicated that she was going through with the wedding, that she had forgiven him for the cake incident in which he had been an innocent victim. Hadn't she?

Nick cautioned himself not to assume anything until Hazard had the wedding band on her finger and said "I do."

"Oh my God!" Nick gasped as he frantically searched his pockets. "What did I do with them?"

Rich frowned. "What's wrong?"

"Do you have the wedding band and marriage license?" Nick asked wildly.

"No, you didn't give them to me. Don't tell me that you already lost them! I'm supposed to be taking care of the ring," Rich grumbled. "Now you're going to make me look bad."

Nick dashed down the aisle, headed for the door. He had left the box with the ring on the bedroom dresser, and he couldn't remember where in the hell he had stashed the marriage license for safekeeping!

"Nicky, you come back here this very instant!" Velma wailed. "Don't you dare run out on Amanda!"

"I'll be back," Nick called over his shoulder, on his way out the door.

Amanda was frustrated when she closeted herself in the Sunday school classroom to change clothes. She had come down to the wire and still hadn't been able to identify Frank Lemon's murderer. She had nothing. Yet, she was thoroughly convinced that Frank's death was no accident.

Grumbling, Amanda unrolled the garment bag and tossed her windbreaker pants aside. Particles of sand dribbled onto the floor as she uplifted, and unzipped, the garment bag.

"Good grief!" Amanda chirped when she saw the dress Velma had selected for her. She committed an awful sin by cursing, right there in church. She stared at row after row of delicate ruffles and dainty lace that was stitched from the waistline to the long hem of the gown. And the neckline! Amanda hadn't exposed that much cleavage in years!

"Hurry up, hon," Velma called from outside the door. "The guests are beginning to arrive." Chomp, chomp.

Amanda groaned when a pair of glass slippers—clear plastic high heels, actually—tumbled from the garment bag to the floor. She was going to look like Cinderella, she realized. What weird fantasy was Velma trying to create here? For some reason, Velma saw Thorn and Amanda as a fairy-tale couple, and she intended to carry the theme through the wedding.

Muttering at her preposterous get-up, and her purple hair that was so brittle that it broke off at each touch, Amanda wormed into her gown. Sure enough, the tight bodice left her looking as if her chest was about to spill from the plunging neckline. Lord, how did she get herself into these messes?

Amanda stuck her foot in the glass slipper . . . and then realization hit her like a brick. She glanced from the granules of sand on the floor to her dirty windbreaker pants.

How had river sand gotten on her pants?

Amanda staggered in her glass slippers when she remembered crawling across the bedroom floor of the cottage, while wearing her windsuit. She must have picked up the sand from the dirty clothes that were strung around the room.

Dirty clothes . . . caked with grease and . . .

"Oh, God," Amanda croaked, her eyes bulging from their sockets.

The clothes—that was the clue she had overlooked in her haste to survey the cottage. She had crawled right over the top of the grimy garments and realization hadn't soaked in. Damn, she was dense! All the clues had been staring her in the face and she had been too distracted with all this wedding business to reason out who had bumped off Frank.

Two meals on the expense accounts . . .

Two sets of shoe prints in the sand—a man's and a woman's . . .

Two pair of tennis shoes in the office of Lemon's Used Cars . . .

A burned fuse under the instrument panel of the big red truck . . .

The steering wheel tilted to the "down" position . . .

When the clues dropped neatly into place, Amanda knew who lived in the cottage on Frank Lemon's property.

She knew why the shoe prints had been in such odd disarray.

Wheeling around, Amanda scooped up the veil to conceal her hideous hairdo, then poked her head around the edge of the door.

"Thorn!" Her frantic voice boomed down the hall, drowning out the quick-tempoed beat of the organ music that Billie Jane Baxter was performing for the waiting guests.

To Amanda's dismay, Thorn didn't appear—his brother, Rich, did.

"You called, Cinderella?" he said, and grinned as he took in the diving neckline and cascade of ruffles and lace.

"Where is your brother? I need to see him immediately."

Rich waggled his eyebrows. "Sorry, Hazard, but your *need* for Nick will have to wait until the honeymoon. Can't put the cart before the horse, as they say."

Amanda glared impatiently at Rich. "I want to talk to Thorn. Where is he?"

When Rich shifted awkwardly, then glanced down the hall, Amanda frowned suspiciously. "He's not here, is he, Rich?"

"Well, he was here, but he left," Rich said helpfully. "He—"

Fuming, Amanda slammed the door in Rich's face.

Thorn, the big rat, had bailed out on her! Damn it, Harjo must have told Thorn about last night's kiss. And someone must have told Thorn that Harjo's Blazer had been parked in her driveway all night. Obviously, Thorn had gotten mad and left.

Of all the nerve! Thorn had no right to be upset, because he had done the horizontal two-step with the cake lady. And now he had the audacity to leave Amanda at the altar just because of the incident with Harjo? Talk about double standards!

"Well, fine," she muttered. "I'm out of here. Besides, I have a killer to track down."

Amanda snatched up her purse, and whizzed out the door, serenaded by Velma's repeated wails of "Come back, come back!" and Rich's "Hazard, wait a minute!"

Amanda hit the door running. In the gathering darkness, she saw the Watts brothers—who were in the parking lot, decorating her jalopy truck with shoe polish, shaving cream and strings of beer cans that were attached to the back bumper.

When Amanda bounded into the old truck and switched on the ignition, Cleatus and Cecil Watts gaped at her.

"What are you doing, 'Manda?" Cecil asked.

"Surely you aren't running out on the chief . . . are you?" Cleatus questioned anxiously.

Amanda didn't bother to reply. She gunned the old truck and sped down the street, accompanied by the sound of beer cans banging against the pavement.

This might not be her wedding day, but it sure as hell was going to be the day she tracked down the killer who left Frank Lemon dead in the driver's seat!

Nick caromed around the corner to see Velma, Rich, and the Watts brothers staring south. "What's going on?" he asked as he pulled to a stop.

"Amanda took off, all decked out in her wedding dress," Velma yowled. Mascara bled down her plump cheeks with the stream of tears. "She wanted to talk to you before the wedding and Rich told her you had left the church. Then she blazed off in her truck. My wedding plans are ruined!"

Nick glowered at his brother. "Thanks a lot. Why the hell didn't you tell her where I was?"

"I tried, but she didn't give me a chance to explain," Rich defended himself. "She slammed the door in my face, then burst out the back door before I could stop her."

Nick stared grimly at his brother. "Was Sam Harjo with her?"

"No, she drove off alone," Cleatus reported. "We didn't even have time to hitch all the beer-can streamers to the bumper before she roared off."

Nick stared down the dark street. He had to catch up with Hazard, had to explain that the kiss between him and the cake lady meant nothing, had to explain that he had left the church because he had forgotten the ring and the license.

Damn it, he was going to make Hazard listen to him! She wasn't leaving him here at the church with hundreds of guests to stare at him with their pitying looks!

If Hazard intended to back out on him, then she was going to have to tell him, right to his face.

In determined strides, Nick returned to his truck. His foot mashed the accelerator all the way to the floorboard. Tires squealed. Nick roared off, leaving Velma wailing behind him.

"Oh my God, now what are we going to do?" Velma blubbered.

Beverly Hill burst from the back door of the church, flapping her arms like a duck preparing to go airborne. "Aunt Velma! Like, you have got to do something and quickly! Nicky's mom and Amanda's mother got into a shouting match in the sanctuary, while the ushers were trying to seat them. They started pulling each other's hair, calling each other *snob* and *country bumpkin!* Now they are rolling around in the aisle, hissing and snarling at each other. The guests are taking bets on the outcome of the fight!"

"Great, just great," Rich muttered. He stared at the church, then glanced at Nick's retreating truck. "Well, I guess Mom will have to fight her own battle. I better go after Nick. If the scowl on his face is any indication, Prince Charming intends to track down Cinderella and hit her over the head with her glass slipper."

When Rich charged off in his car, Velma wheeled around to face Bev: "Go tell the guests to hop in their cars." Snap, pop. "No matter where the bride and groom end up, the wedding party is not going to be far behind. Those two yahoos are not going to weasel out of this wedding ceremony, not if I have anything to say about it. I've spent two weeks making these arrangements and they are not going to be for nothing!"

"But what about the mothers of the bride and groom?" Bev questioned.

"If they want to stay here and slug it out, then let them. We have to follow Nicky and Amanda!"

In a swirl of silk and chiffon, Velma galumphed toward her car to give chase. By damned, this wedding was going to take place, even if Velma had to drag Nicky and Amanda back to the church by their heels and nail their feet to the altar!

Fourteen

Amanda ignored the racket of aluminum cans bouncing on the road behind her. Her thoughts were focused entirely on the clues she had overlooked—until this evening. She should have figured out the murder scheme the moment she saw those shoe prints in the sand, then saw the men's and women's shoes sitting in the office of Lemon's Used Cars. She was definitely slipping, she decided.

She should have known what the killer had cleverly arranged when she picked up the left shoe from the bottom drawer of Irene's desk and the right shoe that was out of place in the restroom. But, because she was a creature of orderly habit, Amanda had simply put the shoes in their proper places to make matched pairs. Geez, one of the pivotal clues had been hiding in plain sight and she had overlooked it!

In a cloud of dust and pelting gravel, Amanda zipped down the road. Her headlights flared on Floyd's house, then on Ima's. She whipped into the driveway of the small cottage that sat on the edge of Frank's property. Holding up the layers of ruffles and lace of her gown, she bounded from the truck. Her glass slippers pelted the sidewalk and her veil whipped in the wind as she hurried to the door of the cottage that was silhouetted in the darkness.

Before Amanda could raise her hand to knock, the door whipped open and an arm shot out to grab her. Amanda found herself crushed against Freddy Lassiter's long, lean body.

"Well, well, Cinderella, looks like you took a wrong turn on your way to your wedding," Freddy smirked at her.

Amanda grimaced when a pistol barrel pried her ribs apart. "Good ole, easy-going Freddy," she muttered. "I figured I would find you here. You almost pulled it off. Then you hung around long enough to look innocent, and even offered me information. I fell for that ploy like an idiot."

"I had to watch what I was doing, when dealing with someone as shrewd as you," Freddy said. "You have a reputation for finding clues that regular cops overlook."

Amanda glanced down to see the suitcase sitting by the door. "I suppose you're planning to hightail it out of the county, now that things have simmered down."

"Yeah, but it looks like you'll be coming with me, Cinderella. I'll have to be sure that you don't leave one of your glass slippers behind to tie me to your disappearance. You're going to have an unfortunate accident, after leaving Thorn at the altar—"

Freddy's voice trailed off into a scowl when he saw the cloud of dust billowing on the hilltop.

Amanda found herself dragged to her truck, her hands hurriedly tied to the door handle with her wedding veil.

"Nice hair, Hazard," Freddy snorted as he gunned the jalopy. The old truck sputtered, then purred as Freddy blazed down the driveway, making his getaway before Thorn's truck reached the bottom of the hill.

The moment Freddy topped the next rise of ground, he switched off the headlights, then turned a sharp right at the country intersection. He drove past the thick clump of cedar trees that lined the road, concealing the truck from sight momentarily. Then he whizzed off, hoping Thorn wouldn't notice the abrupt change of direction.

Amanda tried to wrest her hands free and grab the steering wheel, but Freddy had secured her improvised handcuffs tightly. Damn, things weren't working out as she had planned. She had hoped to take Freddy by surprise, then calmly talk him into giving himself up, but he had heard her coming in the old truck, with its bad muffler and beer-can streamers. He had panicked when he'd seen Thorn's truck speeding toward him.

At least Thorn hadn't abandoned her completely, Amanda thought to herself. At the last minute, he may have decided not to marry her, but at least there was enough history between them that he didn't want her to come to harm. She would try to remember that, just in case she ended up like Frank Lemon—dead in her own driver's seat.

Amanda knew the only way to save herself was to get Freddy talking so he wouldn't have time to plot out his next move.

"I must admit you really had me going when you swiped Irene's left shoe and Ernie's right one," she said as calmly as she knew how. "That was incredibly clever of you. Those tracks in the sand had me confused."

"Yeah, I thought that was pretty clever," Freddy said as he glanced in the rearview mirror to monitor Thorn's position. "Knowing your talent for investigation, I didn't think we should take any chances, so I set up Ernie and Irene by wearing one of his shoes and one of hers. I figured those two lovebirds deserved to catch the heat if you got wise to what happened to Frank."

"But you overlooked the fact that I could tell a left shoe from a right shoe print in the sand. I knew there was something strange about the tracks the moment I saw them—"

Freddy cut a sharp left, causing Amanda to bang her head against the side window. He glanced over his shoulder to see Thorn's headlights through the fog of dust.

"Damn, that Thorn is a regular bloodhound, isn't he?"

"Yes, he is," Amanda agreed. "So you might as well pull over. Thorn is nothing if not relentless."

"Not a chance," Freddy said determinedly. "I made it this far and I sure as hell don't intend to quit now . . . oh, hell!"

Amanda glanced over her shoulder to see what had upset Freddy. A stream of headlights were trailing behind Thorn's truck. It looked as if all the wedding guests had saddled up and ridden off like a posse.

Velma's idea, Amanda predicted. The Amazon beautician refused to see her wedding plans foiled.

Calmly, Amanda stared at Freddy who had begun to sweat profusely.

"Why did you do it, Freddy?" she wanted to know. "Was it because Frank wouldn't give you a respectable cut of the profit he was making on stolen car sales?"

Freddy nodded curtly, his eyes glued to the dark road ahead of him. "The son of a bitch made me take all the chances of getting caught stealing vehicles and driving them out to the country. Hell, I didn't even get a meal out of the bastard for all my troubles. He was too busy panting over that bimbo he was stuck on.

"Frank helped me dismantle the cars, but he was never around in the heat of a tense situation that could land me in jail again," Freddy muttered resentfully.

"Did he threaten you if you didn't stick with the original deal?" Amanda asked as the clunker truck sped over hill and dale.

"Yeah, he kept reminding me that I was the one with the police record. Frank swore he would sick Deputy Payne on me if I didn't continue the car theft scam."

"So," Amanda said thoughtfully, "sometimes you dismantled and burned and other times you stole vehicles, loaded them in the U-Haul that Frank rented on a monthly basis, and then hid them behind the pond dam so you could take them apart at your leisure. The stolen parts were placed on wrecked vehicles that Floyd and Sally Jean could pick up for little or nothing at salvage and auto auctions."

"Damn, you are good, aren't you, Hazard?" Freddy smiled wickedly. "Too bad you won't be around to give your statement to Deputy Payne. Not that he would be interested in your conclusions."

"Why wouldn't Payne be interested?" Amanda asked. She braced her glass slippers on the floorboard when Freddy swerved around the corner of the section, doubling back toward his house.

Amanda had the uneasy feeling that Freddy had been doing entirely too much thinking, though she had been launching rapid-fire questions at him. Unless she missed her guess—and she was pretty sure she hadn't—Freddy intended to drive around the section, without the headlights to give away his location. Then he planned to lose himself in the wedding procession that trailed behind Thorn. In the darkness, and the thick cloud of dust, the wedding guests wouldn't realize that Freddy was *behind* them.

"Freddy, you didn't answer me," Amanda persisted as Freddy floorboarded the old truck. "Why doesn't Payne want to know what really happened?"

Freddy smiled wryly at her, then refocused on the road. "You mean you haven't figured out his angle, Hazard? I'm disappointed in you. I've been hearing what a whiz you are at investigation and how we have to be careful what we say and do around you."

"Did Deputy Payne get a dinner out of Frank?" she wanted to know.

"Nope." Freddy careened around the corner and gunned the engine. He focused intently on the stream of cars driving west, then slowed down so he could pull in behind the last car in the procession and flick on his headlights.

Amanda glanced back, watching Thorn's truck back up

in the distance, circle the intersection and switch directions. Clearly, Thorn was having trouble figuring out where Freddy had gone, since he had been driving without headlights and taillights.

Amanda inwardly grimaced. She may have been too confident in thinking she could come out of this situation alive. If Freddy managed to leave the wedding procession driving in circles, like a dog chasing its tail, she could most certainly end up dead in some obscure ditch filled with tall weeds!

"Where the hell did that clunker truck go?" Nick muttered aloud.

Trying to follow the truck without taillights in the darkness wasn't easy. Twice, Nick had made a wrong turn, rolled down the window and pricked his ears to the sound of aluminum cans clattering.

Well, at least Hazard had tried to contact him before she got herself in a scrape, Nick consoled himself. Problem was that he had left the church and she refused to delay her never-ending crusade for truth and justice. Even if Hazard had decided to bail out of the wedding, because of that damned cake-lady incident, she *had* tried to let him know where she was going. He would try to remember that before he bit her head off—if she was still alive so he could give her hell!

Hurriedly, Nick picked up the microphone attached to his CB. "Benny? Are you back in that procession that is following me? Come in!"

"I'm here, Chief," Benny Sykes came back. "What the devil is going on?"

"I think Hazard figured out whodunit, but she's managed to get herself into trouble, as usual. I had the old truck in my sights, but now I've lost it. I don't know where the hell it went, so keep your eyes peeled."

"Keep my eyes peeled. 10-4, Chief."

Nick replaced the mike, then stared into the distance. When he saw a set of headlights flick on, he increased speed. "Clever of you, pal," he said, as he put the pedal to the metal and roared off in a cloud of dust and flying gravel.

"Did you stick a burned-out fuse under the instrument panel of Frank's truck before you made that sensational leap into the sand?" Amanda quizzed Freddy.

"Nope, didn't have to," he replied. "It wasn't functioning when I checked over the truck earlier that afternoon."

Amanda could tell that Freddy had begun to relax, now that he was bringing up the rear of the wedding procession. His tight grasp on the steering wheel lessened. He thought he had it made in the shade.

Good, thought Amanda. Now that Freddy had let his guard down, she would have the chance to strike. All she had to do was bide her time, wait for an opportune moment.

"So, you're saying that this was a premeditated plan to lure Thorn into a chase and send Frank flying into the river."

"Yep, and it worked superbly until you got suspicious." Freddy glanced sideways at her, then frowned. "Just what tipped you off, Hazard?"

"The steering wheel," she replied as she coiled her legs beneath her on the seat, assuming a casual position—or so she wanted Freddy to think.

"The steering wheel?" he parroted, bemused.

"Frank kept the steering wheel tilted to the 'up' position to accommodate his round belly. You forgot to switch it up before you made your escape leap."

Freddy scowled in disgust. "Damn, I forgot about that. I should have left it where it was when I got in."

"Don't feel bad," she said. "Every criminal gives himself away, somehow or another. The average Joe wouldn't have noticed the change."

"Yeah, and if you weren't so damned smart, you wouldn't be in the fix you're in now," Freddy reminded her. "Sorry, Hazard, but you know entirely too much. I have to admit that I kinda like you, but when it comes down to sparing you or saving my own hide, I'm sure you'll understand that you'll have to be sacrificed to keep me from going back to jail."

"You could turn evidence and implicate Floyd and Sally Jean," she suggested. "You could plea bargain, you know."

Freddy chuckled. "You never give up, do you? Well, thanks, but no thanks. I'd rather take the money, change identities and find somewhere else to live. As for you—"

While Freddy was completely off guard, trailing along behind the wedding procession, Amanda swiveled her legs up and struck out with her glass slippers. The heel of her right shoe hooked on the steering wheel. The other sharp-pointed heel spiked Freddy's hand.

Freddy howled and drew back his hand instinctively. The clunker truck swerved across the road, headed for the ditch. Cursing ferociously, Freddy grabbed the wheel before the jalopy slammed, head-on, into the corner fence post. The truck broke through the barbed wire, and wires snapped, then coiled and tangled around the front wheels.

"Shit!" Freddy hissed when he saw Thorn's truck speeding toward him, tipped off by the conspicuous swerve into the ditch.

Freddy leaped from the truck and took off across the wheat field at a dead run.

Amanda strained to break loose from the wedding veil handcuffs, but she was stuck like glue. There was nothing she could do but wait until Thorn arrived to set her free.

To her irritation, Thorn did little more than glance at

her as he plowed through the ditch and gunned the engine in hot pursuit of Freddy. Sure enough, Thorn was pissed about Harjo's kiss, Amanda decided. Thorn wasn't speaking to her, though he cared enough about her safety to chase after her when Freddy took her hostage. Even if she and Thorn weren't on speaking terms for the next hundred years, she would have to remember to send him a thank-you note for coming to her rescue.

"Benny, the suspect is fleeing on foot across the wheat field," Nick said into the mike. "Block his path at the west fence."

"10-4, Chief," Benny replied.

Nick didn't know who the hell he was chasing, but he could see the man's silhouette in the high-beam headlights . . .

"Hell!" Nick swerved the truck when the suspect wheeled around to point a gun at him. The discharging bullet zinged off the fender of the four-wheel-drive truck, but it didn't discourage Nick from giving chase. He had been in worse scrapes, while working for OKCPD and the Narc squad. This was a piece of cake in comparison.

When the suspect took off running again, Nick mashed on the accelerator, intent on sideswiping the man.

"You've got him now, Chief!" Benny yelled over the CB.

Nick kept one hand on the wheel while he reached behind the seat to grab the lariat he always carried in his truck—in case he had to rope a contrary calf that broke through a pasture fence. The moment Nick pulled alongside the suspect, he took a swipe with the coiled rope. He saw the silver of the pistol reflecting in the headlights, saw the spitting end of the gun bearing down on him. Nick slammed on the brake.

The shot whizzed past the windshield and thudded in the wheat.

When Nick recognized the suspect, he muttered under his breath. Obviously, Freddy Lassiter was involved in Frank Lemon's death. Otherwise he wouldn't have taken Hazard hostage, then tried to shoot Nick out of his pickup seat. Freddy had become panicky and desperate and he was fighting to save himself from arrest and inevitable conviction.

"Give it up, Freddy, there's nowhere to run," Nick called out.

"Oh, yeah?" Freddy raised the pistol and took aim.

Nick scowled in irritation as he hurled the rope at Freddy's gun hand. Freddy ducked away from the flying coil of rope. Nick bounded from the truck before Freddy could come to his knees to fire off a clean shot. Nick kicked the weapon from Freddy's hand with the toe of his white, patent-leather boot, then delivered a punishing blow with his fist that discouraged Freddy from getting up after he was knocked flat.

"You damn fool!" Nick bellowed at Freddy. "If you have any hope of getting out on parole in the next thousand years, you better stay down!"

"Damn that Hazard," Freddy muttered out the side of his mouth that wasn't bleeding and swollen. "She ruined everything."

"That's what she does best," Nick grunted. "She sure as hell ruined my evening."

Benny Sykes whizzed across the wheat field. The squad car ground to a halt, rocking on its suspension springs. The headlights beamed on Prince Charming and the downed suspect.

"Good work, Chief," Benny said as he scurried forward. Hurriedly, he cuffed Freddy, then hoisted him to his feet.

"As for you, Freddy," Benny snapped. "You're going

to have to sit and fry in your own grease for a while. If you think I'm going to miss the wedding of the decade, just to haul your butt to jail, then think again. You're going to spend the next couple of hours in cuffs and leg irons, in the back seat of my car."

Nick glanced over his shoulder toward the jalopy truck that was stuck in barbed wire. In dismay, he watched Sam Harjo's Chevy Blazer pull up to check on Hazard. From the look of things, there might not be a wedding.

Glumly, Nick grabbed his discarded lariat, coiled it neatly, then tucked it behind the pickup seat. The time of reckoning had come, Nick mused as he climbed behind the wheel.

In grim apprehension, Nick retraced his path through the field to confront Hazard.

"You okay, Hazard?" Harjo asked as he opened the passenger door of the truck.

Amanda, who was still tethered to the door latch, fell off balance. Harjo scooped her up in his arms before she plunked to the ground in a tangle of ruffles and lace.

"Hold on, doll face, I'll have you untied in a sec."

Hurriedly, Harjo unwound the veil, then set Amanda to her feet to examine her for injuries.

"I'm fine," Amanda insisted.

Harjo stared over her head, watching Thorn approach. "Here's you big chance, Hazard. Who's it going to be? Him or me?"

"How about neither of the above," she said huffily.

Harjo frowned, then stared pensively at her. "You don't want either of us? But what did I do to upset you?"

Amanda scowled at the handsome commish. "You know perfectly well what you did, so don't play stupid."

When she heard the truck grind to a halt, and the door creak open, she rounded on Thorn. "And as for you—"

"I can explain," Thorn said, effectively cutting her off in midsentence.

"It didn't mean a thing, right? Just a last fling, right?" she sputtered. "I suppose it's okay for you to fool around with the cake lady, but I'm not allowed the same privilege, right?"

Thorn opened his mouth to reply, then frowned. "What the hell are you talking about?"

"Don't play stupid, either, Thorn," she gritted out. She glanced down the road to see the compact car zigging and zagging around the procession of vehicles that had stopped on the road. "We have a decision to make before Velma gets here, and she's barreling toward us as we speak."

"I didn't tell him, Hazard," Harjo spoke up. "Is that what you think I did? Well, I didn't. That was personal and private and I didn't say a damned thing about it."

Amanda winced as she stared at Harjo, knowing what Thorn was going to ask before the words were out of his mouth.

"What didn't he tell me that is personal and private?" Thorn growled, then swore colorfully. "Never mind. I can guess! Damn it, Hazard, how could you!"

"How could *I?*" she retaliated indignantly. "How could *you!*"

"Me? All I did was sit there like a slug while the cake lady kissed me. I didn't participate, not even for a second." His arm shot out accusingly. "But you and Harjo!" Thorn spewed several more epithets as he shrugged off his white jacket. "Here, Harjo, you want to play Prince Charming? Fine, be my guest!"

When Thorn hurled the coat at Harjo, then wheeled around to stalk off, Amanda's heart missed several vital beats. He was walking away! He thought she and Harjo had shared more than a steamy kiss in the seat of her jalopy?

"Hold it right there, Thorn," she yelled at him.

Thorn pivoted on his heels of his patent-leather boots. "Go ahead, Haz, say it to my face. Let's get it over with," he shouted at her.

Amanda halted in front of him, then glanced back at Harjo who held the white jacket. Her gaze swung back to Thorn who stood rigidly in front of her, staring at her with those penetrating midnight-black eyes.

"All Harjo did was kiss me," she said quietly. "That was all, and for the very first time since I've known him, I'll have you know."

She saw Thorn wince as if he had been slapped. The sweet, dear man was jealous and his male pride was smarting. Good, then he knew how she felt when she heard about the cake-lady incident.

Amanda smiled wryly as she took a step closer. "And do you know something, Thorn?"

"No, at the moment I don't know a damned thing except that I'd like to plant my fist in Harjo's face."

Amanda moved ever nearer, until mere inches were between them. "I wanted to tear out the cake lady's hair at the roots and scratch out her eyes."

Thorn blinked. "You did?"

"Did you take her home with you?" she asked him point-blank.

"No, absolutely not. My only house guest was my brother who snored up a storm on the couch."

"Thank God everybody's all right!" Velma trumpeted as she lumbered across the road, clutching the hem of her silk and chiffon gown so it wouldn't drag in the dirt. "Can we go back to the church now?" Crackle, chomp.

Amanda never took her eyes off Thorn. "Well, Prince Charming? It's your call. Marry me now or lose me forever."

A slow smile worked its way across his lips. "I'll get

my jacket, Cinderella. You grab the veil to cover your hair."

When Thorn sauntered off, Amanda smiled to herself. She knew she had made the right choice. As much as she admired and enjoyed Sam Harjo's company, he could never be more than a close friend.

That was, quite simply, the way it was. Long ago, feminine instinct had told her that this sexy country cop was the man for her. Through the ups and downs, the ins and outs, nothing had changed. And although Mother insisted this was the second mistake Amanda had made in her life, Mother didn't know what the hell she was talking about!

"Looks like I'm the odd man out," Harjo mumbled. "I guess you win the prize, Thorn."

Nick accepted the white jacket Harjo handed to him. "You know, Harjo, in spite of everything, I still like you. Of course, I would like to take off your head for kissing Hazard while she was wearing my engagement ring."

Harjo shrugged a broad shoulder. "And like I said before, I expect you would have resorted to the same last-ditch attempt, if the boot was on the other foot."

"Yeah," he openly admitted this time. "I would have."

"Come on!" Velma called impatiently. "This wedding procession is getting restless!"

Nick spun on his heels to return to his truck. Hazard had retrieved her wedding veil and waited inside the cab.

"Did you and Harjo clear the air?" she asked as she fluffed her ruffles, then tugged at the plunging neckline.

"Yes," Nick confirmed as he started the truck.

"Good. I like Harjo . . . but I'm crazy about you, Thorn."

Twenty-four hours of knotted tension drained from Nick. "Good, because I'm still crazy about you, too. And the only reason I left the church was because I forgot to pick up the wedding band and marriage license."

"And the only reason I left the church was because it finally dawned on me who had bumped off—"

When Hazard's voice dried up, Nick glanced at her. "Now what's wrong?"

"Thorn," she said, very slowly, very deliberately, "I don't think we can close this case yet, because something still doesn't add up."

"Damn," Nick groaned. "Now what?"

"Let me drive," she insisted, scooting toward him.

Nick started to protest, but Hazard had that determined look in her eyes. He was not going to argue with her—not now. This wedding still hadn't taken place. He decided to save the arguments until they were legally bound.

"Okay, Hazard, but don't wreck my truck. It's the only vehicle that we have between us that still runs."

When Hazard slid beneath the wheel and zoomed off, Nick fastened his seat belt. Wherever they were going, at least they were going together, he consoled himself.

Fifteen

Amanda sped around the corner of the country intersection, then pointed a purple-tipped finger at the CB. "Call the sheriff and have him meet us at the church."

"Why?" Thorn questioned.

"Because the sheriff needs to bring in Floyd and Sally Jean Lemon for questioning. Floyd lied to me when he said he was no longer working with Frank. He is in on the car-theft ring and he was furious with Ernie because he left those counterfeit bills of sale in Frank's desk where I could find them.

"The sheriff also needs to haul in Ernie and Irene for tampering with the ID numbers on vehicle registration forms and car titles. Ernie is the one who ran me off the road, in hopes of discouraging me from continuing my investigation. He had Freddy replace the grille and front bumper of the car he was driving."

Thorn blinked, stunned. "The entire Lemon clan was in on this auto-theft scam?"

"Yes," Amanda confirmed. "All but—"

Amanda's thoughts exploded in her mind when she remembered her conversation with Freddy during the chase. During those tense moments, when she was trying to keep Freddy talking, hoping to distract him so she could attempt to escape disaster, she hadn't paid close attention to what he said—or rather what he had unknowingly revealed to her.

Hell, I didn't get a dinner out of Frank, not even once.

I should have left the steering wheel up when I got in.

Deputy Payne didn't get a free dinner, either.

I've been hearing what a whiz you are at investigation, and how we had to be careful what we said and did around you.

I didn't think we should take any chances.

We . . .

I'm going to take the money, change identities and find somewhere else to live . . .

The money . . .

Amanda gunned the truck. She had one more stop to make before she returned to the church.

"This isn't the way back to town," Thorn pointed out.

"I know, but we have to make an important pit stop. Get on the horn and call the sheriff so he'll have time to get to the church when we do," she ordered hurriedly.

Thorn called police headquarters, requesting that Janie-Ethel patch him through to the sheriff.

While Thorn spoke to the sheriff, Amanda's mind whirled in twenty different directions at once. Her first instinct about Frank Lemon's overnight trips had been correct, she assured herself. The receipts for meals confirmed it. But she had let herself be convinced that Frank had nothing else going except his illegal theft ring. Wrong!

"Why are we stopping here?' Thorn asked as Amanda veered into the tree-lined driveway.

"Because the mastermind behind Frank's cleverly staged murder is walking around scot-free."

"This better not turn into another fiasco, because I'm not packing hardware," Thorn muttered. "All I had to defend myself against Freddy was a lariat."

"And a fine job you did of it," she complimented him.

"Not to worry, Thorn, you can handle this situation. Just follow my lead and everything will be dandy."

"Yeah, right," Thorn said, and snorted. "Do you know how many times you've said that to me and things didn't turn out dandy?"

Ignoring the question, Amanda led the way up the sidewalk to ring the doorbell. After a moment the door opened.

Ima Lemon stepped back, startled. "What are you doing here?"

"Wrapping up loose ends for your estate taxes," Amanda said as she barged inside without invitation. "Grab your purse, Ima. You need to come with us."

"I do? Why?" Ima's nervous gaze darted this way and that.

"Don't even think about it," Amanda advised as she whipped off her veil, then wrapped the netting around Ima's wrists.

"Are you mad? What do you think you're doing?" Ima shrieked.

"Thorn, escort the widow to the truck, please," Amanda requested. "We're working on a short clock here, you know."

To his credit, Thorn didn't bother her with questions. He simply did as he was told. His behavior assured Amanda that he was going to make a model husband.

"I'll have both of you behind bars for this, don't think I won't!" Ima screeched as Thorn shoveled her out the door. "My lawyer will sue the pants off you."

"Calm down, Ima," Amanda said as she closed the door behind her. "You'll have your chance to speak to your mouthpiece in due time. I must admit that you almost fooled me with your sentimental comments. I was even flattered when you insisted that you wanted no one but me to handle the estate taxes and dealership accounts. You almost took me in when you tried to win me over. You came very close to getting away with this."

"Getting away with what? What are you raving about? I haven't done anything to warrant this demeaning treatment," Ima snorted indignantly.

When Thorn glanced uneasily at her, Amanda knew he was having doubts about her reasons for apprehending Ima Lemon. But Amanda was determined. She gestured for Thorn to stuff Ima in the truck, despite her convincing protests.

Amanda slid beneath the wheel, then backed from the driveway. "Now don't go blaming Freddy for this, because he did his best not to implicate you. He just got a little careless with his *I's* and *we's*."

"Freddy?" Ima's tone of voice changed from indignant to wary.

"Good ole Freddy, your part-time gardener, the ex-con who held his own personal grudge against Frank. Freddy was willing to make extra money when you decided that you'd had your fill of Frank's indiscretions."

"This is preposterous," Ima huffed. "I don't have to listen to this nonsense!"

"Come off it, Ima," Amanda said as she followed the gravel road toward town. "Frank was cheating on you and you found out about it. I saw the receipts for meals—meals for two—on the expense account for his *supposed* business trips. You decided you'd had enough of his philandering so you hired Freddy to put Frank out of your misery, once and for all. You dissolved Frank's blood pressure medication in his drink so he would pass out, but you wanted to make sure Frank didn't pass out somewhere on the road and do nothing more than wreck his truck and put a bump on his noggin."

"This is all wild speculation and there is not one bit of truth to it," Ima objected.

"If Frank had blanked out while driving, there was a

good chance there would be barbed-wire scrapes on the paint," Amanda went on. "But there weren't, because I looked the truck over thoroughly after it was impounded.

"Since Thorn had already stopped Frank for drinking and driving, all you had to do was wait until the interaction of whiskey and medicine knocked Frank out cold, then do with him what you wanted."

"You really should write fiction," Ima sniffed. "That is the most ridiculous story I ever heard. I never tampered with Frank's whiskey or medication. And yes, I will admit Freddy did mow the lawn, but I didn't conspire with him. I loved Frank! I have always loved Frank, 'til death did us part!" Her voice rose to a yell.

Thorn glanced at Amanda again. She could tell by his expression that he was falling for this sentimental crock Ima was dishing out.

"Oh pl—ease," Amanda snorted. "Save the melodramatics. I saw your personal bank accounts, remember? You, not Frank, withdrew a thousand dollars the day before he died. I'm sure the money will be found on Freddy's person, or in the cottage, when the sheriff makes his search. Freddy said that he planned to take the money and leave town. He wasn't referring to the cash in Frank's wallet, because you told me yourself that no money was missing."

"I was planning to buy new furniture," Ima said in a rush.

Amanda smiled cattily. "Really? Paid for in cash? Yeah, right. People do that all the time."

Apparently, Thorn was beginning to believe that Amanda was on the right track, because he turned toward Ima and said, "You have the right to remain silent. You have the right—"

"Oh, shut up," Ima snapped at him.

"When Frank passed out after his evening meal, I suspect, you phoned Freddy," Amanda continued. "The two of you hauled Frank to the truck, but Freddy switched the steering wheel position without thinking. Then Freddy drove around to locate Thorn. You knew he was on night duty because Benny Sykes was on R and R. And, of course, with Deputy Payne sniffing around Loraine, you knew he wouldn't be suspicious of you, because he was eager to have Thorn's job and remain in your good graces.

"Payne made the perfect pawn, and so did I," Amanda said with a self-deprecating grimace. "You all but told me to check the business accounts closely, because you *wanted* me to realize that your son-in-law, whom you have absolutely no use for, was involved in the theft ring. You wanted Ernie punished for two-timing Loraine, just as you wanted Frank punished for two-timing *you*.

"Then, after Freddy lured Thorn and me into that high-speed chase, he made his leap to safety, wearing one of Irene's tennis shoes and one of Ernie's. You picked Freddy up and returned home. It was a clever scheme and you didn't have to ask Freddy to make a mess with a pistol or knife that would have the police asking questions. Unfortunately, there were just enough clues to lead me back to you, Ima."

Amanda knew the instant Ima realized none of her protests could counter the truth. The widow slumped defeatedly in the seat, her head downcast, her bound hands clenched in her lap.

"That son of a bitch," Ima hissed hatefully. "He has been carrying on with that floozy, who is fifteen years younger than I am, for over a year. He didn't think I would find out about her. He didn't think my sister would tell me when she saw the two of them together, because we rarely speak to each other these days. But Sally Jean leaped at the chance to tattle on Frank.

"He charmed me away from Floyd all those years ago and made me the other woman in my sister's life. Then *I* was the one he cheated on with that hot-to-trot Williams woman!"

Ima stared at Amanda, her eyes glistening with angry tears. "Do you know how it feels to have your husband call you by another woman's name while he is so drunk that he can't even remember who he's with?"

Amanda looked straight at Thorn and said, "If my husband ever does that to me, I won't hire a hit man to dispose of him. That would be letting him off too easily. I will take him for all he is worth—financially—reduce his reputation to cinders, see that he is ostracized by everyone in his hometown, make him an outcast of—"

"We get the point, Haz. No need to belabor it," Thorn mumbled.

"I still think he deserved it," Ima spat bitterly.

"He probably did," Amanda agreed as she pulled into the church parking lot. "Unfortunately, hiring a hit man to bump off your husband is still a criminal offense." She glanced questioningly at Ima. "So . . . do you want Thorn to finish reading your rights or do you prefer to let the sheriff deliver the spiel?"

When Ima requested to see the sheriff, Amanda ushered her away.

"As for you, Thorn. I'll meet you at the altar in ten minutes." she said over her shoulder.

"I'll be there. Just make sure *you* are, Hazard."

Amanda hand-delivered Ima to the sheriff, presented her report that cited Deputy Payne for mishandling the investigation. She told the sheriff about Payne's rude behavior and harassment when she encountered him at the parking lot of Watts's Auto Repair Shop. She also informed the sheriff of Payne's torrid affair with a married woman, while on duty. The sheriff assured her that Payne would be dealt with properly and would never show his face in Vamoose again.

Well satisfied and vindicated, Amanda strode into the

church. She didn't miss her cue for the bridal processional, either. She was there to take Daddy's arm and walk down the aisle, carrying a bouquet of passion pink roses tied with Prussian purple ribbon.

Thorn was standing at the altar, just as he said he would be, decked out in his Prince Charming tux. It was a perfect, fairy-tale wedding . . .

Except for the great white rat of a groom's cake that split down the middle and fell on the floor, because Beverly Hill forgot to turn on the air-conditioner so the icing wouldn't melt.

Amanda lounged on her lawn chair, enjoying the tropical sun that glistened off the crystal-clear blue waters that lapped against the sandy-white beach. Palm trees swayed in the balmy breeze and the four-piece band played Reggae music. A floppy-brimmed straw hat concealed Amanda's bad hairdo. She held a frozen strawberry daiquiri in her purple-tipped fingers. The luxury cruise ship was anchored at sea, and Thorn was by her side.

All was right with the world, Amanda thought to herself.

"Ah, this is the life, Thorn," she said, then sighed contentedly. "I could get used to waking up at my own leisure, pampering myself all afternoon and dining out day and night."

"Me, too," Nick murmured as he basked in the sunshine. "How did you do it, Haz?"

"How did I do what?"

"How did you figure out that the entire Lemon clan was involved in the auto-theft ring? How did you figure out who had Frank bumped off and why?"

Amanda smiled at him. "Pure feminine brain power and strict attention to detail."

Nick turned his raven head to stare at Hazard's voluptuous figure, encased in a skimpy black bikini. She had the cake lady's synthetically enhanced body beat all to hell, he noted appreciatively. "I never did thank you properly for getting my job back and sending Payne packing."

"You didn't? Then what's that stuff we have been doing every night for the past four nights all about?"

"That was just me working my way up to a grand finale of a thank-you," he said, then waggled his eyebrows and grinned rakishly.

"It gets better?" she asked. "Don't know how that could be, Thorn. Far as I'm concerned, your nightly performances have been absolutely perfect."

The compliment had Nick beaming like the tropical sun. "Come on, Hazard," he urged, grabbing her hand. "I don't think I can wait until tonight to thank you again."

Sure enough, he couldn't. The newlyweds beat a hasty retreat to their deluxe cabin on the cruise ship, and still had time for a swim before they sailed off to their next port of call . . .

Dear Readers,

I hope you enjoyed accompanying me through my latest investigation of *Dead in the Driver's Seat.* I'm sure you will understand if I take some time away from Vamoose to enjoy this picturesque paradise in the tropics. I don't plan to return home until my disastrous hairdo grows out. But never fear, dear readers, I will be back in small-town America, doing my part to see that truth and justice are never compromised.

Warm regards from the Bahamas!

Yours truly,
Amanda Hazard-Thorn, CPA

THE MYSTERIES OF MARY ROBERTS RINEHART

THE AFTER HOUSE (0-8217-4246-6, $3.99/$4.99)

THE CIRCULAR STAIRCASE (0-8217-3528-4, $3.95/$4.95)

THE DOOR (0-8217-3526-8, $3.95/$4.95)

THE FRIGHTENED WIFE (0-8217-3494-6, $3.95/$4.95)

A LIGHT IN THE WINDOW (0-8217-4021-0, $3.99/$4.99)

THE STATE VS. ELINOR NORTON (0-8217-2412-6, $3.50/$4.50)

THE SWIMMING POOL (0-8217-3679-5, $3.95/$4.95)

THE WALL (0-8217-4017-2, $3.99/$4.99)

THE WINDOW AT THE WHITE CAT (0-8217-4246-9, $3.99/$4.99)

THREE COMPLETE NOVELS: THE BAT, THE HAUNTED LADY, THE YELLOW ROOM (0-8217-114-4, $13.00/$16.00)